MYSTERIES *of* MARTHA'S VINEYARD

A Light in the Darkness

MYSTERIES *of* MARTHA'S VINEYARD

A Light
in the
Darkness

RUTH LOGAN HERNE

Guideposts
New York

Mysteries of Martha's Vineyard is a trademark of Guideposts.

Published by Guideposts Books & Inspirational Media
110 William Street
New York, NY 10038
Guideposts.org

Cover and interior design by Müllerhaus
Cover illustration by Greg Copeland, represented by Deborah Wolfe, LTD.
Typeset by Aptara, Inc.

Printed and bound in the United States of America
10 9 8 7 6 5 4 3 2

A Light
in the
Darkness

CHAPTER ONE

Well, Priscilla..." Priscilla Grant gazed out over the Atlantic Ocean and hauled in a breath of sweet sea air. "You are definitely not in Kansas anymore." The sound of waves, rolling steep and wide along the craggy shore forming the eastern property line, rose up to her. She inhaled again and tried to calm her pounding heart. She was really here. She was really doing this.

She turned back to her late aunt's—no, *her*—seaside cottage and studied its weathered, sea-blue clapboard siding and white trim, the windows flanked by white shutters and garnished with flower boxes. Rose-toned geraniums and neon pink-and-green elephant ear rose from the boxes while deep purple lobelia spilled down the sides. The splash of color brought life to an otherwise austere yard, a yard that begged for attention. She'd have to give the yard some thought, but right now she had to give thought to a great many things. All in good time.

The lighthouse, impossible to ignore, loomed over the cottage and cast a shadow of graceful authority.

She owned a lighthouse. An old and very valuable lighthouse.

Disbelief swept in, and she pushed it right back out.

The tower itself was a crisp white, capped by a black lantern room ringed by a railing. A small window, halfway up the lighthouse, was also trimmed in black. The lighthouse, which, as Priscilla understood it, was now maintained by the Coast Guard, served as a noble sentinel on the shoreline of Martha's Vineyard, lighting the night sky in fine tradition.

Gazing at the ocean, Priscilla felt her nerves begin to calm. She'd spent her whole life in the relatively small world of her Kansas farming community. She'd lived in the same farmhouse since she was a kid, helping first her father, and then her husband, Gary, work the fields of wheat, corn, and soybeans. She and Gary had raised their thirty-two-year-old daughter, Rachel, on that farm, and eight months ago, Priscilla had held Gary's hand and whispered her undying love and goodbyes as he slipped from this world. One last breath that ignited so much change.

And now this.

The sight made her smile, and after burying a beloved, smiles were few and far between, so it surprised her a little. It felt rusty, like when turning on the hose on those first days of spring, but natural too. Like the hose, it had once been used on a regular basis.

Just a month ago, she'd learned she had inherited this cottage from her aunt Marjorie Latham. Priscilla shocked everyone who knew her, especially Rachel, by deciding to leave the farm, the only life she'd ever known, and move to the East Coast.

Gary would be proud if he could see me now, she thought and knew the truth of her words. It was time to find out what else life had in store for her.

Rachel's ringtone signaled another call from her daughter, but Priscilla left the phone tucked in her purse. She didn't have anything new to talk about yet. She'd get her suitcases moved into the cottage, take a good look around, and unpack a little. Then she'd call Rachel back. Her daughter meant well, but she had a worry streak.

It was time to break that pattern. To begin anew. Rachel had texted and called throughout the day to check on her mother. A little of that was more than enough. Priscilla needed some time to herself to discover her new home.

She rummaged through her bag until she found the envelope from Aunt Marjorie's lawyer that contained the house key. Then, straightening, she fit the key into the lock.

"What do you think you're doing?"

Heart racing, she spun and dropped her purse. A man stood on the sidewalk a few yards away, his arms crossed and his face dark with disapproval. His short-sleeved shirt and pants were the same shade of blue, a uniform of some sort.

"Nothing!" she yelped like a guilty child.

His frown deepened. "This is private property."

"I know," she replied in a more dignified tone. "It's *my* property actually."

Surprise lifted the man's eyebrows and loosened his arms, but he still seemed unconvinced. "Since when?"

"Since my aunt Marjorie died and left it to me," she said, gaining confidence. "It was my grandmother's cottage before that, and *her* grandfather's before that, and I don't know how many Lathams more. We've been here for ages. I'm Priscilla Grant, by the way."

The man relaxed and smiled at her. The smile brightened his hazel eyes, and Priscilla found herself smoothing her chin-length hair. "Well, that explains a lot. I'm very sorry for the misunderstanding." He extended his hand, stepping forward to greet her. "I'm Gerald O'Bannon, captain of the local Coast Guard station. One of our radio outposts is just down the shore from your lighthouse, and as I was driving past, I saw your car. A lot of people have been poking around Vineyard Haven and Tisbury the last few days, and I thought you were another treasure seeker."

She bent to pick up her purse. "Please don't worry about it. I'm glad someone was looking after the place for me." She paused as his words registered. "Did you say another *treasure seeker*?"

His smile widened. "Ah, you *are* new in town. If you'd been here more than a day, someone would have told you all about it by now." He paused, letting the suspense build, and Priscilla played along.

"Told me what?"

"Last week the *Boston Globe* printed a story about Martha's Vineyard's most popular buried-treasure legend. During the Revolution, the son of a local blacksmith made off with the Redcoat payroll. He managed to hide it before he got caught, and the British were never able to recover it. The *Globe* reporter spent a few months researching the claims and convinced himself the legend was possibly true—that Nathaniel Claybrook really did hide a chest full of British gold, and that it was most likely hidden on this side of the island. As you can imagine, enthusiastic would-be millionaires have swarmed the Vineyard, looking in every likely spot. They've poked around the wildlife preserves and along any stretch of seashore they can sneak on to with metal detectors. I'm amazed at how quickly this thing escalated. The lure of a deserted lighthouse or any aged structure seems to draw their interest. Judging by what the past few days have been like, I'm pretty sure it's going to get worse before it gets better."

They both looked toward the lighthouse before Priscilla turned back, skeptical. "There's no way that lighthouse existed during the Revolutionary War."

Gerald laughed. "You're right. It wasn't built until eighty years later. But it's a nice thought, isn't it? Treasure hidden in a lighthouse?" He checked his watch. "I'm on duty in fifteen minutes, so I'll leave you be. Again, I'm sorry for startling you."

She reached out to shake his hand once more. "It was nice to meet you."

"You as well, Priscilla." His eyes sparkled. "I'm sure we'll bump into each other now and then. Welcome to the island."

Priscilla smiled her thanks and waited as he walked to the white SUV parked at the end of her driveway. A bright red stripe emblazoned the car door, and the words *Coast Guard* were inscribed a little farther back.

When he was gone, Priscilla turned back to the cottage. The side door unlocked with a soft click, and she stepped into a dark, slightly musty hallway. She fumbled for the switch.

Light flooded the entry and spilled into the adjacent kitchen and living room. Priscilla gazed around with appreciation. She hadn't visited this fairy-tale cottage since she was a child, yet it mirrored her vague memories. The mismatched furniture hailed from different eras but partnered with the sunny yellow walls, white trim, and bright Cape Cod curtains for a charming effect.

She dragged her two suitcases inside, one at a time, until she had them both standing next to the four-poster bed in the larger of the two bedrooms. She considered unpacking, filling the small closet and antique tallboy dresser with her belongings, but first she wanted to explore the rest of the cottage.

She started in the living room. Some objects she remembered from long ago—the painting of the lighthouse above the fireplace, viewed from the ocean during a storm, and a porcelain swan she had coveted as a child—but many items were new. The bathroom boasted a claw-foot tub and a black-and-white tile floor. The spare bedroom, though small, looked inviting with its quilted bedspread, antique dressing table, and gingham curtains. In the kitchen, she found some lovely old tea tins, and the fridge and oven were, thankfully, fairly new.

Between the kitchen and small dining area was a gorgeous Hoosier cabinet, a must in nineteenth-century kitchens. A wide, flat wooden counter offered workspace above two deep, wide bins, one for flour and one for sugar. On the opposite side, a small cupboard door opened to reveal old-style baking pans and a few new ones as well. The upper part of the antique cupboard held Johnson Brothers china and beveled glasses behind glass-fronted doors. She opened one door and lifted a plate.

These were the exact plates she remembered from that long-ago visit. The elongated table had extended into the living room, with one of these quaint, wintry plates tucked in front of each chair, perfect for a New England setting. The sturdy cabinet seemed to bind old and new together in timeless beauty.

On the kitchen counter to the left of the stove, Priscilla spotted a bright yellow envelope with her name on it. Inside was a greeting card with a picture of the island along with a handwritten note, which read:

Priscilla,

Welcome to Martha's Vineyard! We did our best to spruce up the cottage for you. We're so excited to have another Latham cousin living so close. We look forward to getting to know you better. Once you're settled, give one of us a call. We'll show you around the island and treat you to brunch at our favorite seaside café.

Happy homecoming!

Your long-lost cousins,
Joan, Gail, and Trudy

Under each name was a phone number, solidifying the fact that she had family here.

That knowledge brought comfort. Her last visit occurred when she was eight, and she hadn't kept up with the Latham side of the family at all. Though their names sounded familiar, she had only vague memories of Joan, Gail, and Trudy. Still, she looked forward to meeting them. It was a relief to know she had some ready-made connections on the island. Meeting new people had never been her forte, making her move east more of a challenge, but what was life if it offered no challenge? Gary had taught her that and so much more.

She set down the card and continued her exploration. At the back of the kitchen, a door revealed a set of stairs leading downward. Priscilla was surprised to find a cellar. She hadn't expected one this close to the shore, but she supposed the bluff on which the lighthouse stood made it possible.

Suddenly apprehensive, she flipped the switch just inside the door. A single bare light bulb illuminated the musty space. Smaller than the footprint of the house, it had probably been built to serve as a root cellar or pantry. Spiderwebs decorated the lower reaches, a clear sign that the cousins had given the ancient basement a wide berth. She decided they were smart women and closed the door. She could attack the basement...and the webs...another day.

Another door, painted white, stood at the far side of the living area. She wrinkled her brow as she crossed the room and tried the handle. Locked.

Locked meant there must be a key someplace, but where? She went back to the kitchen. A small key rack with two tiny drawers hung just inside the back door. An old-fashioned skeleton key lay atop the narrow shelf. An old key for an old door? She picked it up and retraced her steps. She inserted the key into the mysterious door's lock, and when she heard metal on metal, her success inspired another smile, less rusty this time. She tugged the door firmly, and when it resisted, she tugged harder. It sprang forth at the added force, revealing a narrow stairway leading up. To what? She flipped the single light switch. She'd never thought about the cottage having an attic, but as she mounted the steps, that was exactly what she found. Steep eaves narrowed the headroom, and stale air filled the space around storage boxes in every shape she could imagine.

Peering past the boxes, Priscilla focused on a large sea chest against the far wall. The time-weathered wooden chest was so big, she could have curled up inside it.

She went straight to the chest and knelt down. She expected to find a lock, but all she had to do was lift the brass latch and push. The hinges creaked in protest against the heavy lid, but the chest opened.

Priscilla held her breath as she took in the contents. She noted three stacks of books in various sizes and colors. She lifted the one nearest her, a slim clothbound volume, and opened it to find a journal of some sort, cursive writing filling the lined pages. She squinted and tilted the pages until the light hit them full-on and she could make out a few lines.

It was a lighthouse logbook dated 1933. The keeper had kept notes about passing ships, messages received, and repairs made. She set the clothbound journal on the floor next to her and lifted a leather-bound journal from the chest. This log was from 1928. The entry she turned to documented a storm that had kept the lighthouse keeper up all night. She reached back into the chest and pulled out a stack of five or six more journals. She imagined spending a few hours in her cozy armchair, a cup of tea at her side, with her own personal slice of history in her lap. The fact that, as the present owner of the lighthouse, she was now part of this history made her pause. "Oh, Gary," she whispered, "if only you were here to discover all this with me."

She was about to close the chest lid when she noticed a unique journal halfway down the center pile. It was larger than the others and bound in dark, rich leather, embossed with a vine pattern. It looked old. *Really* old. Priscilla hesitated for a moment, suddenly wondering if she should be taking these logs straight to the nearest museum instead of pawing through them. But curiosity got the better of her.

The leather felt dry enough that she worried it might crack. She settled back on her heels and laid the logbook on her lap, running her fingers over the tooled design. She slowly opened the cover to see tall, spidery handwriting stretching across yellowed paper. She didn't dare try to turn the page, certain it would rip or crumble to dust in her hands, but she lifted the journal, trying to angle it into the light so she could find a date. Something fell out of the back of the logbook, bouncing off her leg and landing on the floor with the bright *ting* of metal. Priscilla nearly dropped the journal but managed to carefully close it and set it back in her lap.

She picked up the object. A coin. She raised it to the light and was shocked to find it was gold instead of the silver she'd expected. The coin's face showed the profile of a portly man with a garland of leaves in his hair like Caesar. She brought the coin closer to her face and squinted to make out the letters circling his head.

GEORGIVS III DEI GRATIA

Georgius III. George the Third? King George the Third?

Her hand shaking, Priscilla turned the coin over to find the image of a coat of arms. It was surrounded by a string of letters that made no sense to her, but her gaze was arrested by the date at the top.

1775.

What, exactly, was it that Gerald O'Bannon had told her about Nathaniel Claybrook and the Redcoats' stolen gold?

CHAPTER TWO

Take a breath. Put the coin in a safe spot. Unpack.

The sensibility of the mental advice wasn't lost on Priscilla. Revolutionary mysteries were the fodder of children's books and educational TV shows. They didn't actually exist, did they? Not in Kansas anyway, settled long after the British had been sent packing.

The logs and coin said otherwise, but she needed time to process this information. On a practical level, she would require food at some juncture. Her local map listed a Stop&Shop down the coast, and the nearby town of Tisbury was home to lots of small businesses. She needed to walk away from this and take time to acclimate herself with the town, the shops, the people.

But first, food and unpacking, mundane chores that would allow her time to think.

She plopped the first suitcase onto the bed, unwound the lengthy zipper, and lifted the top. She withdrew her serviceable navy-blue dress. As she did, a small jewelry pouch slipped from the folds and on to the floor. Twin gold earrings popped out. One stayed put alongside the velvet sleeve, but the other rolled across the bright-toned rag rug on the polished hardwood floor. She retrieved the earrings and the pouch, refusing to think about gold, then immediately lifted a summery top with a gold chain tie-on neckline from her suitcase.

More gold.

The thought of that lone gold coin and the history of the land, the Lathams, and the lighthouse intertwined in her head. If that gold was hidden somewhere on the island and a piece of it lay here in her antiquated cottage, logic suggested the bulk of the treasure could be here as well. And that Coast Guard captain—handsome Coast Guard captain, she admitted to herself—said folks had been searching on her property. Perhaps there was more to this story. In an area so rich with American history, there had to be a place to learn about it. She'd look into it when she drove into town. For the moment, organization and shopping were key. Perhaps the prosaic job of stocking food shelves and a refrigerator would push buried treasure from her mind.

She settled the empty luggage into a corner and slipped her purse over her arm. Grabbing her keys, she headed for the door facing the road.

Three faces peered through the wide-paned glass.

She screeched and they screeched, but theirs were notes of delight.

"She's here!"

"It's her!"

"Priscilla, it's us! Joan, Gail, and Trudy!" The blonde pointed to herself when she said the third name. "Welcome to Vineyard Haven!"

Priscilla opened the door and was instantly engulfed in a trio of hugs and a round of exclamations, most of which came from

Trudy. Gail looked thrilled to meet her. Joan stayed back slightly but appeared pleased as well.

When Trudy grabbed Priscilla in a third hug, Joan rolled her eyes. "You'll scare her right back to Kansas with your antics, sister dear. By the look on Priscilla's face, she hasn't seen the likes of us before." Joan offered the warning in a calm, steady voice with no malice. "You might want to tone it down."

"Oh, she'll get used to us in no time," Trudy insisted. Her bright smile and anxious-to-please expression put Priscilla in mind of a puppy she and Gary had raised nearly twenty years before. The golden Lab mix had been sweet, kind, and good, but he had little desire to sit still for long and had been a total washout as a hunting dog. Still, Buford had been a trusted friend for nearly fourteen years. Trudy's blonde bob, merry blue eyes, and her bubbly gestures matched the pup's. "Were you going out?"

"To town," Priscilla told them. "I need to buy some food, and I want to learn my way around." She held up her map of the island. "This makes me look like all the other tourists out there. I want to be able to toss it away and act like a local."

"You will in no time," Gail promised. Her voice was firm and direct, stronger than Joan's and less effusive than Trudy's. She was taller than the other women, like Priscilla, and her brownish bob of chin-length hair framed a fuller face with blue-gray eyes. "Once the summer crush ends, about 60 percent of the people disappear. And then it drops another ten or fifteen thousand when the leaves fall."

Priscilla frowned. "They wait for the leaves before they leave?"

"Leaf peepers," Joan explained. She moved toward the door and swung it wide. "Girls, let's let Priscilla get her shopping done, and we can talk to her later." She shifted her attention back to Priscilla. "Can you join us for dinner tonight at Gail's place? We're marinating chicken, and I've skewered fresh squash and tomatoes from the garden. Patio tomatoes," she added as if it mattered. "The real ones won't be ripe for weeks, but I find those little container plantings are a lovely treat in July."

"What can I bring?" Priscilla asked immediately. Gatherings back home were generally potluck, and she remembered that being a New England tradition as well.

"How about some fresh fruit?" Joan suggested. "That would be lovely and easy while you get your bearings."

"I'll do it." Priscilla followed them out the door and then paused. "Oh, wait."

The trio pivoted, almost in unison.

"Where does Gail live?"

"Oh, what are we thinking?" Trudy made a face while Gail pulled a Post-it from her purse and jotted down an address. "Do you have a GPS?"

"I do, but I've been through enough weather traveling east that I made sure to buy a map as well," Priscilla said. "The GPS wanted to take me up some obscure mountain road during a bout of bad weather in central Pennsylvania. I realized then and there that while there's good to be said about technology, there's good to be said about an old-fashioned laminated map as well."

"You are a wise woman," declared Gail. "We always need to have a plan B. Just in case."

"Plug this address into your GPS or just check it out on the map," Trudy added as Gail handed over the sticky note. "It will bring you right to Gail's door. It's a quick trip down Old Lighthouse Road and take a right on to Fairfield. You can't miss it."

"What time is good?"

"Six thirty, if that's good for you," Gail told her. "My dad lives with me. He would be your uncle Hubert, your mother's brother, but everyone just calls him Hugh. Dad doesn't take well to change—he's not exactly what you'd call easygoing—so six thirty is about as late as I dare plan a meal."

"Six thirty works for me," Priscilla told her.

"That gives us time to sit and talk," Gail added. "There's something special about a summer's night when the breeze calms down and all the boats come back to shore."

It did sound special, and the girls' arrival offered a pleasant respite from Priscilla's agitation over the coin. She didn't get agitated as a rule. Why start now, with a new plan afoot?

She'd approach the mystery of the coin like she would anything else, with a simple, straightforward plan of attack, starting with the town historian. If Tisbury didn't have one, she'd find someone associated with the schools or the library. Although what kind of historic New England town wouldn't have a vested historian?

She found that hard to imagine as she drove toward town. She spotted the Stop&Shop but drove right on by, heading into town instead. She'd park and walk around the town, then do her shopping. That would leave her plenty of time to get a fruit bowl ready for tonight. The thought of supper with her cousins invigorated her.

She had to search the busy town for a parking space and wondered how such a cozy island could handle the influx of tourism. People thronged the streets, and the roads patterned out in multiple directions around her.

She glimpsed the tall masts of sailboats in a nearby harbor, and the wooden walkways sported rope railings, like docks along the water's edge. Nautical symbols dotted signs and mailboxes, while shades of blue, green, gray, and white dominated the neighborhoods, with the occasional maverick splash of yellow, pink, or purple. It almost made her wonder if there was a paint code. The thought seemed to fit the antiquity of the town.

She shrugged her purse up over her shoulder as her phone began to vibrate in her pocket. She withdrew it, saw Rachel's number, and accepted the call. "Rachel, how are you?"

"The same as I was four hours ago. How are you, Mom? Are you there? Did you find it all right? Are you lost?"

"I'm fine," Priscilla assured as she walked toward the busy business district. "I'm here, I've moved my belongings into the cottage, and I couldn't be less lost if I tried. It's difficult to get lost on an island. The very nature of the geography is self-limiting. But just in case, I have a map." She patted the pocket of her purse with a confidence she didn't quite feel.

"I hear people. Is it busy there?"

"Right here, yes. And you'll have to come visit, darling, once I'm settled. The cottage is cozy and quaint, a quiet seaside setting. Here in town, there are people everywhere. It's quite crowded. Quite a difference, isn't it?" She'd never minded the solitude and quiet of their Kansas farm. It seemed right, up until Gary died. And then nothing was right, and the silence pressed on her like a ship's anchor, locking her into one place while life passed her by.

"Are you okay exploring the town on your own, Mom?"

"Other than the tens of thousands of tourists, yes." Did she sound cryptic? Possibly, because where was it written that the daughter should become overprotective of the mother? "I'm exploring the town, then I'm going to grab some groceries, and then I've been invited to supper with my three cousins."

"You found cousins already?"

"They're enthusiastic," she admitted as she walked, looking this way and that. The town's busy beauty called out to her, and everyone seemed amazingly cheerful, but why wouldn't they be? The charming setting, highlighted by picture-perfect weather, green grass, thick trees, boat whistles, and bright white sails dotting the water seemed joyous. And the smell of fresh fudge from Murdick's Fudge Shop made her downright hungry. "They stopped by this morning, and they got the cottage ready for me. Lovely ladies. I think."

"And they're not mad that your aunt left the cottage to you and not one of them?"

Rachel's question hit home. Why *had* Aunt Marjorie done this wonderful thing? Was it because Priscilla had lost Gary? Was it an attempt to bring her back to family, or was there some weird family history behind her reasoning?

Priscilla had no idea. Perhaps it was as simple as two sisters loving each other and Aunt Marjorie having no children of her own. Still, family loyalty was a far cry from leaving someone a unique oceanfront property valued at seven figures. A property that might have a stash of gold buried on it somewhere.

She shushed that thought instantly and answered Rachel. "I expect they have places of their own, honey. Remember, my mother's family lived here for generations. Lathams are part of the landscape. I've just added one more."

"Except that's not home," Rachel whispered. "Wheatfield is home. The farm. The land. At least it was."

Priscilla couldn't do this. Not again. Not here, not now, surrounded by people. Talking about the past pulled her into it. It had been a good life, she recognized that, but everything was different now. Rachel had moved away from the farm years ago and was now a top-level project manager for a telecommunications corporation. She visited a few times a year, but she was busily engaged in her own life, just as it should be. Staying in that rambling farmhouse alone wasn't an option for Priscilla, and she recognized that as soon as she opened the lawyer's initial letter.

"Paths change, darling. Sometimes they have to because we're given no choice." As she spoke, she noticed a small, plain sign arrow, pointing through the maze of streets. Historical Museum. Just that. Nothing more. She made the left turn and aimed for a sunny yellow Queen Anne Victorian tucked slightly off the road,

right at the curve. "I have to go, darling. I just spotted the historical museum, and I need to meet the curator. Rachel, you've always
loved history, and you're going to love this place when you visit. It's
steeped in old but embraces the new. I'll give you a call back as I
get settled. Love you!" She hung up quickly because though
Rachel had a good heart, she liked to wrangle.

*She lost her father when you lost your husband. You share a deep
loss. Doesn't that make her feelings normal?*

It did.

But that didn't help fill those empty days on the windblown
Kansas prairie. She hadn't sold the farm yet. She wanted to test the
Massachusetts waters first. See what fit. But if this worked out,
wouldn't a young couple love to raise their family on that sweet farm?
The farmhouse should be filled with life again, as it had been for
years. She hurried up the walk, past a larger sign that said Welcome
to East Shore Historical Museum. Curator: Mildred Pearson.

She climbed the wide, pale gray steps and crossed the old-
fashioned porch to the front door of the converted house. The
door swung open as Priscilla approached, and a young woman
with a little boy emerged. "Oh." The young woman looked surprised when she almost smacked Priscilla with the storm door as
the boy squalled in her arms. "I'm so sorry, I didn't see you."

"I want to stay here! I want to stay here and play! Why don't
you ever let me do what I want?" the boy shrieked in anger, reaching for the door around his mother's shoulders.

Priscilla moved to one side to avoid his flailing arms and legs.
"A history lover, I take it?"

The young woman made a face mixed with dismay and humor. "I think it's more likely that he wants more of Candy Lane's cookies. She provides them for the History Tea every Monday afternoon, and Ryan is determined to eat the entire plate." She gathered the boy in more securely as she headed down the walk. "Nap time!" she sang out, which inspired another round of protests from the indignant child.

A History Tea?

Intrigued, Priscilla stepped through the door into a wealth of yesteryear. The historians had converted each room of the house into a distinct time period of wall coverings and furnishings. Historic photos decorated the walls, while quaint room settings filled each space, as if she'd walked into another dimension. The rooms displayed a plaque advising the relative historical date. An 1812 parlor. An 1850s dining room. A 1790s pantry, lined with painted wood shelves and kitchen necessities of the time. Gazing at the multitude of hand-cranked, labor-intensive devices, Priscilla felt lazy by comparison.

She heard voices coming from the kitchen. She followed the noise and paused in the doorway. So did the chatter. Three women and one man sat around a small table, and all stared at her as if having a stranger walk in on Monday tea was against the order of things. "Good afternoon," she said.

A tall, thin woman stood up. Smooth gray hair, pinned up, made her seem even taller and thinner than she was. She wore a long dress, in keeping with the antique displays, and wore no makeup on suntanned cheeks. The coloring meant she didn't spend every day inside the museum. She moved forward. "Hello." She stuck out a hand. "Mildred Pearson. I look after the museum."

"Priscilla Latham Grant," Priscilla told her as she accepted her handshake. "I've just moved into my aunt's cottage…"

"The lighthouse on Bailey Point?" The man's brows shot up, along with a look of interest. "The lighthouse has a new owner? Since when?"

"Since she left it to me?" Priscilla suggested with a hint of humor. "I haven't been back to the Vineyard since I was a child, and I'm hoping to learn more of the area history. And the light-house's history," she added. "I figured here was the best place to start, but I can see you're busy."

"Not too busy to share a love of history and cookies." Mildred lifted a plate and offered it to Priscilla. "If you want to connect with history, try these. Rosemary shortbread cookies lightly dusted with powdered sugar. They're melt-in-your-mouth delicious."

Priscilla tried the cookie and couldn't hold back a smile. Nor did she try. "These are amazing! You said they're made with rose-mary? Who would think to put rosemary in a cookie?"

"They're love cookies." Another woman smiled as the man rolled his eyes. "Rosemary is the herb of love, they say, so Candy calls these her love cookies."

"And why wouldn't she?" said the third woman. "Everyone in town loves them. And her."

"If you want to be in on the news in town, stop by the bakery," the man spouted, not looking one bit happy about cookies or his-tory or baking. "The gossips gather there daily. If it's old news you're looking for, bearing the intellectual qualities of true history, Mildred and I can help you."

His words put a funny look on Mildred's face, but she shielded it quickly. "I'd love to talk to you about our history. The town, the island, the Latham family. I find the whole thing absolutely fascinating, Priscilla. Can you come by tomorrow morning?" She tipped her head slightly, waiting for Priscilla's answer.

"I'd be glad to. What time?"

"Nine is good, if that's not too early."

It wasn't, so Priscilla nodded.

"We open at ten," Mildred explained. "That will give me an uninterrupted hour to fill you in. Would you like to stay now and have tea with us? We're nearly done, but you're welcome to join in."

It sounded marvelous, and what better way to meet fellow history lovers than over cookies and tea? But she didn't have time. "I'd love to, but I can't today. I've got some shopping to do, and then I'm meeting my cousins for supper. And I'll need more time to settle in, I expect. I just arrived."

"Then welcome." The second woman stood. Where Mildred seemed tall and almost regal, this woman was small and athletic-looking. She reached out quickly to extend her hand in greeting. "I'm Sheila Weller, from another old-time family, and this is Franklin Mayweather. He's a history professor—"

"On the mainland. Dartmouth," the professor cut in. "Just summering here, enjoying fair respite from the grind of educating today's young minds."

Priscilla had never thought about teaching college courses as a "grind" kind of position. Birthing cows? Fixing balers and tractors and monster-size wheels in inclement weather? That was a grind. But she offered a polite nod. "How nice."

"It is indeed lovely to meet you, Mrs. Grant." He stood like the others, but his handshake wasn't firm like Mildred's or sporting like Sheila's. It was fleeting, as if he feared he might catch something.

"And this is Carrie Nash. She's working on an advanced degree in marine biology but has a penchant for history too."

"And a love of the Vineyard." Golden-haired, young, and pretty, Carrie shook Priscilla's hand quickly. "Nice to meet you, Mrs. Grant. I love sailing by the lighthouse. The romantic in me wonders how many women must have prayed beneath that light, hoping it would guide loved ones home. No small number, I suspect."

"I expect you're right." Carrie's words inspired an image of women and children waiting for their menfolk to return to harbor. Shipwrecks were rare in modern times, but they were a regular occurrence in the eighteenth and nineteenth centuries. "Thank you for the cookie and for sparking an idea," she told Mildred. "I think I'll check out this bakery while I'm in town. What did you say the name was?"

"Candy Lane Confectionery. On Beach Street. You can't miss it."

"Lovely. I was going to take fruit to our supper tonight, but I think I'll grab dessert instead. Fruit is fine in its place, but pastry wins the day."

"Gail's a chocolate lover, Trudy is an equal opportunity dessert aficionado, and Joan has a keen eye for Candy's cream puffs." Sheila listed the cousins on her fingers as she spoke.

"Perfect!" Priscilla hadn't had a cream puff since the Terhunes had closed their family diner back in Wheatfield. She thanked everyone again and hurried out the door. She was about to make a quick left toward the business district when Franklin Mayweather called her name from behind.

She turned, surprised. "Yes?"

"I just wanted to take a moment to welcome you to town, Mrs. Grant. Personally."

Personally?

He smiled, or tried to, but the smile seemed as tepid as the earlier handshake.

She longed to make a face at him and be on her way. His grandiose manner, the way he stretched out words as if unwilling to speak plainly and simply, and the handshake were all annoying. "Thank you, Professor. I'm sure I'll see you around."

"I could perhaps stop by the lighthouse and advise you on some of the more interesting history."

Not in this lifetime.

Out loud, she said, "I think my talk with Mildred and some old-fashioned personal investigation will suffice. But thank you." She moved on before he could say more and made it a point not to look back until she rounded the corner. When she did make the turn, she sneaked a look backward.

The professor was staring after her, frowning. One hand stroked his chin as if trying to solve a problem.

Priscilla quickly ducked around the yellow masonry building marking the corner.

He'd followed her out of the museum and then invited himself to the lighthouse. Why?

You are single and in possession of a very pricey property. Two good reasons.

She stood still as that reality sank in. She was single, and her property was valued at a price far beyond Biblical rubies, which meant...

She would have to be on the lookout not just for historical gold diggers in search of Revolutionary booty. She'd have to be aware of romantic gold diggers too. Priscilla Grant couldn't believe she even had to think such a thing, but common sense said otherwise.

It was a ridiculous situation, and when she got home tonight, she'd give Gary's picture a good scolding for leaving her to handle all of this on her own.

And then she'd blow him a kiss, turn out the light, and try to sleep in a new bed, in a new house, with a cache of gold possibly hidden somewhere nearby.

But first: cream puffs.

CHAPTER THREE

Y ou've been to Candy's!" Trudy spotted the white box in Priscilla's hands that evening and looked delighted. "Now I know you're one of us. Do I dare ask what's inside?"

"I was told these are Joan's favorite," answered Priscilla as she handed the box to Gail.

"You didn't." Joan put a hand to her chest as if overwhelmed by Priscilla's thoughtfulness. "Cream puffs."

"I can put them right into the fridge, unless we want to prove the saying right and eat dessert first." Gail paused, waiting for their answers.

Losing Gary at such a young age—well, young for these times, Priscilla amended—had taught her to enjoy life's simple moments. Her loss reminded her that God's time line prevailed. Not hers. She raised her hand. "I vote yes to eating dessert first."

The cousins grinned in agreement. "Dad will be delighted," said Gail. "Priscilla, come meet him. He's in his chair, ready for one of his favorite shows, but I know he wants to meet you."

Priscilla followed Gail into a comfortably crowded living room, which opened to a lovely back porch overlooking a shady yard.

"Dad, Priscilla's here. She brought cream puffs from Candy's place."

The elderly man skewered Priscilla with a tough-guy look. "Gail said you were back in town. I wasn't inclined to believe it. But then if someone goes around leaving you a monster-size bequest, I suppose that's reason enough to come back east."

Gail's cheeks turned pink. "Dad. Priscilla barely even knew we existed. Kind of. And don't be rude," she scolded softly. "Show her your nice side, or she's likely to think you mean it, and even more likely to take this cream puff right back."

A twinkle brightened his narrowed eyes. "I do like cream puffs from Candy's, and there's no sense risking a loss like that. And while I can understand that Miss Priscilla here didn't remember much about her East Coast family, her mother had to come from somewhere. And that somewhere was here. Priscilla." He stood slightly and offered his hand. "Nice to meet you again."

Priscilla accepted the handshake with a smile. "Uncle Hugh, it is a pleasure to see you again. It's been a long time."

"That it has. But you're welcome back here, and I'm glad there's someone with some youth and gumption looking after the light-house property. And I'll enjoy this." He indicated the cream puff on the plate. "Thank you for thinking of it."

"You're welcome. And I…"

"Have a nice visit." He sat back down and didn't move his gaze from the game show. Clearly the amenities were over.

"We've been dismissed," Gail whispered, and Priscilla had to agree. "He's a little crusty around the edges…"

Joan rolled her eyes, and Trudy bit back a laugh.

"Okay, quite crusty when he wants to be, but he's got a good heart."

"Like father, like daughter," Joan agreed. "And in twenty years we might all be a little feistier than we are now. He's blessed to have you."

"Well that goes both ways," offered Gail in a matter-of-fact tone. "When my marriage fell apart years ago, he was right there helping me fix this, do that. He ran the kids around from school and sports so I could work. Our lives would have been very different when Brett walked out if my parents hadn't been here, willing to help. I'll never forget that. But now I have something else on my mind." She lifted the box and took a deep breath. "Dessert."

"We're such radicals." Trudy laughed as she withdrew four gold-rimmed china plates from Gail's cupboard. "We've got paper plates for supper, but cream puffs are deserving of the very best, don't you think?"

"Yes," said Joan. "Priscilla, this is such a wonderful treat. I only allow myself to go to Candy's once a week because the temptation meter goes off the charts, and at our age we have to start making choices with a little more care."

"I'm not going to think about age and choices." Trudy cut the string on the box and lifted the lid. "Not when this box of deliciousness is staring me in the face." She set the cream puffs on to plates as she spoke. "Priscilla, what made you think of this?"

"I stopped into the history museum to ask a question or two..."

"And Monday is History Tea day," noted Gail.

"Exactly, which led us to talking about cookies, then the bakery, followed by dessert, and here I am. And I noticed something interesting today." Three sets of eyes looked her way—blue, brown, and blue-gray. "I felt like I could tell the people who belong here, the ones who actually live here, apart from the tourists."

"Well, of course you can," said Gail as if the influx of tens of thousands of people didn't add layers of confusion to the setting.

Trudy didn't look one bit surprised. "The locals have a way of acting that sets them apart. Which can be good. Or not," she added with a meaningful look.

"But is it weird that I noticed it my first day here?" Priscilla wondered. She made a little face of concern. "It took me by surprise because I'm a fish out of water too. And yet I didn't feel that way as I roamed through town, surrounded by tourists and friendly shopkeepers."

"Because you're a Latham," Joan said softly. "You're one of us, and time and distance can't erase that, Priscilla."

"Maybe that will help you get your bearings more quickly," added Gail. She picked up her plate and headed for the yard. "In any case, I'm glad your wanderings brought you to Candy's bakery. Let's sit out here, listen to the birds, and get to know each other better."

A cool breeze, banked sun, and the company of three smiling women anxious to welcome her back to Martha's Vineyard.

Priscilla couldn't think of anything better.

Priscilla easily parked her car in the half-empty municipal lot at 8:55 the next morning. Folks meandered here and there, and the waterfront was already teeming with life, but the streets weren't nearly as crowded as they'd been the previous day. She climbed the steps and tapped lightly on the museum door.

"Right on time." Mildred opened the door and stepped back to give her room to come in. "I like punctual folks. Those that respect others' time are more likely to respect them altogether. Come back into the kitchen. Coffee or tea?"

"Coffee, and thank you."

Mildred led the way and put a pod of ground coffee in a one-cup brewing system. "I didn't think I'd like this contraption when someone donated it to the museum kitchen," she noted, and her wry look hinted that she'd been bested by convenience. "First, because it's blatantly modern in an antiquated setting."

Priscilla was pretty sure the convenience made up for just about anything because she loved her single-pod brewing system, but she found Mildred's penchant for propriety almost enchanting. And maybe a little amusing as well.

"I fussed about it originally because I'm not a big fan of change, and that's more my problem than anyone else's," Mildred admitted as she took mugs from an old-fashioned cupboard. "I figured folks had been making coffee in pots for centuries. Why change? And then"—she pressed her lips into a firm line as if perturbed by her findings—"I realized that this machine gives me a perfect cup of coffee every single time. And that was reason enough to love it, right there." She set Priscilla's coffee down, set hers on the opposite side of the table, slipped on to the old-fashioned wooden bench, and said, "So, Priscilla, your grip on that book is so tight, it's got me wondering what's brought you to the museum twice on your first two days in town. And please, for the love of all that's good and holy in God's great universe, do not say 'gold.'"

Priscilla said it anyway. "It *is* gold, Mildred. Moreover, I believe it's *the* gold." She set the old logbook down and withdrew the coin from its center pages. She slipped it across the table and watched Mildred's eyes go wide.

"This is British coin." A short, tight whistle of surprise underscored Mildred's reaction. "Dated 1775."

"Yes."

Mildred tipped the coin to examine its edges. Her eyes narrowed before she lifted her gaze to Priscilla's. "Are you saying that you've been in town one day and found the treasure that went missing more than two centuries back?"

"I found this one and only coin," Priscilla told her. "It was tucked into this journal. I was examining some of the lighthouse keepers' notes in the attic, and it slipped out. Could it be a coincidence?"

"The lighthouse has an attic?"

"Small and stuffy, but yes. Is that a surprise?"

"Marjorie wasn't big on visitors, and the Preservation Society wanted her lighthouse in the worst way. But she wasn't about to give it up, and no amount of money could tempt her otherwise. There wasn't an attic in the cottage drawings, so maybe it was accessed later. Not everyone wants the world to know and approve every little thing they do in a historic home," Mildred added. "It would be some coincidence to have you stumble on one of the very guineas reported to have been stolen and hidden all those years ago. And why one gold coin, hidden in one book?"

"Why, indeed?" The deep male voice at the open back door startled both women.

Priscilla sloshed her coffee on to the table, and Mildred made the coin disappear in rapid fashion as she turned. "Franklin, this is unexpected. You knew I was meeting with Priscilla this morning. Why are you here?"

"Perhaps for that very reason." Dressed in a tropical-colored floral Hawaiian shirt, he puffed his shoulders like a bird preening its feathers and then offered his rendition of a charming smile to Priscilla. His attempt fell short of the mark, and she fought a grimace. "Where did you say this coin was found?"

Priscilla hadn't come to the museum to make a public announcement. She'd come for advice, and the sudden presence of the professor made her uncomfortable. "Perhaps I should leave." She stood.

"No." Mildred stood too, but while she said no to Priscilla, she turned to face Franklin Mayweather. "This is a private meeting, Franklin, and I don't appreciate you sneaking up to the back door to eavesdrop on conversations."

"As a lover of history . . ."

Mildred shut him down. "Respecting privacy outweighs any appreciation for the past," she told him firmly. She folded two strong arms across her chest and nailed him with a dour look.

"If you wish to see the museum or me later, make an appointment."

Surprise, then chagrin, changed the professor's features. "I beg your pardon, ladies. I had no intention of becoming a nuisance. I'll take my leave."

He offered a slight, dignified bow and left, but Priscilla was pretty certain he meant to be a nuisance and that he wanted to know more about her, the lighthouse, and the gold. With a growing appreciation for her new financial status, she was pretty sure her simple clothes and flat shoes weren't the attraction, and the oaf hadn't yet tasted her roasted chicken or double dutch brownies.

She sighed and sat back down. "He heard."

Mildred nodded. "He did, and he's developed an unseemly interest in this gold since the story broke, which makes me wonder if he's in financial difficulties or is just a lover of mystery. I can't deny that I've often wondered about the cache of gold myself. Where it was put, if it's been found, and how no one has stumbled across it in all this time."

"Are you familiar with the lighthouse's history?" Priscilla asked.

"I am. The population has grown significantly here, especially in the past decade, but I've familiarized myself with the original dwellings and land deals. What are you wondering?"

"The chest holding these ledgers and notebooks and the coin." She leaned forward and spoke softly in case the professor decided to lurk outside one of the open windows. "It's large, and the stairs to the attic are narrow. It couldn't have been brought up there in the normal fashion, and there are no windows. How did it get there?"

"Perhaps a late addition narrowed the stair?" Mildred folded her hands, perplexed. "The current town board would require a permit to do any kind of addition, and I've never noticed one on file except when the garage unit was added on the south side of the driveway. With historic properties, there's quite a process to make significant changes, but something could have been done before the zoning laws went into place or prior to its being declared a landmark property. It's curious, isn't it?"

It was because who would intentionally build a stairway too narrow to remove the contents of the space above? "Do you suppose the gold might be hidden in the wall?" she whispered, hardly daring to say it out loud in case someone walked by or the professor lingered outside. "Or beneath the flooring? Did Aunt Marjorie live there alone for a long time?"

"All her life," Mildred answered. "It was willed to your grandparents from your great-uncle, and Marjorie loved the place. They gave her life's use or something like that, so it might be that she felt she had to leave it to you. Or more likely she had remorse because of the family rift. And she had money enough for a good while. The Lathams have always had an eye toward good investment, and they owned a fair share of island real estate and mainland stocks. But I must admit you've got me wondering. A wall that didn't used to exist, a closed-in attic, and a coin from the time in question. That's certainly reason enough to rouse one's curiosity, isn't it?"

It was.

The clock struck ten in the town square just as the doorbell rang. The museum was about to open to the public, and Priscilla didn't want anyone aware of the reasons behind her visit. "Mildred, I'm trusting you to keep this to yourself. Please." She tucked the coin into her purse and the book into the innocent-looking grocery satchel she'd brought along. The last thing she wanted to do was call attention to herself or the antiquated ledger.

"And that's exactly what I intend to do," Mildred assured her. She paused before opening the front door for visitors. "You don't know me yet, Priscilla."

Priscilla angled her head in acknowledgment.

"But you'll find that in everything I do, I have the best interests of the town at heart. I've lived here all my life. I've been part of this place from my first breath and will be until my last, although I'm hoping that won't be for some time yet," she admitted. "My father was a town historian, and his father before that, and I even have a Native American story keeper in my maternal heritage. Keeping some stories quiet and revealing others is in my blood, and I have no intention of setting this town on its ear any more than this series of newspaper articles has already done. But having said that"—she leaned closer and kept her voice soft—"I'd love to help solve this mystery. Not because of the money involved." Her shrug indicated that money wasn't a big deal to her. "But resolving a piece of island history would be wonderful, wouldn't it? Although there's always a vestige of romance in the unknown, and folks do like to let their imaginations wander, don't they?"

"There is a lure, I admit," Priscilla whispered, "but I'm a little bothered by the thought of treasure seekers at my cottage, snooping around the lighthouse property. Things like this weren't the norm on the Kansas prairie, and I'm not quite sure how to handle it."

Mildred smiled. It wasn't a harsh smile, but it wasn't an easy one like Trudy's either. "I understand. I would suggest day by day."

"There's something we can agree on." Priscilla moved to one side as Mildred opened the door to admit ticket holders. "Thank you, Mildred."

"You are most welcome."

Priscilla slipped out to the right while visitors came in through the left. She glanced around, deciding what to explore in town, then walked around the back of the museum on a hunch.

A flash of vibrant colors at the edge of the trees blocking the museum from the narrow road beyond confirmed her concerns. Unless Martha's Vineyard had become a summer home for rainbow-toned exotic birds, that flash of color in the trees meant Franklin Mayweather had hung around in his Hawaiian shirt, hoping to learn more.

A prickle of unrest raised the hairs along the nape of her neck. Why was he snooping? Was he a simple treasure seeker or something more sinister?

The quaintness of the island town mocked her thoughts, but even a farm girl understood the attraction of big money to some. Her property plus the possibility of a hidden stash of gold might make her quite the catch.

She pivoted and set a quick pace for the street. To find out more, she needed to know more, and there was no time like the present to do exactly that.

CHAPTER FOUR

Priscilla walked through the main doors of the brick-and-clapboard public library and paused. The streets were filling with sightseers and tourists, and the stately library seemed quiet by comparison. A nicely dressed woman with walnut-toned skin and soft black hair approached from the side while two younger women worked behind the broad wooden counter. "Can I help you?"

"I hope so." Priscilla waved a hand toward what she thought was east from inside the library. "I'm Priscilla Grant. I just moved into the Latham family lighthouse, and being new here, I'd love to find out some of the history."

"There's a lot of that going on lately," noted the woman with a laugh. "Welcome to town. I'm Clara Lopez, the head librarian. You're Miss Marjorie's niece."

"One of them."

The woman acknowledged the correction quickly. "Of course, there are several nieces from that side of the Latham family, but I meant you are *the* niece. The one who wasn't here with the rest of the family."

It seemed odd that she'd be brought up in conversation at all. Her confusion must have shown as Clara led the way deeper into the library. "Miss Marjorie often talked about her niece in Kansas when we had our little history chats or book club meetings."

"So far, so good."

"She mentioned that she hadn't seen you in a very long time."

"Also true, but why would she be talking to people about me?" It made no sense. Her aunt hadn't sent letters or called. Not even as much as an e-mail, to the best of Priscilla's knowledge. So why would she be a topic of conversation at all?

"Families are funny things," said Clara with a sympathetic smile. "If there's one thing I've learned being *on* the island but not really part of it because my family has only been here for two generations..."

Priscilla winced. "You're still considered an outsider?"

"To some," the librarian acknowledged, "but that's a life lesson in and of itself. Families have a way of falling apart and slipping back together, just like it was when the first colonists claimed this island. History has a way of repeating itself, doesn't it? Which makes it sad that this section of the library"—she tapped the small, hand-carved Local History plaque with one hand—"is underappreciated and underused. Until this week, that is. Since that article about the gold hit the stands, we've enjoyed an upswing in popularity. I only wish it wasn't going to be short-lived because big old libraries like this might become the relics of the past before we know it. Can I help you find something, Priscilla?"

Priscilla set her purse and the canvas bag with the logbook on the table, then thought better of it and picked them both back up again. What if someone had been listening at the museum? They could have followed her over here. She reached into her purse to reassure herself that the coin was still there, and when her fingers touched the smooth, cool edge, she breathed easier. She'd have to find a good hiding spot for the coin at the cottage, out of sight and hopefully out of mind. The implications of the coin and the professor's odd behavior were beginning to weigh on her, and when things weighed on her, Priscilla knew exactly what she needed.

Chocolate.

But that would have to wait, so as Clara pointed out the local history shelves, Priscilla bided her time. When Clara walked back to the midsection of the library, Priscilla slipped the coin into a zippered side pocket of her purse.

Then she slung the purse over her head to carry it cross-body, like a messenger bag, with the zippered side firmly tucked against her hip.

You're acting paranoid. Stop it.

She ignored the mental scolding. She was not paranoid, she decided as she examined the first of several volumes Clara had set on the table. She preferred the term *cautious.*

The carousel table had a computer station at each nook. She hadn't thought to bring her electronic tablet, so she logged into the public computer in front of her. First things first. She went to the *Boston Globe* site and brought up last week's article about the Revolutionary gold. Brandon Scott had researched his story well, and the Google search indicated that patrons had retrieved this page almost two dozen times in the past seven days. Add that to the people searching on their own devices and smartphones...

Brandon Scott had piqued a lot of interest in the hidden gold. As she read his article, Priscilla began to understand why.

The historical evidence seemed clear enough. Nathaniel Claybrook had stolen the money box from a Redcoat encampment. The reporter had tried to pinpoint the exact area, with little luck. Old British records named multiple encampments on the island and mainland, but none of the eighteenth-century names existed today. Howarth Knoll. Bennett's Field. Bainbridge Hook. Bardsley's Point. Holmes Cove. Morris Point. As she examined a library-cached historical map, not one of those names came up on the screen, and a Google search turned up nothing.

So where was the British army outpost that year? And how could she find that crucial information if the reporter was unable to pinpoint it? She had the trunk full of logbooks in the attic, but they were from more recent times, so how could they be of help?

She drew her brows together and went on reading.

Old records indicate the most likely spot for the encampment was Howarth Knoll, a strategic point along the northeast shore. If that was the military encampment, logic suggests that the gold was hidden within a mile or so based on the timing. The military log reports that Claybrook was caught within hours of the theft, questioned, jailed, and subsequently hung for his crime. Transporting a wooden box of gold coin would be no easy task, and even with some sort of wagon, roads were rough and a wagon would be noticeable. This leads me to believe he carried the heavy treasure, or possibly dragged it on some sort of pallet. That option would be less noticeable, especially if drawn through sand. Further research begs the question: Did Claybrook plan this theft? Or did he happen upon it left untended while British troops enjoyed too much Massachusetts ale?

A small map showed a wide outcropping into the water and set above. Scott pegged this as the most likely spot to be Howarth Knoll, and when Priscilla drew a line northwest with her finger, her cottage and the lighthouse stood just within the mile marker, making it as likely a place as any other.

Was Brandon Scott's research accurate? Assuming it was and she'd already found one piece of similar coin, where could the rest be?

She sat back and thought hard.

She opened up a new document and began making notes. She listed possible hiding places and realized she didn't know her new property at all, so that became first on the list. She needed to familiarize herself with the cottage, the lighthouse, the shore, the attic, and yes...she winced a little, remembering the size of those spiderwebs arching from beam to beam...the basement. Brandon Scott had uncovered the theft and poor Nathaniel's outcome. He'd been hanged by the angry British troops, and their payroll, desperately needed, was never recovered. Or if it was, no one was the wiser, and someone walked away with a great deal of money. If that was the case, there should be some local evidence. A grand house built on limited funds, or a pricey business endeavor.

Or…and this sent a shiver of consternation down her spine…it wasn't found, and it might be sitting on her land at this moment.

"How's it going?"

Priscilla clicked off the screen quickly when Clara's soft voice interrupted her search. "I didn't hear you come over."

"We wear soft-soled shoes so we don't disrupt patrons as they work or read," Clara explained. "You do know that you can borrow most of these books and take them home with you, right?"

"Aren't they research books?" Priscilla asked.

"The ones labeled as research have to stay here, but a lot of these are simply coded as history or local author, and those are all available to borrow. If that would be easier than sitting here," she added.

It made sense. She could take the books home, grab chocolate on the way, and see if she could unlock a little more information. As she stood, she asked, "The reporter who wrote the article about the hidden gold? Brandon Scott."

Clara nodded.

"Did he research things here? At this library?"

"He did, but he used other sources as well. And a lot of online information too. It's amazing how much you can access with a stroke of the keyboard, isn't it? Someday all this might become obsolete." Her gaze wandered the lovely library, and Priscilla looked around too.

"You think we might lose libraries? Seriously?"

Clara shrugged. "With the push toward a paperless society, many things are possible. Why have money tied up in big buildings with shelves and utility bills and payroll if folks can access it all for free on the Internet? A full 21 percent of our funding was slashed for the current year, and we're looking at more cuts for next year. That means less staff and fewer hours open. Once you start cutting services, it's like putting a nail in the coffin. Things tend to go downhill from there."

"I noticed that it's quiet in here," Priscilla replied. "I assumed it was because of summer and how busy the businesses are."

"It's a double-edged sword. The locals work extra hard to make money during the season, from May to October, and there's little time to visit the library when you're putting in long, hard days. And by the time things calm down, a lot of people head south for the winter. The decrease in population is sharp."

"But they pay yearly taxes on property. Surely that must help."

"It does, and we've actually had an increase in population, but people don't use the library the way they used to. Kids do online research at home, and there are Internet services that let you borrow books for free or a nominal cost." She breathed deeply. "Things are changing, and it's hard to see because I look around this historic library," she said, pointing to the old-time photos and mementos lining the walls of the history section, "and I see generations of people, dating back to Revolutionary times, helping their community learn and grow as one."

"I'd never thought of this," Priscilla admitted as they moved back to the main desk, centered in front of the double glass doors. She hadn't frequented her local library since Rachel graduated from high school. She bought books as needed, and other than a rare event, hadn't bothered stopping by the library for anything in years. "I'm going to make it a point to become a regular patron," she declared as one of the young women signed her up for a library card. "I can't believe that such a wonderful place might become a relic."

"We'd appreciate it," said the younger desk clerk. "If they cut payroll any more, we won't be able to offer the programs the town has come to love, and how sad would that be? It's almost as if there's a conspiracy to make us nonessential."

Conspiracy? Mystery? Hidden treasure? Why had she imagined Martha's Vineyard to be quiet and colloquial? Clearly a mistake on her part.

She accepted the books and bid the library staff goodbye. As she walked back toward her car through crowded streets, she pondered their words. Why would a community want a lovely place like the local library shut down? It made no sense. Especially if the population had increased over the last decade like she'd been told. That kind of an upswing should bring in more tax dollars, not less.

She turned up the walk to Candy's bakery and entered the busy shop. Tourists tended to flock to the left inside the bakery, eyeing the prepackaged items bearing nautical themes. Lighthouses, sailing ships, fishing rigs—the package designs were well-aimed toward a come-and-go public. The right side of the shop held a dozen café-style tables with four chairs each. Like yesterday, several tables were filled with locals.

It wasn't that they looked different, she realized, but they sounded different, a little more "Boston" than the opposite side of the room. And they weren't in a rush to go anywhere or do anything as they sipped their coffees and munched on sweet goods from the bakery counter.

"Next?"

Priscilla moved forward, and the sprightly woman behind the counter smiled. "You're back! The gals must have liked the cream puffs."

"You remember me from yesterday with how busy you are?" Priscilla was surprised and pleased. "That's quite impressive."

"Well, as soon as you left, I had three locals explain who you were, why you're here, and where you live," the woman told her. "You've created quite a stir because it's unusual for someone from outside to inherit one of the local properties. And such a nice one too! I'm Candy, by the way. Candy Lane. And this"—she swept the busy establishment with a smile of pure love—"is my place."

"It's so nice to meet you!" Priscilla exclaimed. "The gals loved the cream puffs, and I'm pretty sure I won Uncle Hugh's heart when we gave him his. And yes, folks tend to talk, no matter where they are, that's for certain," Priscilla said, and then she pointed to the tiered racks lining the wall behind Candy. "Would you wrap me up one of those cranberry muffins there, without nuts today, but I also need two chocolate chip cookies to assuage my growing need for chocolate."

The woman lifted a muffin with a wax paper wrap and nestled it into a bag while another clerk did the same with the two cookies. "Here you go. That will be three dollars and fifty cents."

A small price to pay for her breakfast and nerve-soothing combo.

She handed over the money, and as Candy handed Priscilla her change, she asked, "Do you run the counter often? That's a little unusual, isn't it?"

"There are two ways to look at that," Candy assured her. "I oversee all the early baking and make sure everything is up to snuff when we open those doors, but if I spend my whole life in the kitchen, I miss out on so much. It's a treat to be out here, meeting people and greeting the customers." As she handed Priscilla the twin bags, she leaned a little closer. "And I do love to chat with folks. The locals keep me up-to-date on everything that's going on..."

"Like quests for gold and new folks in town."

She laughed lightly, and Priscilla decided she liked the baker. And someone with their fingers on the pulse of everything going on could prove valuable in her quest for information.

"Well, I'm mostly laughing at the gold-diggers and treasure seekers, but the plus side of that is every one of them gets hungry and most have a sweet tooth. So if they're hunting along this side of the island, they'll likely stop in here and buy a few of this or a box of that. So let the quest for old gold begin!"

That was a smart way of looking at the current situation. Priscilla nodded in quick agreement as she pocketed her change. "Good for the imagination and great for the economy."

"Exactly."

Priscilla turned to leave as more people streamed through the heavy glass door. Three sets of guilty eyes from the locals' side of the bakery darted from her down to the tabletop holding their coffees and a selection of cookie crumbs. She kept moving, exiting through the open door.

She'd never been the new girl in town. She'd been part of the fabric back home, woven into the warps and weaves of the Midwest tapestry, but here she was an anomaly.

She didn't like being singled out because then she had to wonder what they were saying. What they might be thinking. And wasn't that silly because why would she care?

Rachel's ringtone sounded. Priscilla withdrew the phone as she approached her car. "Hi, darling. How are you?"

"I'm fine, but I wish you wouldn't turn off your phone," Rachel scolded instantly. "I've been trying to reach you, and it went right to voice mail."

"Rachel, you know it's impolite when people allow personal phones to interrupt meetings, so I turned if off like anyone would do. Simple courtesy, my dear. And now I've turned it back on, and here you are."

"You had meetings? With whom?"

Of course she'd want to know, but there was really no reason she shouldn't know. And yet it almost made Priscilla feel like she needed to report her comings and goings. "The town historian, and then I had a research session at the library."

"Are you bored, Mom? Because you can always come back home. That option is open as long as you don't sell the farm."

Bored? With all the hints of old money and new puzzles surrounding her? And the constant sound of the ocean, lapping the shore to her left?

"I'm the opposite of bored, Rachel. I'm beyond intrigued by how amazing this place is. You'll love it, and you'll wonder why we didn't move east long ago."

"Dad would have never given up his farm."

That was absolute truth.

"And I loved growing up on the farm. It was home, Mom."

Priscilla heard the whisper of guilt-inducing whine in her daughter's voice and chose to ignore it. "And now I've got a new home here, and it's delightful. And the pièce de résistance? A fresh cranberry muffin in my hand."

"That's the shining moment of your day?"

"It is so far," Priscilla declared. "Listen, darling, I've got a lot to do, but I will love showing you around when you head this way. After I've found my way around, of course."

"I love you, Mom." Rachel's sigh indicated it might be a little difficult to love her mother at this moment, but Priscilla let that go too.

"Love you too! Bye!"

She settled herself into the driver's seat of her car, newly determined. Rachel didn't think she'd make it here. Rachel didn't see her as a strong person.

The realization hurt, more so because it held a grain of truth.

She'd always wanted to be a strong person, and in some ways she was. Being a farm wife, managing the books, and helping with birthings and lambings—none of that was easy. And she'd been an excellent 4-H leader, thank you very much. But for several decades, she'd been repeating her life, season by season, until the years blurred behind her.

No more.

She couldn't let Rachel's doubts undermine her new chances. She'd been in a low-energy state back on the farm. For months after losing Gary, just getting up and putting one foot in front of the other pained her. Soul-weary pain, realizing she was absolutely, totally alone on a two-hundred-acre farm with nothing to do but watch the wind blow through dried, brown plants.

Her soul had felt like those plants. Old and dry and dusty.

Now it didn't.

The sea wind touched her cheeks and her brow through the open car window. She watched the wind push through banks of green grasses, making them bend and wave along the dunes.

She'd faced her own personal Rubicon, burying her husband so early. They'd had so many plans. To travel, to see things, to sell the farm and enjoy some time together to just be.

But Gary hadn't really wanted to sell the farm, and as years ticked by, she realized he might never reach that point. Now the matter was moot.

She squared her shoulders and eased out of the parking spot. She steered the car down the narrow lanes of the lot. Before she turned on to the road, she stuck her hand into one of the white bakery sacks, but she didn't reach for the one containing the almost-healthy cranberry muffin. She went straight for the chocolate because no matter what Rachel thought or what those townsfolk were hobnobbing about in that bakery, she intended to "make it," just like Mary Tyler Moore had in that super cute show way back.

She might not look like the actress, but she embodied that same indomitable, hat-tossing spirit, and no one was going to take that away from her.

She headed east toward the bluffs, munching a chocolate chip cookie as she went, and felt instantly better until she crested a rise and saw a crowd of strangers poking around her property. One person reached out and boldly tried the door as if to go into the cottage. *Her* cottage!

Priscilla pulled on to the shoulder, screeched to a halt, and jumped out of the car.

CHAPTER FIVE

W hat are you doing?" Priscilla demanded as she raced across the curved country road. With the way these people had parked, she couldn't even access her own driveway. "Who are you? Get away from my door!"

The man on the porch pulled back, but she'd seen him grab the handle and turn it as if he had a right to be there. "We heard the lighthouse was abandoned."

"You heard wrong." She braced her hands on her hips and stared him down. "Who are you, and what is your business here? And even if the cottage *were* empty, it belongs to someone, doesn't it? Everything," she scolded in her best Sunday school teacher voice, "belongs to someone."

"You live here, and you haven't heard there might be gold hidden someplace on the eastern shore?" asked a woman. Doubt darkened her words. "Then I don't think this can really be your place."

Now she had to justify her presence to complete strangers? What kind of town was this? "I can call the police and have them run you off. Maybe that will be more convincing. Hey, you! You, there!" She stormed across the yard edging the road as two young men—teens, she thought—came creeping around the lighthouse's curve, poking and prodding a metal detector along the bottom. "Get out of here. This is private property!"

The boys looked up, exchanged glances, and paid her absolutely no attention.

The sound of a car engine approached, and when it came over the rise, she recognized the crisp red stripe against the bright white paint. The Coast Guard vehicle came to a quick halt, blocking the two cars parked haphazardly in her driveway.

Gerald O'Bannon climbed out, looking tall, strong, and very authoritative, and Priscilla was never so glad to see an official-looking person in her life. He aimed a calm look of understanding her way, lightened by just enough humor to say he wasn't worried about the strangers lurking around her house. Then he aimed a darker look at the insurgents. "Are you having a welcome-to-the-island party, Mrs. Grant? I must have missed my invitation in the mail." He scowled from person to person as he turned, scouring the area. "Have any one of you people been invited on to this property by Mrs. Grant?"

Several of the trespassers exchanged nervous looks. The boys tried to creep backward now that Gerald was on the scene.

The man who'd tried her door was now leaning against a car with careless nonchalance. "We were told the place was vacant."

"Vacancy doesn't give people the right to trespass, does it?" The captain folded his arms across his broad chest and braced his legs apart, just a little. Enough to show strength and an unflappable attitude.

Another man spoke up. "It seems to me that if you're going to enjoy the added revenue of setting up a series of articles about buried treasure, then you have to put up with the inconveniences that go along with it."

"I most certainly do not." Priscilla faced the man fully and couldn't quite believe those words had come out of her mouth. She wouldn't call herself timid, exactly, but she'd always shied away from standing up for herself, perhaps because there was rarely need to do so back home. Now she was, and it felt good. "I'm not required to endure any inconvenience whatsoever, and if any of you trespass on my property again, I'll file charges against you. Take your crazy ideas and your quest for an easy paycheck elsewhere. There's nothing to be found here."

Guilt hit her midsection because it very well *might* be here, but these people didn't have the right to come on to her property and start breaking into her home, hunting for something that was clearly not theirs.

It's not really yours either.

Oh bother. She knew that, of course. And she'd never cared for money. Anyone on a farm realized that value lay in the acquisition of land, not necessarily in the annual exchange of goods. But if she did find the gold, as unlikely as that seemed, she could make sure it went to good use. Something noble and good for society as a whole or even for the island. And maybe a nice pair of walking shoes.

The people began edging away. Most of them didn't face Gerald or her directly. The boys slipped off down the beach, probably to annoy someone else with their quest. The adults quietly accessed their cars and left once Gerald eased his vehicle up the road to allow them room to maneuver. In less than three minutes, she was left alone with Gerald O'Bannon.

She took a deep breath and wasn't quite sure if she wanted to faint, cry, or invite the captain in for coffee.

Coffee won. "I've just come from the bakery, and I have a cranberry muffin I'd be glad to share and a chocolate chip cookie I might be more inclined to hide away."

His smile said he found her honesty amusing.

"Would you like a cup of coffee? And if you say yes, let me warn you that I have a deep curiosity about a town that spurs travelers to go on a treasure hunt and bother innocent people, then seems surprised when things like this happen."

He sighed, ran his hand across the nape of his neck, and followed her inside. She tucked her purse away, determined to hide the guinea in some obscure place before the end of the day, then came back into the kitchen. "Do you use cream, Captain?"

"Gerald, please. Just Gerald. Yes, to cream. And I want you to know, Mrs. Grant..."

"Priscilla. Please," she added, so she wouldn't sound bossy. Bossy middle-aged women were far too prevalent in farm country, and maybe everywhere, but she wanted to put the brakes on that trend. Somehow sounding bossy in a new place stepped over a boundary, like moving next to an airport and then complaining about the planes.

"Pretty name." He said it easily, not as if he was flirting with her, but as if he really thought it was a pretty name. "It's an island name. Did you know that?"

"I knew there were Priscillas before me, but while my mother loved history and Martha's Vineyard, she didn't bring up the subject of her family often. A simple mention tended to set my father off, and my mother preferred peace." She set the two coffees on the table. She didn't see a sugar bowl, so she poured sugar into one of Aunt Marjorie's mugs and added a spoon. "I wasn't born on the island."

"No, but your mother was, and it's nice that she gave you an old island name even though you were halfway across the country."

"I think it was her way of feeling connected to her roots here." She offered him a humorous look. "There certainly weren't any other Priscillas in our part of Kansas. None that I knew of anyway."

He laughed softly. "I expect not. Still, this whole lost gold thing wasn't set up by Tisbury or the island. The Vineyard is busy enough every summer and fall, so to deliberately try to make things crazier would be foolish. And with the exception of a small number of rich folks, almost everyone on the island makes their living off the tourist industry while quietly waiting for them all to leave."

"Seriously?"

He made a face. "Let me say there's a good share of people who like the island to themselves, but they're smart enough to know that five months of busyness supports their mortgage payments the rest of the year."

"Of course. This is very different, Cap—" She paused and corrected herself. "Gerald."

"I expect it is. I've never been to Kansas, but I grew up in Nebraska, and I understand the culture shock. And yet both places seem good. Different, but good."

"But will I get used to it?" she wondered out loud. She sipped her coffee, then pulled the muffin from its sack and broke off a piece, not worrying about a plate or napkin.

He laughed and broke off his own piece of the muffin. "Miss Tilly would be shocked by this."

"Who's Miss Tilly?"

"She runs the historic inn you pass at the edge of the village."

"The Colonial Inn? With the stunning front porch, gorgeous hanging baskets, and gardens to die for?"

"That's the one. She's obsessive about protocol, and eating a muffin off the table would offend her sensibilities."

"Tell me you're not serious."

His expression said he was.

Priscilla put her chin in her hands and frowned. "Is she representative of the town as a whole? If so, I have a slim chance of fitting in here."

He laughed once more, and she decided she liked his laugh. It wasn't too loud or too soft, and when he smiled or laughed, he seemed sincere. "For the record, this island is such a hodgepodge of new and old that anyone can fit in here. We have crazy young artists and sage old folks and a few farms and great businesses. The influx of people has made things tough on some," he acknowledged as he stood. He picked up his captain's hat from the table. "It drove already high real estate prices higher, and that's made it hard on a lot of folks. If your house is paid for, but you can't afford to pay the property tax on it to continue living here, that's a raw deal in anyone's book. And if you're a lifelong resident but can't afford to buy even a simple house, that's tough too."

"I never thought of that. Of how much the taxes are."

"They can tell you the full story at the town hall. Marjorie was the kind of woman who thought ahead in everything she did. If she's paid for this year, then you've got a break. That will give you time to figure things out."

Taxes were a fact of life. She knew that, and their farm was worth a lot of money back in Kansas. But if she used that money to pay her annual taxes, what would she have to live on?

"I've worried you." He sounded sorry.

She shook her head. "More mad at myself than worried because I've only just realized part of my situation here. I was so excited about inheriting the lighthouse that my mother loved that I never gave a thought to two things." She propped her arms on the table, dismayed. "First, that a single woman who owns high-priced real estate needs to be more savvy than one who retires to a simple two-bedroom ranch house in Kansas."

"You're certainly a property owner of means now."

"And second, that I never even thought about the tax structure here. But I'm forewarned now, and I'll check it out online. Today

I'm going to stay right here, do a little historical research, and guard my house."

"If you need help, call me." He handed her a card with his name and phone number. "I'm only ten minutes away, and I was coming by this morning to tell you that when I saw the circus outside."

"Thank you, Gerald." She took the card and saw him to the door. "I appreciate it. And your timing was perfect."

"Purely accidental, but I'm not unwilling to take the credit." He lifted his hat slightly in salute. "I'll see you soon, no doubt."

"Of course." She watched as he walked to his car. When he'd pulled away, she took her keys outside and backed her car into the driveway. She left it there rather than in the side-facing garage near the road. No one would make the mistake of thinking the house uninhabited with a car parked in the driveway. At least no normal person would make that assumption, but she was beginning to wonder if treasure hunting relieved folks of their common sense.

She'd meant to check out the churches in town that morning but had spent more time at the library than she intended. That would give her a reason to drive into town (and get another one of those amazing muffins) in the morning.

She set up her laptop on the table and sent her cousins a group message before she got to work, inviting them for supper. They'd be able to guide her through the logistics of fitting in. She would lay all these practical questions and thoughts at their feet.

If she was going to serve dinner, she needed to buy some food, so she went to the Stop&Shop and filled a cart. Running to the store wasn't her favorite thing to do, so why not stock up?

When she arrived back home with enough supplies to fully stock her shelves and fridge, there were five No Trespassing signs tucked along her roadside property line and a note on her front door.

> A temporary inconvenience while the treasure hunters mob the island. I put four on the water side as well. Hope it helps.
>
> Gerald

His kind gesture made her pause, and her eyes filled unexpectedly. Priscilla wasn't a crier for the most part. Oh, a good Christmas commercial could make her reach for tissues, and she loved sweet movies with happy endings, but the Midwest frowned on crybabies, and so did she.

But for the kind captain to take the time to help her in a new setting and a most unusual situation touched her heart. No one had looked out for her in a long time. It felt good, and not as if he were intruding, but as if he were simply being nice.

She took the groceries inside, put things away, and had an early dinner ready for the gals when they arrived at five thirty. "I know it's early," she told them, "but I had so much to talk to you about, to ask about, and I couldn't wait another half hour."

"The only person in town who would take offense at an early supper is Miss Tilly, but she's so full of quirky things to say that time passes quickly when you're at the inn," Joan assured her. "As for myself, I'm happy with an early dinner. I was over at

Sheila Weller's helping with cranberries today, and I'm ready for food."

"She was at the museum yesterday for the History Tea," Priscilla said as she set out a robust lettuce salad. "She seemed nice."

"Nice and capable, my kind of woman," remarked Gail as she wavered between adding more salad or more roasted potato casserole to her plate. The potatoes won. "I'll have to find out how you make these potatoes, Priscilla. They smell amazing!"

"Midwest meets the shore." Priscilla smiled. "I'm glad to share the recipe, although I think it actually started right here on the island. My mother said her mother used to make these for every family dinner."

"Aunt Charlotte's recipe." The cousins exchanged troubled looks.

"No wonder they smell so good," said Gail, but she didn't look happy when she said it. She looked kind of woebegone, and Priscilla hadn't used a word like woebegone in, well...ever.

"I've made these for dozens of potlucks back home, and they've never made anyone sad before, much less three people at once." Priscilla braced her hands on the back of a chair that needed a couple of screws tightened. She'd have to scour around and find a screwdriver in the morning. "Why do you all look so down?"

"The last time your mother and Aunt Marjorie spoke was over a pot of these potatoes."

They fought over potatoes? "You're kidding."

Joan shook her head. "It was a family Thanksgiving, and we were all just little girls, but there was a terrible row."

"She means a fight," Trudy cut in.

"But not a real fight, like with punches," added Gail. "I'd prefer the term strong disagreement."

"Over potatoes?"

"No. Well." Joan drew her brow down over her nose. "The potatoes weren't the cause, but they were a catalyst."

"An accessory." Trudy offered a solemn nod. "It all began with Uncle Stew."

"Stuart Latham, the congressman?" She'd read about him in a Wikipedia article about Massachusetts.

"Not s-t-u." Joan corrected her. "S-t-e-w. He was a fisherman and not really an uncle at all. He was a good fellow in some ways, but a little light-fingered on the financial end of things."

"A thief? Aunt Marjorie and my mother had a lifelong falling out over a thief?"

"Not a thief, per se," Gail began to explain, but she took the time to take her plate out to the waterfront veranda. Priscilla filled her plate and followed quickly because who in their right mind fought over potatoes?

"He was a thief and a finagler to boot," said Joan, "and he tried to charge your father double for a ferry ride when there was a storm coming. He called it supply and demand, but in reality it was price gouging of folks who needed a safe place to stay. Your father called him on it, and then Stew told him that your mother never meant to marry him in the first place because she was stuck on Billy Manders, whose family ran the whale watches back in the day. Your father took one look at your mother's face and decided what Stew said was true, and he up and left the island."

"Hightailed it right back to Kansas and wouldn't spend Thanksgiving here."

"He left me and my mom here?" Why didn't she remember it this way? She remembered flying back to Kansas with her mother but had no recollection of why her father wasn't with them.

"He did, and our parents downplayed it because it was Thanksgiving and we'd all intended to go to church together, then have our turkey dinner."

"Only Aunt Marjorie couldn't let it go because she had a crush on Billy herself, and he never paid her one bit of attention, but the week your parents came here, Billy stopped by half a dozen times to see your mother."

"No." Her infatuated aunt really thought that Charlotte had a thing with another man, not her father? Oh, the blindness of young love!

"Yes." Gail looked absolutely certain. "When your dad left, Aunt Marjorie held it in until dinner, then let your mother know that she'd been pining for Billy for years and that he didn't care for her or anyone else except your mother."

"And the family became divided over a pot of the best New England-style roasted potatoes I've ever had. Until now," Trudy added. She sighed as she chewed a morsel of potato mixed with bits of cheese, ham, onion, and bacon.

"The family really thought Billy was here to flirt with my mother?" What a preposterous story because her mother had distinctly told her something quite different about Billy Manders.

"Well, we know the truth of the matter *now*." Joan stressed the timing. "But back then such things weren't talked about, and now we all realize that Billy had found a true, Christian confidante in your mother and was able to talk to her. Somehow we managed to turn the blessing of friendship into a family feud, and I think Aunt Marjorie had a lot of years of regret under her belt."

"My mother was a very comfortable person to be around." Her mother had been a kindly, warm person, the kind that folks gravitated to in any situation. "But she wasn't one to grovel for forgiveness. In fact, she often mentioned that when the good Lord was handing out New England pride, the Lathams may have gotten in line twice."

"My dad used to say that too." Gail smiled softly. "When Aunt Marjorie realized the foolishness of her mistake, she felt dreadful because the whole fight amounted to a teen girl's crush and cantankerous behavior and unrequited love."

"This has Arthur Miller and Shakespeare written all over it. The foolishness of melodramatic youth."

"It sure does. The sad part is why they let it go on so long," said Trudy. "It's always better to forgive and move on, isn't it?"

Priscilla nodded.

"We've never served these potatoes since that day." Gail must have decided that was reason enough to take a second helping and did exactly that. "Aunt Marjorie said it brought back too many bad memories. When she got older and understood the truth of the matter, she realized how her thoughtlessness had messed up a family. Yours and hers."

"She never married?"

"No." Joan shrugged. "If you knew her, you'd know that was probably for the best. She had a kind heart and a bulldog growl, and menfolk take kindly to one but not the other."

"I'm astounded." Priscilla wiped her mouth with her napkin. "So why leave me the property when she and my mother died still at odds?"

"Because it was the right thing to do." Joan met her gaze, and when Priscilla frowned, she nodded. "She knew she'd cheated you out of summers on the shore, out of family that would have loved you, out of a childhood and choices you could have made, given the chance. Leaving the property to you was her way of making amends."

"That's a lot of amends." Priscilla swept the open yard leading to the water with a long, slow look. "This place is worth a fortune."

All three nodded.

"And you don't hate her for leaving it to me?" Priscilla had wondered about this, and it seemed like a good moment to ask. "And not splitting it between the three of you?"

"How could we split it?" Trudy drew her brows together, then widened her eyes, surprised. "You mean sell it and split the money?"

"It's a common enough practice," Priscilla noted.

"Not here. And not with Latham lands," Gail assured her. "No, Aunt Marjorie did the very thing she should have, and that was to heal old wounds."

A multimillion dollar piece of property went a long way toward that, Priscilla decided.

"And bringing you back to the island. To the Vineyard. Because you fit here, Priscilla."

You fit here.

The words struck home in one way and not in another, but as the three women gazed at her, for the first time since crossing to the island, Priscilla felt like she could fit here. And that was the best feeling of all. "It's beautiful, sure enough."

All three cousins nodded assent.

"And I am in love with Vineyard Haven."

"It's precious, isn't it?" Joan eyed her potatoes with longing and then set the plate aside. "I've eaten far more than I should have, but those potatoes have been nothing more than a memory for me for decades. It's so good to have them again. And you," she added. She leaned forward and pressed her hand to Priscilla's arm. "To have you here makes this whole thing perfect. But what about your daughter? That had to be hard, to leave her in Kansas."

"It was." Priscilla turned her face into a sea-washed breeze and breathed the fresh, salt air. "When we lost Gary, there was all the fuss and bother you normally get when a good man dies. And then there was nothing. Oh, my friends would stop by on occasion, but being on farms, and having busy lives, and all but one of them still working with years before retirement, meant I was alone much of the time."

"Not a good circumstance in trying times," Joan noted.

"No." Priscilla bit back a sigh. "But a lesson to be learned. I'd spent so much of my life waiting to retire with Gary and do things that I rarely did anything other than the daily normal. And that was over. Rachel's a high-level project manager for a telecommunications corporation in Kansas City, so while she was grieving far away, she was keeping busy. And I wasn't. This"—she swept a glance over the lighthouse and yard—"is better by far."

"Does she miss you?"

Priscilla weighed that question carefully. Rachel was a dear daughter, but the fact was she probably missed the status quo more than her mother. "She misses that normal has been changed. I think she took comfort in the fact that with her dad gone, I was there on the farm, in that big old house, watching over things so they'd look the same when she came to visit now and again. I needed more than that, you know?" All three women nodded. "I needed to start over, so when the lawyer's letter came about this place, I knew it was my chance. I cite that as day one of my new adventure. Rachel sees it a bit differently."

"When she comes to visit, we'll show her the best of the best," declared Trudy. "She'll fall in love with the island and never want to leave. Did it take long to sell your house in Kansas?"

"I haven't listed it yet."

Silence descended over the group as all three women stared at her. "You might not stay?" Trudy's eyes had gone wide. Now they narrowed in concern. "You might go back, Priscilla?"

"Really?" Gail whispered. "But you've only just arrived."

Joan didn't shame her. Instead she set her plate down and folded her hands. "I think that's absolutely brilliant, myself."

"Going back?" Gail looked at Joan as if she might have lost a screw or two along the way, but her words surprised Priscilla too.

"Not going back, but leaving doors open." Joan fluttered a hand toward Gail and Trudy. "How was Priscilla to know what awaited her here? How did she know if she'd like it? What if she'd sold everything off, come here, and it was awful?"

"But it's not," Gail reasoned.

Trudy nodded. "It's not even the least bit awful," she added. "It's amazing, so of course you'll stay."

"Because who wouldn't?" Gail asked as she lifted her plate off the table. "It's a wonderful place to live."

"If you don't mind winter storms."

"And the occasional hurricane-force blow," added Trudy as if that was a sales point.

"And tens of thousands of tourists every summer and fall."

Priscilla leaned forward as her cousins continued listing good reasons to stay and a few to think about. "Here's what I know."

They stopped talking to listen.

"I've never been to a more beautiful place. I've never met a more wonderful bunch of family in my life."

All three ladies preened at her words.

"And I'm staying put here until God tells me otherwise. And so far, so good."

"I'm so glad, Priscilla." Joan got up, crossed the veranda, and hugged her. "So glad you're here and that you're willing to take a chance."

Priscilla raised her glass of tea. "To new beginnings."

"Salute!" The four cousins clinked glasses together, smiling.

By the time the gals left, the kitchen was neat and tidy, and the sun had long since set. Priscilla went to bed tired and happy, as if talking to her cousins had added a layer of concrete to her plans. Having them here, as neighbors, family, and friends, was making this choice much easier than she thought it would be, and that was reason to give thanks right there.

CHAPTER SIX

Priscilla blinked and peered at the clock radio on the table beside her bed. The soft red glow read 3:42, and silence filled the air. Then what had awakened her?

She sat up, listening.

Nothing.

She lay back down, annoyed with herself, then spotted a light, the one she thought she'd imagined in a dream.

This wasn't the arced beacon of the lighthouse. This was the narrow, ground-hugging beam of a high-powered flashlight, pointing here and there across her property.

Someone was out there.

Chills raced down her spine. Goose bumps prickled her arms, and every tiny hair on the nape of her neck rose up in protest.

She reached for her cell phone to notify the police and then realized she'd left it in the kitchen, a habit Rachel scolded her for on a regular basis. Did she dare creep across the house and retrieve the phone? Would she be seen? Was this person dangerous? Or was it simply a local picking his or her way home up the beach in the dark?

Common sense warred with logic. If she called the police on every little thing, she'd be labeled a nag. And what did she know of

Vineyard customs? Maybe folks walked home with flashlights all the time. Maybe she was the abnormal one, applying Midwestern reason to New England tradition.

The light bounced, swept and bounced again, then turned as if heading for the house.

And her.

She swallowed hard, frozen in place, suddenly wondering why she'd left the humdrum existence of her Kansas farm. She knew all the nuances there. She knew folks, and they knew her, and no one went walking about the country roads with a flashlight at three in the morning.

The light paused. So did her breath. Then the light turned, moving east along the yard, then the beach until it disappeared from sight.

She breathed then, loud and deep, several times. She tried to contain the adrenaline rush to no avail.

Someone had been out there. Who? Why? What were they doing here?

Either they'd come from the east and gone back that way, or they'd continued their quest by moving down the curve of the shoreline, heading toward East Chop.

Perhaps they were walking a dog?

That thought made her feel better. Lots of folks walked dogs, and maybe she had an insomniac neighbor. The light hadn't come close to the house, not really. And it had paused here and there, like someone waiting for a pooch on a leash.

She moved to the window now that the light was gone and tipped back the shade, half-drawn.

There was nothing out there.

Now, her conscience scolded. *But there was something out there two minutes ago.*

She looked east and saw nothing. She yawned, thought about going back to bed, then decided that would be futile. The heart-rush had steamrolled her into a full-on state of wakefulness. She'd never fall back asleep now. Dawn would peek over the horizon in an hour. Why not do some research and get a jump on the day before driving into town?

She'd decided she would leave the coin with Mildred rather than risk losing it. If it was in Mildred's possession, then no one need know it was found at her cottage, at least not until the gold was discovered or the furor died down.

She'd see Mildred, stop by the bakery, and check out the other local businesses. She would take time to browse those rows of cute, small shops and get a true feel for the town. If she stayed...

The shocked look on her cousins' faces had shown her how much they wanted her to stay, and that had warmed Priscilla all the way to her toes. So if she *did* make Tisbury her home, she wanted to feel like she was part of the town, not a resident visitor.

She switched on a light, made a stout mug of coffee, and opened her laptop. With a few flicks of the wireless mouse, she maximized pages of Martha's Vineyard history. A little research and a couple of cups of Colombian coffee were the perfect way to start her day. And if she got tired midday, she'd grab a nap and not feel the least bit guilty. And that wasn't a bad thing at all.

"Mrs. Grant?"

Priscilla turned when a distinctly New England voice called her name as she walked along Main Street about six hours later. "Yes?"

"Hello." A woman walked toward her from one of the cozy streets leading to the harbor. The street was lined with old-fashioned facades and small shops vying for tourist dollars, one after the other. "I'm Teresa Claybrook. I run Misty Harbor Tours just up the road apiece."

"Near the ferry landing."

"Yes."

"I saw that on my town map app," Priscilla explained and raised her smartphone as evidence. "Isn't it wonderful to have such information at our fingertips?"

Teresa laughed. "It really is. I wanted to welcome you to Martha's Vineyard. Your historic property is one of the sweet sights of the island, and I was so glad to know it wasn't going to sit empty for long."

"Uninhabited houses are like an invitation to trouble, aren't they?" She tried not to think of her house back in Wheatfield, but the push to make a decision was always at the back of her mind.

Teresa nodded.

"The one thing I've found in my few days here is that this island is filled with wonderful sights," Priscilla went on. "The small towns. Gingerbread homes, the harbors, the shops, the boats, and open fields. It seems like every corner I turn has something charming to see. And you said your name was Claybrook? Are you one of Nathaniel's descendants?"

"I am."

Priscilla did the mental math and frowned. "Except..."

Teresa raised her left hand. "Let me rephrase that. I'm actually a direct descendant of his brother, Edward. Nathaniel never had any children because he died young."

"So my research indicated." Priscilla said the words easily, but this woman had been about to claim a relationship she didn't truly own. Why? To gain favor?

Teresa lifted one shoulder. "Most folks don't know that Nathaniel never made it through his face-off with the British. They hear 'gold,' and the rest of the historical facts fly out the window, so my family is the nearest thing to a direct descendant that we've got here. And the history link encourages business." She gave Priscilla a frank smile. "I heard you'd moved to town, and I was wondering if we could use your lighthouse as an official tour stop. I'd love to add it to my brochures. We've always done drive-bys of all the best old places, including the lighthouses. And we swing by several fancy new spots people of means have erected on the island, but my customers like the historic spots best. It would be great if we could do more than a simple drive-by with yours."

An official tour stop? Priscilla pursed her lips, considering. "You mean a tour bus? Full of people?"

"A minibus with about eighteen people at a time. They'd have a few minutes to get off the bus, wander around, and take pictures. We schedule two or three tours per day during the season."

"Did you do this with Aunt Marjorie?" If she had, surely Priscilla would have heard about it, wouldn't she? Or noted something in the house pertaining to being a tourist stop?

"We were in the discussion phase."

Hmm...

"Marjorie was getting on in years, and I think she worried about the disturbance," Teresa continued. "Understandable, of course. But a younger person like you might appreciate sharing the richness of historical depth we enjoy here."

She'd pretty much called Priscilla young and designated the lighthouse as a prime spot, but on a historic island filled with prime tourist stops, it all kind of sounded like window dressing. Priscilla shook her head regretfully. "I appreciate history as much as the next person, but I like privacy too. Let's leave it at the drive-by visits for the moment, Teresa. I need time to get my bearings," she explained. "I want to get to know the town, and I've already had my share of surprise visitors poking around my house day and night."

"People are poking around?" Teresa lifted her left brow. Interest sparked in her golden-brown eyes. "At night?"

Priscilla rued her words. She didn't need everyone in town knowing that much attention was being paid to her new property, and she didn't want to stir up more talk. She extended her hand, ready to end this conversation. "It's very nice to meet you, Teresa, and thank you for thinking of me and the lighthouse. We'll talk again once I've been here a while."

"Of course." Disappointment shaded the younger woman's voice, but she recovered quickly and accepted the handshake. "It's a beautiful property you've got there, Mrs. Grant. A lovely combination of history and mystery, the very thing our tourists love."

"As do I!" She flashed Teresa a quick smile before resuming her walk to the museum at a brisk pace. On an island of historical note and open places, of course folks would love to stop by and see the lighthouses up close. Lighthouses drew people.

But why would she approach a perfect stranger who had just moved into town? Priscilla had always heard that true New Englanders were more reserved in their manner, but she realized there was probably another factor at work here. A good business-woman did what she had to do to get by in a place where she was required to make twelve months of money in a six-month time frame. Priscilla respected that.

But that wasn't about to include a twice daily stop at Priscilla's lighthouse for a dozen-and-a-half gold-seeking strangers.

She knocked lightly on the museum's back door. Mildred opened it quickly, saw her, and smiled as she stretched the door wider. "Either you love history more than most, or you've got a secret you're dying to tell."

"How do you know that?" Priscilla whispered as Mildred shut the door and then moved around the kitchen and shut the two small windows. "I had to come before you opened to give you this. For posterity. I really don't like having it on my property. I'm afraid it's going to turn into a major draw when people discover where it was found. Unless we can keep it a secret, but it's probably too late for that with the professor knowing." She handed over the gold guinea. "Here."

"For the museum?"

Priscilla nodded.

"This is a wonderful donation, Priscilla, but people will figure out where it came from. The professor is not exactly discreet."

"I expect you're right, but if they know I've donated the coin, then they'll assume there are no others. Don't you think?"

Mildred shook her head. "They're more likely to assume that you've got a huge chest of treasure hidden somewhere on that bluff and come digging."

Well that was the exact opposite of Priscilla's goal. "I don't want hordes of strangers mucking about, peeking in windows and testing my doors like I had yesterday. Things of this sort are not common in Kansas, let me tell you."

Mildred laughed and then stopped when she read the unhappy look on Priscilla's face. "Nor do they generally happen here, although history has a way of creeping up on us when we least expect it."

"I helped with Pioneer Days back in Wheatfield, so I know that's true. But this treasure-hunting craze doesn't want to leave me a moment's peace, Mildred. How can I fix it?"

"I have an excellent solution."

Priscilla perked up. "You do?"

Mildred nodded. "Find the gold yourself."

Treasure hunt? *Her?*

"If you find the gold, then you instantly put a stop to all the nonsense going on now. Mystery over, life goes on."

"I have no need for that kind of money." Mildred's advice did make a great deal of sense though. "But you're right. If the cache is found, then the hunt is over, and I can go back to a quiet, reserved existence and get to know my new town and home better."

"Well, there's something quite boring about the thought of a quiet and reserved existence." Mildred looked positively dour as she repeated the words. "Life's too short to be too quiet or too reserved in my book, but to each his own, I suppose. If I were you, I'd begin at the library, searching town records. And check out the Whaling Museum, it's full of random facts. Do you have Internet at the cottage?"

"I had it installed while I was traveling here. The lawyer saw to it along with turning on the other utilities."

"There's a database online that was uploaded from old microfiche files, and maybe you'll garner a clue there. There's a link to it through the Tisbury town site, under the History tab. Although if that reporter wasn't able to find the answers, maybe the answers don't exist."

"Or he had a job to do and limited time," Priscilla mused. "I don't think I like this, and I'm pretty sure I'm not one bit cut out for it, but I do think you've come upon the right idea. If we solve the mystery, the nonsense grinds to a stop."

"Exactly." Mildred wrote a few notes on a pad of paper and then tore off the sheet. "Here are some web addresses I've used to find information on old Massachusetts history. And they should link you to more specific sites."

"Perfect."

"Well, here's the thing," Mildred went on. "If Nathaniel really hid the gold here, by rights it should still be here. Unless it was found and quietly taken, but that would have been news even a hundred years ago. Everyone has always known about the gold but figured it was long gone. Even back then, if someone had suddenly turned up decidedly more well off than they'd been a few weeks before, people would talk."

"They always do."

"Which is why I think it's still hidden out there someplace. As for finding it, well." Mildred made a little face of regret. "Good luck, Priscilla."

She didn't want luck, Priscilla decided as she headed toward the library.

It felt good to have the rare coin out of her possession. That might seem cowardly to others, but the thought of that coin and what it might mean had weighted her down. Mildred would put it somewhere safe, and her suggestion to settling the problem by finding the treasure made perfect sense if Priscilla happened to be a detective.

But she was no such thing. She wasn't even an amateur sleuth, although she'd loved reading Agatha Christie as a girl. Who hadn't? And if Miss Marple could take on the capital crimes of her hometown, surely Priscilla Grant could find one large, bulky chest of gold.

The thought unnerved and invigorated her as she walked into the library again. She set her phone for a two-hour silent alarm, and when it buzzed a warning midday, Priscilla sat back, pleased with herself. She'd downloaded a complete family tree from a genealogy site and was amazed that it had few holes. Latham branches spread out in multiple directions, leading straight back to the first ships along the Massachusetts shore. Vignettes were tucked into various branches of the 'tree,' noting family accomplishments. A couple of mayors, two congressmen, and a state senator were labeled, as were three library patrons, a Broadway actress, and one nineteenth-century distant cousin who found himself jailed for some kind of moneymaking scheme.

"Are you done for today?"

Priscilla bookmarked her final page and slipped her small notebook into her purse as Clara approached. "I am. That's about all the sitting and neck-bending I can do at one time." She logged out of the computer and stood. "Now I'm off to investigate the town."

"Investigate?" Clara lifted her brows in surprise. "That's an odd term to use."

"I should have said *explore*," she told Clara, making a mental note to be more careful with her words. "I've been to a couple places, and I've managed to stop by the bakery every day, but I'd like to become acquainted with the rest of Vineyard Haven. I think a walking tour is in order on this beautiful day, don't you?"

"It's an ideal day for that, not too hot and not too breezy. Make sure you check out the Harbor Walk. It's filled with stands and kiosks in the summer, and some great artisans have displays there. And the Whaling Museum is there as well."

"I'd enjoy that. Thank you, Clara."

"A pleasure, Mrs. Grant."

It sounded odd to have everyone calling her Mrs. Grant here. Back home in Wheatfield, she was Priscilla. Or Gary's wife.

She swallowed an unexpected sigh that formed around the lump in her throat and hurried out.

Now and again it caught her like that. She'd be moving along, doing just fine, and memories and emotions would rise up to meet her, grabbing hold. She breathed deeply once she started walking, and the clean, fresh, ocean-breeze air helped. And that was another surprise, how the sea air invigorated her. Made her stronger.

She walked toward the business district, then altered her course to wander through the neighborhood streets and past the churches. She'd seen several old-fashioned steeples poking up through the trees, and Priscilla knew one thing: if she was going to find her place in Tisbury, she needed to find a church that felt right. With so many little towns on the island, one of them was bound to fit, but why not start here?

She'd walked several blocks of quaint neighborhoods and passed a couple of churches when a compact brick building caught her eye through the maple trees. She ducked along a narrow street, turned a corner, and found herself facing a red brick church.

It was small and well-kept, but not fancy. No big, flowing gardens marked the pathways, and there was something delightfully simple in the building's honest cleanliness and natural wood door. She climbed the steps near the street and approached the sign attached to the right of the broad door. Faith Fellowship All Are Welcome.

The sign listed service times, and then she spotted something else that made her add their service time to her phone calendar. In Cooperation with Other Area Churches, This Hall Will Provide Shelter for the Homeless from January 1 until May 1. For More Information call 206-555-2626.

A church that was also a homeless shelter? And why would there be homeless people in Martha's Vineyard?

She touched the sign with one hand, then stood back and snapped a picture of it with her phone.

As she turned, a small, shaggy, red-and-white dog darted along the road's edge, slaloming in and out of parked cars. He held his red, feathered tail high, like a flag waving in the breeze. When two cars entered the road from opposite directions, she called to the pooch, hoping to draw him up away from the street.

Her ploy worked but only after he'd crossed the narrow road away from her, then dashed back as if he'd just heard her command. She rushed toward the road as she saw the accident coming but could do nothing to prevent the outcome.

Brakes squealed from both directions. One car careened to the right into a stack of garbage cans from the nearby homes. The other car had nowhere to go. A solid thump made Priscilla's heart jump straight up in her chest. It beat wildly as she dashed across the thin grass into the street.

The dog lay sprawled on its side. It whimpered, moved its head, then laid its head back down.

And then he looked at her. Right at her. He perked up his ear as if he were trying to communicate with her, to tell her it would be all right.

It wasn't all right. She never should have said anything when she spotted the dog. If she'd stayed quiet, he might not have run into the road.

Tears filled her eyes, and this time she couldn't blink them back.

CHAPTER SEVEN

Is this your dog, ma'am?" The driver of the car that hit the dog stooped low, distraught. "I'm so sorry. He came out of nowhere, and the other car was right there. I'm so very sorry."

She shook her head because he wasn't her dog, and yet... what would become of the little fellow?

"He's a stray, I think."

The very New England male voice came from a different man over her shoulder. "He's been about since a while back, lookin' for a bit here and there. It's a sorry shame that it's come to this. He's a likable little fellow. Friendly like."

"It *is* a shame, Tyler." A woman crouched next to Priscilla. "But we can't leave him here, and my car is closest. Maybe Doc Morris will be able to do something."

"A vet bill for a stray don't seem reasonable, Ms. Jones, but it's your dollar."

Another voice joined the growing crowd forming along the road's edge. "I'd like to know who's going to do something about my car." A stout well-dressed woman had climbed out of the vehicle that took out the row of emptied garbage cans. "People are utterly irresponsible about their pets around here, and it's a dangerous nuisance. I suppose you'd like to cover my deductible, *hmm?*" She glared at Priscilla while Ms. Jones and Tyler carried on their own conversation next to the dog.

"We can't let lack of funds stand in the way of doing what's right."

"And the doc's got a good heart, that's for sure."

"Does this dog have an owner?" the angry woman demanded. "Someone needs to take responsibility for this. I could have been killed. We both could have been killed," she went on, indicating the other driver.

Should she call the police? Priscilla wondered. Would an accident with such minor vehicle damage require that? She didn't know and didn't really care because the first thing she needed to do was see to the injured pooch lying in the street.

"Now, Mrs. Banks." The older man adopted a conciliatory tone, kind of sweet but still firm. "It would take more than a few garbage cans to mess up a fancy rig like yours, and this little dog doesn't have an owner, to the best of my knowledge." Tyler faced the woman while Priscilla stroked the dog's silky head. "But I'm real glad you weren't hurt."

"Oh, good grief. That's all I need is sympathy from the riff-raff." She stomped back to her car, climbed in, put it into Reverse, then backed up and drove away.

Priscilla looked from the man's faded gray eyes to his patched, thin-seamed clothing. The woman's clothing was in better shape, but Priscilla was pretty sure a big veterinary bill wasn't in her budget either. "I'll pay the vet bill."

"What?" Ms. Jones drew back, surprised. "It's not your dog though. And the doc might not be able to do much."

"Well, the sooner we get him there, the sooner we'll know. Can you give us a ride?" She faced the woman directly. "I'll hold him. My car's over in the town lot, and I'm new here, so I don't know my way around, and we don't want to waste time."

"Happy to oblige. I'm Ida Lee Jones, and I live just over there." She pointed to a house bordering the nearest side street.

"Priscilla Grant. Newcomer."

"I'll grab my car and be right back."

Priscilla heard the murmur of people's voices around her. She didn't look up. She couldn't make contact with sympathetic eyes, not with tears so close. Why had she called out? Instinct, she realized. But if she hadn't called the dog her way, this never would have happened.

Ida stopped her car behind the accident vehicle.

The first driver lifted the dog into his arms. Once Priscilla was in the backseat of Ida's car, he handed him in. "I'm still sorry, ma'am. Your dog or not, it weighs heavy to hurt something."

She knew that firsthand. She blinked back more tears as she cradled the stray in her lap. "Unavoidable in this case, but thank you for caring."

"I'll close up your place for you, Ida," called out Tyler from the curb.

"Thanks, Tyler. And don't forget to take your pills, all right?"

"You know I forget, so I appreciate the reminder." He waved as the car moved forward smoothly. Ms. Jones looked back through the rearview mirror. "I texted the veterinary so they'd know we were coming. I take my cat there. It's a good place and not crazy expensive. You said you're new here?"

Priscilla nodded. "Just moved in to the cottage at the lighthouse."

"Of course. Miss Marjorie's place. You must be a Latham."

"Her niece from Kansas."

"Do tell." The woman turned right, then left, then right again. "I've never been farther than the mainland for supper and shopping, then right back here to the island, so Kansas could be the moon for all I know. Big farms there?"

The Kansas landscape sprawled with big farms. Priscilla nodded as she stroked the dog's soft head.

"Well, this will be different, I expect. We've got haves and have-nots and some in-betweens, but with house prices and the cost of living here going up, more of the in-betweens are having a tough time. Tyler Bradley's a perfect example. On in years and not much coming in, and that makes things difficult. Not in the summer, so much." She met Priscilla's eyes through the mirror. "But winter's another story."

"I saw that the brick church opens a homeless shelter in the winter."

"And it's a wonderful service, though some don't agree. But giving a few folks a warm bed and a hot meal doesn't seem like a bad thing to me. Course, I grew up without much, so I understand the downside of having too little." She pulled into a paved parking lot. "Here we are. I'd stay with you and take you to your car, but

I'm on shift at the diner in ten. Do you have a way back into town?"

The woman climbed out of the driver's seat and opened the back door as Priscilla answered. "I can call a cousin. Someone will come get me. I'm sorry." For the life of her, Priscilla couldn't remember the woman's name. "What was your name again?"

"Ida Lee Jones. I used to do some work for Miss Marjorie now and again, once she got on in years. She liked the yard kept up, and when she couldn't do it, she hired me on. We had some pretty things going a ways back. Before she got so foggy. And money got short."

The side door of the veterinary clinic opened, and two young people wearing scrubs appeared, pushing a gurney. "Call me, Ida. I'd like to have some yard help. I love working outside but I don't have the eye for what should go where, you know? Give me a shout."

The other woman's eyes lit up. "I'll do that, first thing tomorrow. And thank you."

The male tech took the dog from Priscilla's arms and laid him on the transport gurney. The pup whined softly. No bark. No growl. Just a soft whimper to let them know he was in pain.

Priscilla followed them inside. When she began to cross the hall to the front desk, the young woman called her back. "Don't you want to be with him?"

She did, yes, but surely they'd want to know who was going to pay the bill. Didn't they?

"You can take care of all that later, but right now let's run an assessment."

"I can stay with him?"

"We wouldn't have it any other way." Another man came in, midforties, not too tall, dark-haired, just beginning to gray at the temples. He checked the dog over, making note of several things. The young woman jotted them into a computer, and then he looked up. "I think we got lucky this time."

For the first time in twenty minutes, Priscilla took a breath that didn't cause her pain. "Really?"

He nodded. "I'm going to run some tests, but I think the right shoulder took the brunt of things. It may have popped out but appears to have popped right back in. After the tests, I'd like to keep him for observation overnight, just in case there's more going on than I can see, but I think this fellow will be fine. Just fine."

"Thank heavens!" She choked up again but this time in relief. "I was so scared when he dashed across that road."

"He looks to be about a year old. Has he seen a vet before? Has he had his shots?"

She shrugged. "I've never seen him before today, and one of the people in the neighborhood thought he was a stray. My guess is no. But you can give them to him tomorrow, can't you? If he's going to be all right, he should have his shots."

"They can give him shots at the shelter actually." As the doctor spoke, he gently ran a scanner over the dog, searching for a microchip. Then he shook his head. "No reason to pad your bill, and I'm not finding a chip to tell us where he belongs."

"Shelter?"

The young woman nodded. "When strays are brought in, they automatically get sent to the animal shelter. If they're deemed healthy, they're given shots and put up for adoption."

Adoption? But... "What if he doesn't get chosen?"

The veterinarian grimaced. "Then they get put down. Eventually."

The dog picked that moment to look at her again. He hit her with that same look, as if comforting her and not the other way around. "What if I take him home with me?"

The doctor paused, looking down, but Priscilla thought a tiny smile softened his jaw. "And break protocol?"

"Well, it's not exactly breaking protocol if I claim him before the shelter gets him. So perhaps we should start this conversation over. Doctor, I'm Priscilla Grant, I'm new to town, and this is my dog." She stared at the dog, trying to figure out a name, then smiled. "Jake. He looks like a Jake, doesn't he?"

"He does." The young woman smiled at her.

Dr. Morris added, "It's a good name for an Australian shepherd. I'm not sure if he's a purebred, but he's got the look. Red saddle, white chest, silky fur, medium build, perky ears. They're a smart breed, but they do like their exercise. It's going to be a lot of years before this guy's ready to retire by the fireplace, if you get my drift."

"Then we're a perfect match because I need more exercise." Priscilla stroked the dog's slightly matted head. "We'll do okay together, won't we?"

"And we'll take good care of Jake while he's here, Mrs. Grant."

"Priscilla, please. I like first names."

The doctor stuck out a hand. "Mike Morris. And now that you're the owner of record, we'll be glad to catch Jake up on his shots, but first we're going to set him up for a rest. If he's quiet for a day, the shoulder will be less likely to pop back out. Does working with animals bother you, Priscilla?"

"I was raised on a Kansas farm and then helped run one for nearly forty years. Working with animals comes naturally."

"Perfect. His fur's a mess, but some steady brushing and combing will work that out. They've got pet supplies at Smith Bodfish & Swift. They're a little ways down State Road, just past the auto-parts store. Or you can order online."

"I like to support local business," she told him as they tucked Jake into a kennel in the back with a nursery monitor. Priscilla bent low to give him a last pet. "I'll see you tomorrow, Jake."

His eyes closed, but he gave one quiet thump of his tail, just enough to show he'd heard her words, or at least her voice.

She took care of the registration at the desk, offered her debit card, then called Joan. "Joan, are you available to come get me? I'm at the Southside Veterinary Clinic, and I need a ride back to town."

Joan—bless her heart—didn't waste time. "I'll be right there." Seven minutes later, she pulled into the parking lot. When Priscilla settled into the front passenger seat, Joan turned the car around and headed toward the village. "Should I ask why you're at Dr. Morris's clinic when you have no pets?"

Priscilla told her the story, and Joan didn't chide her for befriending the dog. She smiled and patted Priscilla's hand. "A dog is a great companion. I'm foolish not to take my own advice on this because I lost my Champ about six months back. I told myself I wouldn't jump in and get another dog, but I miss him like crazy. He was a good old boy. I kept thinking that a woman my age had no business going out and getting a puppy because they're so high energy, but now that it's summer, I see it was a foolish thing to do. I can't wait to meet your Jake. A dog on the waterfront is just the ticket, Priscilla!"

"Well, it couldn't be helped. There was no way I could turn my back on him," Priscilla replied. "Having a dog around will be a comfort. Even if he just barks a warning now and again when people are afoot, that would be enough."

"Have there been people pestering you again?" Joan pulled into the full municipal lot and left the car running as she faced her cousin. "More than what happened yesterday?"

"Someone was walking along the waterfront late last night." She shrugged. "Well, early this morning. Between three and four. Maybe someone out walking their own dog?"

Joan's expression went grave. "I wish I could say that was the likely case, but it's not, Priscilla. None of your neighbors are the kind who would be out walking at that hour, and only two of them have dogs right now. Of course, it could have been someone from farther down the beach..."

Priscilla recognized the unlikelihood of that right away. "All the better to have Jake on hand if folks are going to mill around, hunting for what isn't theirs in the first place."

"The lure of easy money tempts all kinds, and not all of them are nice." Joan pursed her lips. "Why don't you come stay with me until this is all over?"

It was a kind offer, but Priscilla had come here determined to flex some muscle, and no way was she going to cave the first week. "I don't think anyone means me harm. They're just out to fatten their pocketbooks. But I'll keep a sharp lookout, and if it gets too scary, I might take you up on your offer. And Joan?"

Joan met her gaze.

"Thank you so much for dropping everything and coming right over. I called you first thing because I knew you'd do that."

Joan smiled. "And I'd say the same in return, so that's a good thing to know about the both of us. Have you gotten your muffin yet?"

"I haven't eaten a thing all day. Can we have lunch together?"

"It's shrimp salad day at the Colonial Inn, so let's go give Miss Tilly some business." Joan pointed up the road toward the gracious inn. "She gets excited when locals stop in, and you must meet her. We can walk to your car after lunch. And maybe a seashore walk too. I can show you around if that would suit?"

"It would be perfect," Priscilla answered. "That's exactly what I was doing when the accident happened. I'd just made it around a few blocks, and I'm eager to get to know the town better."

"Then we'll do a tour after our shrimp salads. And maybe stop at the bakery for dessert. But we won't mention that to Miss Tilly," she added as she aimed the car back on to the two-lane road. "She's got a rift going with Candy over who makes the best humming-bird cake in town, and while it seems silly, hummingbird cake has become an island staple. So the competition is real, and when it comes to cake, the stakes are high at this end of the island."

It seemed like a lot of stakes were high in Martha's Vineyard. Folks were trying to make an annual salary on half-a-year's work. Priscilla appreciated the difficulty in that because parts of farming were the same way, but did that difficulty add weight to the cur-rent treasure quest?

Joan parked in the lot behind the inn, and they walked inside. "Miss Tilly runs a great inn, but she's a little obsessive."

"Gerald mentioned that she's somewhat intolerant of broken protocol. So I've been twice warned."

Joan laughed softly as she reached for the door. "She might cut you some slack because of who you are, but probably not, so gear up, cousin. I promise you, the shrimp salad with a dusting of fresh dill is worth it." She stepped through the door and smiled quickly. "Miss Tilly. Hello."

Priscilla wasn't sure what she expected, but the tiny dynamo that came their way wasn't it. Tilly Snyder was petite and possibly ageless in a Yoda-like fashion. Her dark, graying hair was pinned up in a bun, and she wore a vintage dress that would have done either Hepburn proud seventy years before. Black high heels completed the outfit, and instead of the forties-style single strand of pearls, Miss Tilly wore a necklace of tiny shells, the kind carried in every souvenir and trinket shop near water. The combination worked surprisingly well, and as she drew closer, Priscilla was suddenly aware of her messy hair and worn, comfortable walking shoes.

"Dog hair." Miss Tilly pursed her lips, reached behind a small desk, and opened a drawer. She withdrew an adhesive roller and handed it to Priscilla. "I'm not allergic, but some could be, and it would behoove dog owners to be more aware. Don't you agree?"

Joan kept her gaze down, but her shoulders shook slightly as she laughed, and Priscilla sincerely hoped the shrimp salad was worth the public humiliation. She accepted the adhesive roller and ran it up and down her arms and legs. She hadn't noticed that the thighs of her capris were flecked with Jake's white and roan offerings. By the time she was done, her clothing looked better, and Tilly nodded approval. "Lunch for two, or will Gail and Trudy be joining you today?"

"Gail's helping at Sara's bookstore, and Trudy is sorting and tagging things for the church garage sale, so it's just us today," Joan told her. "Miss Tilly, this is my cousin Priscilla."

"Charlotte's daughter."

"Yes." Priscilla extended her hand. Miss Tilly had to think a moment before briefly touching the tips of her fingers to Priscilla's, and after the dog hair debacle, Priscilla couldn't blame her. "It's a pleasure to meet you. I've heard good things about the inn and your luncheons. And your porches are beautiful."

"A home should reflect the inner soul of the owner. Beauty outside, graciousness within. If you'll both come this way, Hilda will be right with you."

"I think I'll dash to the ladies' room and wash up," Priscilla said once they'd been seated. She slipped her purse on to the chair next to Joan. "I'll be right back."

When she returned from the ornate, Victorian-styled restroom, Professor Mayweather was standing behind her chair. He turned as she approached, and his fake smile made her want to lash out irrationally, a fairly comic reaction. He lifted her purse from the seat and slid the chair out for her. Her skin almost crawled. The hairs on her neck rose in protest again, and when he pulled out the chair next to her and sat down, she had to push aside the urge to run.

"I didn't expect to stumble on to two lovely ladies at lunch today."

He wasn't planning to stay with them, was he? Sitting with them? Annoying them?

"What a pity that I got here early with my assistant," the professor said. A younger man moved their way from a table alongside the opposite wall. "Alan Napier, this is Mrs. Grant. She's recently acquired the Latham family lighthouse. And Joan Abernathy, also from the Latham family. I'm sorry that we already dined or we could have joined you ladies and had a delightful repose. Lovers of history getting lost in time over great conversation."

"Except that Priscilla and I have pressing family business to talk about, and then I promised to show her around town. It's the perfect afternoon for exploring." Joan's gentle words seemed sincere and utterly believable. "So it worked out for the best. Perhaps another time, Professor?"

"Of course." He stood and bowed slightly. "It would be my pleasure. The summer looms long the day, and time shall bide, as ever it has."

He followed his young assistant out of the dining room, and Priscilla turned to Joan, puzzled.

"What did he say?"

"He's been writing poetry for the past decade or more, and every now and again the local paper will take one of his lighter poems and publish it. He fancies himself a contemporary version of Robert Frost, without the farm."

"And not a lick of the physical work that went along with it," Priscilla mused. "A poet and a professor, but with a hidden side."

"Franklin has a hidden side?" Joan leaned forward. "Share what you know, and do not leave out one juicy detail."

The waitress, Hilda, stopped by for their orders, and when she'd gone off to the kitchen, Priscilla leaned closer and explained the professor in hushed detail.

Joan's eyes grew wide. "I can't believe this. Not that he's attracted to you because you're lovely, Priscilla, but that he might be after your pocketbook and not your undying love. Are you certain?" She peeked over her shoulder to make sure no one was nearby. "He had a lady friend in Brighton and popped over there now and again, but that was a while back. And he does seem singularly nervous this summer, more so than in the past, but that could be due to his legal squabbles."

"Legal squabbles? The professor?"

"A big kerfuffle about a college-level history book he published last year. I don't know the details, but it involved a lawsuit for plagiarism, and I heard the university wasn't one bit pleased. But that's all I know."

"I can't imagine a highly regarded college like Dartmouth would take something like that lightly. Ivy League schools have a reputation to uphold."

"He told you he teaches at Dartmouth?"

Priscilla nodded. "When I ran into him at the museum."

"Well, he does in a way. He's over at the state college, the Dartmouth campus. Not the Ivy League school in New Hampshire. Oh, Professor." Joan made a scolding face. "To think of him treasure hunting because you've inherited Aunt's property…" She paused. "It's odd but understandable, isn't it?"

"It's not one bit understandable if you're the new recruit from Wheatfield," Priscilla whispered back. "He gives me the heebie-jeebies, and he's far too interested in my real estate and the possibility of gold therein."

"Money trouble, perhaps?"

"Are professors poorly paid here? Because they make a fair dollar in the Midwest, but the cost of living here is higher."

"Anyone who can spend the entire summer not working and living on the island can't be doing too badly," Joan supposed. "He's been staying in his uncle's place for years. But he does seem more worked up than usual this year. I've only run into him twice so far, and he was even more agitated and pompous than usual."

She opened her napkin and laid it across her lap as Tilly seated more people and Hilda approached with their food. "Nothing a wonderful lunch and homemade Italian cream soda can't put right. And when you try Tilly's pickle chips, you'll be spoiled for life."

Priscilla didn't miss Tilly's nod of appreciation, and when she took one bite of the crisp, red pickles, she had to agree. Odd professors and strange lights aside, Tilly Snyder's watermelon pickles were reason enough to stay on the island forever.

CHAPTER EIGHT

I don't just want a brisk walk, I *need* a brisk walk after eating all that. Which way should we go?" Priscilla asked Joan.

Joan pointed straight ahead. "We'll leave my car here and do a big loop around the business district. That way you'll see the harbor and the vendors and all the little shops. And a few big ones too."

"Do they all close down for the winter?" Priscilla wondered as they headed west.

"Some do, some don't," Joan replied. "Once you're down to the island folk and money gets tight midwinter, it's a different setting entirely. And there's plenty of parking," she laughed as they passed a row of cars packed like sardines in a can along the road's edge. "We try to encourage people to use the buses for touring, but the ferry books up solid for cars, hour after hour."

"I had no idea when I came through," Priscilla confessed. "I assumed there was like a bridge or something."

"Really?"

She nodded. "It never occurred to me, and I didn't want to do too much on the Internet because I wanted to see things firsthand. See what I remembered from when I was a girl. So having to wait for a spot on the ferry was a wake-up call."

"I bet." They turned right toward the harbor, and Joan pointed out places of interest. "There is no shortage of restaurants all across the island, and Tisbury has great offerings. Pubs, cafés, sandwich shops, and of course, seafood is served at almost every one of them. Fried haddock is my favorite, and it's popular among the locals and the tourists." She indicated Fresh Haddock signs in two small take-out restaurants. "And here's the Whaling Museum." She pointed toward a weathered gray-and-white building on the left, slightly uphill. "Now that's a spot filled with old artifacts, Priscilla. The whaling industry was a big part of our history."

"Clara mentioned it at the library. Can we stop in?"

"Sure can." They crossed the street and climbed the steps of the aged building. Joan reached for the door and then paused. "It's closed."

"A popular tourist attraction closed in the middle of the day? With all these people around?"

"I don't understand." Joan gazed around, perplexed. "It's supposed to be open. The hours are posted."

"Is this a public museum? Or private?" Priscilla asked.

"Private, and that's part of the problem," Joan said. "Old Mr. Oglethorpe owns it. It was his uncle's before him, and they just kept adding artifacts and information about the whaling trade. The town wanted to buy it when he started having health issues because it's a crowd-pleaser. Folks don't understand what kind of work it took to make a living and keep people warm and fed and dry in the old days. Every day a struggle."

"We're somewhat spoiled by comparison."

"Well, we'll have to try it another time," Joan supposed. "I'll call the mayor and find out what's going on. It wouldn't seem like a big deal, but the Whaling Museum is pictured on all the tour guides and maps. It's a big part of our history. To have it closed when it should be open will make folks mad, especially if they've purchased online tickets."

"That would be disappointing. Oh, Joan. Look." The harbor splayed out before them like a New England seaside print. Sailboats dotted the water, and docks stretched out in straight lines away from the wide concrete walkway. From their slightly elevated position, the view was magnificent. "This is amazing, isn't it?"

"It never gets old, Priscilla. You'd think it would, but it doesn't. And how many places can you say that about?"

"Too few." Priscilla breathed in the scents and sounds of the busy harbor. Summer-clad people thronged but not in a push or rush. They moseyed from this spot to that, relaxed and carefree. "I wonder what this looked like a hundred years back."

"Or two or three. We're young by European standards, but I'm inspired by the hard work it took to carve a nation out of such raw beginnings. And now we enjoy all this." Joan smiled as they descended the wide gray stairs. "Every once in a while I wonder if I would have been strong enough to make it in the old days. Would I have had the vision to see what could be?"

"I used to wonder the same thing on the prairie," Priscilla confessed. "It took raw courage for the pioneers to face that land and win. I'd like to think we would have been strong enough, Joan."

"I like to think it too, but I'm pretty fond of things like this." Joan led the way into Candy's bakery as they made their way back to their cars. "And on a hot summer's day, I'm mighty glad to have Candy do the baking. Which means I might not have made it after all. What's going on?" she wondered as she held the door for Priscilla.

Two small circles of people spoke in hushed, worried tones to the right of the wide, clean, busy bakery counter.

One of the women came their way. "Have you heard?"

Joan shook her head. "Priscilla Grant, this is Mavis Dunlop. She lives on my street. Mavis, Priscilla is my cousin from Kansas, she's moved into Aunt Marjorie's place. What's happened?"

"The Town Board has installed a committee to look into the library."

"The library?" Joan frowned, puzzled. "I don't understand."

"A feasibility study," Mavis stressed. "Joan, they're trying to save tax dollars. And they're talking about shutting the library down altogether because no one uses it. Ben Whipple had the nerve to call it archaic. As if a library is a useless convenience."

"We've got to stop this." Another woman spoke up, and the voices rose in indignation. "It's ridiculous to think that a town like ours can't afford a library. And just think of those three women out of a job."

"Joan, you should be in on this," added Mavis. "The Lathams have been big library patrons for a long time."

"There's even that beautiful plaque for Llewellyn and his wife and mother in the front alcove."

"That library isn't just a part of our history," lamented another woman. "It holds our history. I've got to go, I'm due back at work, but I can't believe Ben would pull a stunt like this when he knows the locals are so busy working."

"Which might be exactly why he did it now," Joan told them. "Ben's got big ideas, but there's only so much we can ask the middle-income locals to pay for, and we shouldn't have to sacrifice our library to meet his goals. Are they holding a board meeting?"

"That's just it." Mavis scowled. "They're in recess for the summer, except for emergency sessions, so he just slipped this in like it was any old Wednesday. I heard Clara left the library in tears, she was so distraught, and who can blame her?"

"We'll gather together and talk this out," Joan promised. "And don't despair. Ben's flexing his muscles and calling for a committee, but he can't single-handedly dismantle the library and the board won't go for it. My guess is he's looking to stir up trouble enough so that he gets folks talking."

"Well he can mark that as a success," griped an older man.

"Once we're talking, he'll stir the pot to tip things in his favor. He's been like that since he was a kid, running for eighth-grade class president. He didn't win then, and we'll make sure he doesn't win now. But what a dustup he's created," she added to Priscilla as they placed their order at the counter moments later. "Our mayor has a personal agenda, most of which is to become a state legislator. He's young and boisterous and shrugs off history as 'old guard' nonsense. The island establishment doesn't like him, but most of them are in the other towns. He got himself elected by promising lower taxes, but if tossing things like the library aside is his plan, he's got a fight on his hands."

"Clara seemed worried about the library when I saw her earlier today, but I had no idea it might come to this."

"Scare tactics," muttered Joan once they thanked Candy and moved out of the store. "He's trying to bully people into his way of thinking, but I'd hate to see it catch on."

"You think it could?"

Joan pointed west. "That sweet old neighborhood where your pup got hit this morning?"

"Near the Fellowship Church, yes."

"There are a lot of people there who are having trouble paying their way these days. They might have lived on the island for generations, but when you're on a fixed income, tax and food money are hard to come by. Property values have skyrocketed the past twenty years, but that means the property taxes have spiked too. So the older folks are either doing reverse mortgages to keep their homes and pay their taxes..."

"Losing equity every month."

"Or they're going without things like food. Heat. Clothing."

Tyler's thin-seamed clothing came to mind. "All to afford living expenses. I would have never imagined that here."

"Our cost of living has risen. We've got some lovely farms here. We'll have to take you around to see them. You'll appreciate them more than most. But they can only grow so much during our short growing season, and everything else has to be ferried in."

"I've never thought of that. I'm so used to being on the mainland and having most everything a short drive away."

They'd gotten to Priscilla's car. She hit the fob button to unlock the doors, then stopped.

Her back window on the far side was shattered. Pebbled safety glass lay scattered across her backseat.

Her glove box lay open with the contents strewn about, and the covered storage in the center console between the front seats stood open and empty.

"Priscilla!" Joan jabbed her phone as she called 911. "Is anything missing? I can't believe this!"

"There was nothing to take," Priscilla answered as she rounded the car. "I have my purse, I don't keep anything in the car, and my research bag is in your car."

She stopped. Her heart skipped a beat. "Do you suppose they were looking for my notes?"

Joan shook her head quickly as a walking officer approached them. "How much could you have found in a couple of days? And who would even know you were looking?"

Two faces came to mind. The professor's. And Clara Lopez, the helpful, job-threatened librarian who'd left work crying several hours before.

Joan met the officer near the front bumper. "Ed, this is my cousin Priscilla Grant. She's just moved into the lighthouse. We had lunch together and went for a walk, and this is what we found when we got back. Priscilla"—she stepped aside to let the officer through—"this is Ed Sequeira, he's one of Tisbury's finest."

"I'm real sorry about this." He looked genuinely concerned as he snapped pictures with a camera phone. "Is there anything missing?"

"Not that I can see, but I don't keep anything in here. Just a couple of maps and car information. A handful of change for tolls. I can't imagine how no one saw this happen though. With the town so busy."

"These lots fill up early, and then there's no one in here unless people happen to be coming for their car at the same time. It only takes a moment to bust out glass like this with the right tool. After that, it just looks like someone looking for something in their car. Easy enough to get away with, I'm afraid." The officer's explanation made sense. She wished it didn't.

"So this happens often?"

"No, almost never. Crime like this is rare here. Most folks know that the tourists are our bread-and-butter, and they give them a wide berth. Did you have something someone might be hunting for, Mrs. Grant?"

"No." She wasn't lying. Not really. She'd given the coin to Mildred, and her research bag was in Joan's vehicle. "Maybe just someone down on their luck, hoping to score a find."

The officer swept her four-year-old SUV a look of doubt. "If that was the case, there are more upscale vehicles in the lot."

"Perhaps betting I hadn't set the alarm system?" She waved toward several pricey models across the row. "That BMW and Audi would probably sound the alarm if someone tried this on them."

"You could be right."

He didn't look convinced, but she let it go as the auto-glass repair shop texted her a reply. "The repair service is going to meet me at my place. I'd better go."

"I'm going to stop by my house and then come right over," Joan told her. "We'll talk."

"Yes." It felt good to have someone she could trust nearby. She drove back to the point, distraught, and was halfway there before she remembered her research notes were in Joan's car. She pulled into the driveway.

The beauty of the shore stretched out before her. Even with the neglected garden plots and thinning grass, the lighthouse and the keeper's cottage created a postcard image of times gone by.

But doubts assailed her as she crossed the driveway and let herself in through the side door. Maybe Rachel was right. Perhaps she was biting off more than she should. She'd made the trip thinking only of the positives, but who expects treasure hunters to go berserk?

Not her, certainly.

The house smelled unusually musty as she walked in. She crossed into the kitchen and came to a complete stop again.

Her heart froze solid in her chest, and at that moment she was sure Rachel was right: she didn't belong here, in a place where folks wrecked other people's homes, searching for something that may or may not exist. The torn-up floorboards in her cozy living room were reason enough to pack her bags and leave on the next ferry.

Priscilla stared at the mess, hands shaking. The antique braided rug had been tugged back, a lamp had been knocked over, and the central floorboards of the room were pried up. An earthy smell rose up from the basement below as old air battled a fresh ocean breeze for dominance.

She pulled out her phone and hit 911 as quickly as she could with shaking fingers. Who would do this? Who knew she'd be out for a while?

The professor came straight to mind. He'd seen them at the inn. He knew they'd just arrived and that they were taking a walk. Did he use that time to slither over here and mess up her home, searching for long-lost treasure?

He was interested. She knew that for certain, and he'd been more interested when she met with Mildred at the museum, but was he capable of this? And what about Clara? This morning's news threatened her livelihood and her family.

The operator picked up her distress call, and in less than five minutes, two patrol cars rolled into her driveway. Different officers from before. At this rate, she might get to know the entire Tisbury Police Department by the time she'd been here a week. Despite well over fifty years on the planet before coming to Martha's Vineyard, she'd only had to call the police exactly once—when an elderly man T-boned Rachel's car nearly fifteen years before. Here on the island she'd found herself contemplating police help twice and had just filed a report in the village for her vandalized car. She'd driven home, subdued and distraught.

Now she was neither. Now she was old-fashioned Midwestern mad. This was *her* house, *her* land, *her* car, and *her* future. No way was she going to let some two-bit gold monger mess this up. If this person wanted a fight?

They just got one.

"Looks like he came through this window." The younger female officer pointed to the waterfront side of the living room. "You can see it's been tugged back down, almost fully in place. And it looks like someone tried to jimmy this door." She crossed to the narrow door leading to the attic. "See the scores along the edge here? They look new, as if someone used a file to try and pry open the door. Those old locks don't give up easily, do they?"

The floor and the attic, access to the two places she'd mentioned to Mildred. "Are you going to dust it for prints?"

"In general we save that for major crimes."

"Ah." Priscilla nodded, pretending that made sense. "So when I'm dead in my bed, then you'll dust for prints. How silly of me not to think of that."

"She may have misspoken, Mrs. Grant." The older policeman scrubbed a hand over the back of his neck. "We'd be glad to get a tech team out here, but likely as not, it's some visitor wanting to get their hands on that blasted gold that probably doesn't even exist. And very few locals have a record of any kind, so the prints wouldn't give us much to go on if there's no one to match them to. Visitors come and go every day."

"So you can do nothing? There'll be no investigation?"

"Oh, we'll investigate all right." He waved toward her neighbors in either direction. "You're in the open here, so someone might have seen something. Your neighbors are a little far off to be much help, and that buffer of trees makes seeing things from the north next to impossible, but we'll check it out, sure enough. They might have run into the same bit of trouble as you, come to think of it."

Priscilla doubted that. For some reason, the lighthouse and cottage seemed to be a money-grubber's draw. As the pair left to interview the neighbors, the auto-glass repairman showed up. Once Priscilla put him to work, she walked toward the water, ruminating on what she knew so far.

The gold had existed. A young colonial had given his life in exchange, a harsh price to pay, and Brandon Scott's article claimed the gold's current value would be close to two million dollars, a tempting treasure.

Not everyone on the island was well-set financially, and the lure of a fast prize could draw interest, despite the police officers' lack of concern. A cache of gold coin worth seven figures was worth substantial risk to some, even bodily harm to others, a fact she didn't take lightly.

But why was the lighthouse being targeted?

She withdrew the notebook from her purse, sat down on the bluff, and jotted some notes.

1. Contact Brandon Scott and question locations and links to Latham family and the lighthouse.

2. Delve into library's local research files for pertinent historic information.

3. Examine logbooks in attic to find out more about lighthouse keepers.

4. Make list of possible suspects.

5. Investigate basement. Buy breathing masks and long-handled dusters. And bug spray. And swatters.

6. Seek cousins' advice.

Eyeing that last notation, she realized how blessed she was to have good family nearby. What if she didn't? How would she handle this, alone, in a new setting?

But she wasn't alone, and that was something to rejoice about.

CHAPTER NINE

Her phone rang just as she closed the notepad. It was Rachel's ringtone. She picked up the phone and said hello quickly.

"Mom, what's wrong? You sound upset. Is everything all right?"

Normally Priscilla would brush off Rachel's questions because Rachel always had questions. But not this time. A combination of the dog's plight, the ransacked car, the break-in, the officers' lackluster attitudes, and a touch of acid stomach upset made her blurt the truth, which she instantly regretted. "My home's been broken into, and someone's made a mess of my hardwood floor."

"A break-in?" Rachel sounded stunned, and rightly so. "Mom, are you all right? Have you called the police? Is someone there to help you? I can't believe this is happening, and you're so far away! Mom. You need to sell that place and come home. For heaven's sake, you're a Kansas farm wife, not some seasoned East Coast shore dweller. Come home. Please."

Priscilla keyed in on three words. *Kansas farm wife.*

Yes, that was true. She'd been a Kansas farm wife for nearly forty years, and she'd been a good one. But as the gulls swooped, dived, and called overhead, Priscilla knew something else.

She wasn't *just* a Kansas farm wife.

She never had been. She'd longed for a chance to go places and do things. To see things, different things. Season by season, Gary had stayed tied to the farm. He lived his dream, and she couldn't fault him for it, but by living his, her thoughts of adventure had been thwarted.

It suited when she had a husband by her side, with work from dawn to dusk and after, because they were a team. But it didn't suit now, and she knew it would never suit her again. "Rachel, don't fuss. It's not as rough as it seems." It was, but she was not about to admit that to Rachel. Good thing she hadn't mentioned the car too. "You caught me at a bad time."

"Only if you call having your house broken into a bad time. Mom…" Rachel paused, then spoke in a more subdued voice. "You can't possibly mean to stay there when someone is targeting you."

"Not me. My house. And the lighthouse. And possibly the bluff I'm sitting on." She yanked out the notepad with one hand, tucked the phone under her chin, and scribbled "investigate lighthouse thoroughly" as number seven on her list.

"I don't believe what I'm hearing."

"Well, believe it, but don't fret over it. I've got two investigators from the Tisbury Police force heading this way." She might be fudging their rank some, but they were investigating—kind of—so it wasn't really untrue. "And I'm fine. More mad than anything. And I've got myself a dog now, so things should get better. Nothing like a four-legged friend to let me know what's what."

"A dog." Rachel's voice took a steep downturn. "You got a dog?"

"Well, he kind of found me, but it seems we're a match. They think he's an Australian shepherd, not a breed I know much about, but a sweet little fellow who met with some bad luck. You know how much I love animals." She deliberately did not tell Rachel about the poor dog's circumstances because that would drive the melodrama over the edge for her numbers-loving daughter. "Why would that upset you? You loved Buford."

"Because that's the kind of thing people do when they're going to stay someplace."

"Rachel." The officers were moving her way, so she slipped her notebook back into her purse and stood. It made no sense to argue about this with Rachel right now. "I've got to go talk with the police again. No worries. I'm in good hands here, darling. Just like you are there. And notice that I don't pester you about anything."

"Because no one is breaking into my townhouse or lurking outside my doors," Rachel shot back. "Mom, this could be dangerous."

It could be, but Priscilla wasn't ready to call it quits. Not by a long shot. The very idea that she'd been targeted twice in a matter of hours meant there might be good reason to suspect the gold was somewhere on the lighthouse property, and she intended to find it if it was. "Every place takes some getting used to, doesn't it? You hated the city at first. Remember?"

"Yes." She said it reluctantly, but at least she admitted it.

"Rachel, I've got to talk to these investigators. I'll call you later, all right? Love you!" She hung up as the officers drew close. "Any news?"

The older one shook his head. "Nothing. No one saw or heard anything on either side, which isn't a surprise, since the intruder didn't break any glass. Can we send Tommy Townsend over to fix that floor for you, ma'am? He can do the window too. You'll need a new lock on it for sure, but it might be in your best interests to have those waterfront windows replaced if it's affordable. There's some water damage to the casings and the framing, which makes it easy for someone to force the window up from outside."

"The new locks wouldn't be enough?" She studied the twin windows from her vantage point.

"Well, it wasn't today. A lock is only as strong as the wood holding it," he explained. He pointed out the softened wood along the sides as they moved closer. "Rotting wood is never a good thing, but in this instance, it allowed the intruder a fairly easy entrance into your house. Tommy does windows for one of the big window companies on the mainland, but he's pricey. It might be cheaper to have the mainland sales rep come over and write you up."

"But Tommy is a local contractor of good reputation?"

The male officer nodded. His look of approval indicated he got her drift.

"Send Tommy my way. I had no idea the windows were compromised. The paint job hides it well. And my floor needs help, ASAP."

"Tommy had suggested to Miss Marjorie that she'd want to replace those windows, but she was kind of old school. Maybe getting tight on money too," he added. "She had one of the locals paint everything last year and thought the paint added protection from the saltwater breeze."

"Which is true, but it's no guard against intruders," added the young woman.

The pair of officers took their leave and headed back toward the village.

Priscilla eyed the house, drew a deep breath, and walked in. She refused to be afraid of her own house, even though it had only been hers for a very little while. She called Joan, Gail, and Trudy and invited them over for dinner and conversation. The cousins needed to be aware of what was going on, and they might be knowledgeable about the lighthouse history themselves.

And then she started another list.

1. Dog supplies for Jake
2. Get floor fixed
3. Get windows replaced
4. Solve the gold mystery and get on with life

She studied the list and then tacked it onto the narrow strip of wall next to the refrigerator, where she'd see it every time she went for a snack.

But there was no time for snacks now. She was going to take a flashlight upstairs to the attic and start her research. One way or another, she was going to find out what was going on in Misty Harbor, and if that meant solving a Revolutionary War mystery, that was exactly what she intended to do.

By the time the cousins arrived, she'd extricated two boxes of materials from the attic and had set them up in chronological order in the spare bedroom.

Trudy was the first one in the door. "Priscilla! Are you all right? I can't believe this kind of thing is happening to you. I'm so mad right now, I could spit nails!"

Trudy grabbed her in a hug, effusive as ever. Gail wore a sterner countenance. "Joan said she wanted you to come stay with her until this all gets cleared up or at least calms down, and I have to agree, Priscilla. Staying here could be dangerous. Either someone knows something or thinks they know something, and that's just as dangerous, if you ask me. For whatever reason, you and this property seem to be at the center of this treasure hunt, and we can't have anything happening to you."

"Not with you being new and all," Trudy added.

Joan pinned her with a skeptical look. "So it will be all right for her to be bothered once she's been here a while?"

"Well, the island is a little eccentric, and she needs to know that. My guess is it's quite different from the Kansas prairie."

"You can say that again," declared Priscilla, and she pointed toward the spare room. "I've got old logbooks lined up in there, and I plan to examine them to find out more about this lighthouse, the keepers, and the blasted gold that's interrupting my daily life. I made a tater tot casserole—not summer fare but easy— and I figured if you gals know anything about the lighthouse, you might share it with me. The sooner I find things out, the sooner I can move on."

"Your floor." Joan eyed the damaged boards and gaping hole that provided a view into the craggy, musty basement. "Oh, Priscilla, I'm so sorry about this."

A sharp rap sounded on the back door.

Silent, the four women stared at one another until Priscilla moved toward the door. "Coming." She opened it and breathed a sigh of relief. "You must be Tommy."

"I am, ma'am, and you must be Miss Marjorie's niece. Heard you had some trouble, and I've come to fix things up for you. Ah, Gail." Tommy's eyebrows shot up, and Priscilla was pretty sure he flushed when he spotted that particular cousin. "Good to see you."

"And you, Thomas." Gail used his full name, but not as if they were distant acquaintances. More like calling him Thomas was a comfortable thing to do, and wasn't that a note of interest? For the moment, however, romance was the last thing on Priscilla's mind.

"Let me show you into the living room, and you can get to work. I'm glad you were able to make it over here so quickly."

"Well, Bill and April from the police department let me know right off, but I was at the inn, working out a plumbing problem for Miss Tilly, and when you get to know Miss Tilly, you realize that one problem invariably leads to another and another. But I'm here now."

She showed him the damaged floor, then the two windows and the scraped door casing. He thinned his lips and got straight to work on the floor, easing the scarred floorboards back into place as best he could. He examined the outside of the house while she and the ladies got plates and silverware out, and then he came back in. "I'm going to do two things."

Priscilla nodded.

"I've got those floorboards back in place, but for a full fix, we'll need to have three new boards installed and the floor refinished, and that's a bit of change out of the pocket."

"Isn't everything these days?" Joan wondered, and Tommy nodded.

"Then there's the windows, ma'am." He frowned and rubbed his jaw lightly, then shrugged as if he couldn't help what he was about to say. "I'll write you up two estimates, one for the insurance company for the window that was jimmied..."

"I haven't gotten insurance yet," Priscilla confessed. "I meant to do it over the past few days but hadn't gotten to it yet. And I expect Aunt Marjorie's policy doesn't transfer."

Worry marked Joan's gaze. "We'll have to see if it does, but the deductible might be high. Auntie always had a bit put by to take care of things, so she didn't mind a high deductible. And maybe the insurance depends on when she paid the last premium. If she paid for a full year, you might be all right."

"Well, and then there's the rest of the windows. I told Miss Marjorie she should replace them, but she was getting tightfisted and refused. I'm going to write you up an estimate to replace all the windows. There's not a one of them that fits solidly anymore, and your aunt has been having them sealed each year, but a sharp east wind plays havoc with old windows this close to the water."

"All of the windows? Really, Thomas?" Gail leveled him a serious look because everyone knew that window replacement was no minor expense.

He looked uncomfortable, as if he might feel guilty about the recommendation, but he stood his ground. "Lucky there aren't too many, being a small house and all, but yes, all of them have rot and should be replaced. The small ones aren't too bad, pricewise." He pointed to the kitchen window and the bedrooms beyond. "But those windows along the front are steep, and they're in a bad way."

What choice did she have? "You write up the estimates, and I'll see what's what. No sense trying to make a decision before I have the facts, *hmm*? And what do you think about the door here?" She ran her fingers over the nicked and scraped casing. "There's no real damage, so I can smooth that out and repaint it, don't you think?"

He eyed the door, then her. "I'll leave a sheet of sandpaper, and I expect there's touch-up paint in the garage. This door stood solid, didn't it?" His voice took on a note of pride.

"It did. The police noticed that as well."

"My daddy built this door. And that little staircase behind it."

"Really, Thomas?" Gail asked the question, but all three cousins looked surprised.

"There used to be one of those fold-down ladders to the attic space. And a hatch hole, right here." He pointed up to a smoothly finished ceiling over their heads, and all four women looked up. "My dad said Miss Marjorie hated that hatch and ladder, so she hired my father to put in the staircase. It's small because he only had that much room to work with." He splayed his hands in a narrow span. "She was insistent, and he was handy enough to do the work and make it nice. When he told her folks wouldn't be able to drag big things down those stairs, she said that wasn't her problem. She got sharp-tongued now and again." He smoothed his hand over the door once more. "It's good to know that his craftsmanship stayed true to form when they tried to pry open that door."

"It's a nice memory, Thomas." Gail smiled at him as Joan and Trudy moved back to the kitchen area.

"It's not something we talked much about. Even back then, folks were getting up in arms if you made changes to old places. But my dad, he figured if a body owned a place, they owned it. And that was that. I almost forgot." He reached into his shirt pocket and withdrew an aqua pen. "I found your pen in the grass along the front windows."

"My pen?" Priscilla reached out and then withdrew her hand. "Where did you say you found it?"

"Just south of the forced window, in a tuft of grass the mower didn't quite hit. The color made it blend."

"That's one of Teresa's pens," noted Trudy. "She gives them out all over, and she's so proud of that color she picked. Sea-blue-green it's called, and it's a good match for a waterfront business, isn't it?"

"You've been to Teresa's then." Joan took the pen from Tommy and set it on the counter. "She's gone all over the island trying to set up new stops for her touring business. A good share of visitors seem inclined to do their own thing these days, so where she used to schedule six tours per day, she's down to a few, and those aren't always full. Trying times, for certain."

Teresa had just gotten herself added to Priscilla's "persons of interest" list. Decreased work, passing herself off as a direct descendent of Nathaniel Claybrook, and a company pen dropped into a random tuft of grass near a forced entry.

Priscilla didn't hold much with coincidence, but she held her tongue now. Teresa would have been working midday, wouldn't she?

But with only a few tours per day, the midday hour might be the perfect time to get away from the cozy side street office alongside the shop boasting the best lobster rolls in town. Could it have been Teresa who broke into her house? Priscilla didn't know, but one way or another, she intended to find out. She'd add "check into Teresa" to her to-do list once Tommy was gone. No sense letting the whole island know what she was doing. "I met her on the street this morning," she said out loud, "and she was wondering about adding the lighthouse to her list of stops."

"Oh, Auntie would turn over in her grave," said Gail. "She wanted no part of strangers traipsing around on her property, and Teresa tried to muscle her into it more than once, especially when she found out that Auntie was getting short on money."

"But Aunt Marjorie would have none of it," added Trudy. "She said her privacy was worth some sacrifice, and she sent Teresa right back to the village. Told her a drive-by with a pause to take pictures was fine because she didn't control the road, but by golly she controlled the rest of the property and had no intention of making it a thruway stop to line someone else's pockets."

That sounded a little harsh to Priscilla, but maybe her aunt had to be strong to face down Teresa.

"I'll get on then," said Tommy. "I'll drop by with the estimate first thing, Mrs. Grant."

"Priscilla, please. And if you're busy, you can e-mail it to me." She jotted down her e-mail on a slip of paper and handed it to him.

He nodded. "Priscilla, then. Nice to meet you, but I wish it was under better circumstances. Things like this give the island a bad name it doesn't deserve."

"Thank you, Tommy."

He dipped his chin and walked off, but not before he glanced over his shoulder at Gail.

She had her back turned, and Priscilla didn't miss his look of disappointment, but when Joan and Trudy had moved toward the side door with their plates, Gail gave a quick look and wave over her shoulder.

Tommy's smile said more than words ever could.

Gail turned back, saw Priscilla watching, and sighed. "Tommy and I have a mutual arrangement."

Priscilla was old enough not to want to know the details of anyone's mutual arrangement. But that didn't stop Gail.

"He lives with his mother, and I live with my father, so we're both caretakers for an elderly person, and they've been sweet on each other for years but too old to think of things like marriage.

But while they've been flirting, Tommy and I have been flirting too, and I'm afraid it's going to mess up everything."

"What could it possibly mess up?" Priscilla lowered her voice to match Gail's soft tone but wasn't sure why. "What's wrong with two single people flirting? Or falling in love?"

"That's just it!" The normally unflappable Gail waved a hand toward the door. "He can't leave his mother, and I can't leave my father, and how can we combine the awkwardness of two stubborn old folks, neither of who will leave their homes? So it's a standoff, and I can't say a thing in front of Trudy or Joan because they'll just die laughing at the silliness of it all. But it's not silly. Not to me, and not to Tommy. But the old ones are stubborn as can be, and we're supposed to honor our father and our mother, but in this case, there are days I'd like to shake the pair of them. Except other than that, they're the sweetest old folks you'd ever care to meet. So it's a conundrum. You met my dad. You saw how set in his ways he is. His chair, his shows, his nap time, his food. He doesn't vary much, and the thought of combining households might kill one or the other, and then how do Tommy and I live with that?"

"Another conundrum." Priscilla frowned. "It's hard to force someone's hand when they're in advanced years because if they suffer a downward turn..."

"Then I have to live with that on my conscience. I can't do that. Neither can Tommy, and it's so discouraging. We try not to think about it, and of course that makes us think about it all the more."

"Do your parents know?"

Gail frowned. "What?"

"Your father and Tommy's mother. Do they know you're interested in each other?" Priscilla pressed. "It might be wise to tell them. Let them think on it a little. They might be stubborn, but if they knew their choices were keeping the two of you apart..." She lifted her shoulders in a shrug. "They might take that into consideration. And I bet the four of you could have fun together. Something to think about anyway."

"I will," Gail promised. She pasted a bright smile on her face as they walked through the door to the covered patio area facing the water. Looking at her, no one would suspect she'd been disturbed moments before. Did everyone in town have secrets like this? That made Tisbury and Vineyard Haven more like Wheatfield than Priscilla had expected.

CHAPTER TEN

Priscilla sat down at the patio table and withdrew her notepad. "This is going to be a working supper." She pointed to her windows and her front room as supporting evidence. "We've got our job cut out for us. If I'm going to stay here and be comfortable in my own home, I need to solve this mystery and get on with life, and I need your help," she told them. "You gals have lived here all your life. You know the towns and the history and the locals. I've made myself a list of things to check up on. I'd like to start with any information you might have about the lighthouse and this gold. What can you tell me? And how would you ladies like to scour that lighthouse with me? After supper, that is."

"Exploring the lighthouse would be awesome." Trudy waved her fork that way. "Auntie hasn't let anyone in it for years and years, so who knows what we'll find? Every now and again the preservation society would stop by, give it a once-over to make sure there was nothing rotting, and they'd check it off their list and be on their way. But I'm no history buff, Priscilla, so I'm not much help with that, I'm afraid. Old stuff isn't my thing."

"One of you must know something. Don't you?" Priscilla tapped her notebook with a pen, but not Teresa Claybrook's pen. She'd slipped that right into a plastic bag once Tommy had left the room. He'd probably smeared any chance of good prints they might have gotten, but it was good to be on top of things. Just in case. "I thought history was big here."

"It is, and my mother could have filled in a lot of blanks because she was always delving into old things, but I never paid much attention." Apology laced Gail's admission. "I barely passed high school history, and that's a shameful thing for a Daughter of the American Revolution to admit, isn't it? It doesn't interest me one bit, so I'm no help, Priscilla. But this casserole is amazing. Really, really good."

"I love living in a historic village," added Trudy, "but the only thing I know about the lighthouse is that it's been in Latham hands for generations. How that might tie into the gold hunt is beyond me. I considered the gold story to be a legend until that reporter began spewing all those facts."

Priscilla turned toward Joan, less hopeful, but Joan surprised her. "I'm the history buff among us. You've got the lighthouse logs, don't you?"

Priscilla pointed toward the corner of the house. "In the spare bedroom right now. I lugged all the earliest ones down from the attic."

"It's such a silly thrill, to be able to explore parts of this place that were always under lock and key," Gail said. "That little door has always been locked up tight, just like the lighthouse."

"To keep nosy little girls out of historic records, I expect." Joan exchanged knowing looks with her cousins. "Remember how we liked to snoop around and she'd tell us to mind our own business?"

"We were curious little critters, for sure." Trudy tried another bite of the casserole and gave a blissful sigh. "Priscilla, you are a true cook, the only one among us, and I hereby issue a decree stating that you are not allowed to go back to Kansas for anything other than a short visit because I would miss your cooking. And your company. And all the fuss and bother too," she added, smiling. "We haven't had good dustups like this in a long time."

"Except that I don't want my cousin hurt," cut in Joan. "Enjoying the added elements of crazy is fine from a distance, Tru, but unfortunately Priscilla is up close and personal because it's her place they're targeting. That can't be comfortable for anyone, but especially if you're new in town."

Trudy winced. "Good point. Sorry, Priscilla. But this dish is amazing."

"It was a family favorite in the Midwest too." Priscilla began to add something else, but Joan interrupted her.

"How about if you and I go through the ledgers and logs together? I'm working mornings at the hospital, so if you're around for the afternoons, we can pore over them and see if we can find anything of note."

"I'd help, but we've got the church sale coming up, and you know that's intense," Trudy said.

Gail and Joan offered matching grim nods.

"Why is your church sale intense? Are they low on funds?" Priscilla asked Trudy.

"We're even on funds but high in competitiveness," Trudy told her. "As silly as it sounds, my church competes with the Wesleyan church to see who can sponsor the bigger sale each summer. We beg for donations for months, then organize them all, and then the pastor donates the remaining items to the mainland shelter and mission to take a tax deduction that strengthens our winter bottom line. Which is all well and good except that an old argument between the two communities over a shared fence between the properties began an all-out war."

"Between two churches, which is ridiculous in and of itself," spouted Gail.

"It is, but Grace Community Church did refuse to pay its share of the fence upkeep."

"Because it wasn't their fence, Tru," Joan pointed out and then shook her head. "Never mind, it's been argued back and forth for decades. You and me discussing it now won't change a thing."

"Decades?" Priscilla asked softly.

Gail frowned. "Unfortunately yes, and that kind of contention probably makes Wheatfield seem pretty attractive again, doesn't it?"

"Except that we had a similar situation, only it was a shared tree in our instance. One pastor wanted it down, the other loved it, and what a feud it began."

"When people of God throw the gauntlet, it's a sad moment in any time or town," said Trudy.

"Sad, but unfortunately normal because folks do tend to want their way, don't they?" Priscilla closed the notebook without making an entry. "So, Joan, you don't mind helping? I'd love to work with you in the afternoons. And I should be bringing Jake home tomorrow, so we can work together, the three of us."

"Jake?"

"Who's Jake?"

Priscilla filled them in on the dog and then withdrew a set of keys from the rack inside the door. "Are we ready, ladies?"

"More than ready. I can't believe we're lighthouse exploring." Trudy rinsed the handful of dishes and set them on the counter. "We can do dishes later. Let's check this out while the light's still good."

They crossed the driveway and gathered around the lighthouse door. Priscilla plied one key after another into the lock. When the fourth key made an audible click, she pushed the door open with a confidence she didn't quite feel. "We're in."

The door creaked softly but swung easily. The four women entered the broad, circular, brick-lined space, but before Priscilla let the door swing shut, Joan slipped a small garbage can between the door and the frame. "Just in case. Old locks and old doors aren't the most trustworthy pairs."

"Good idea." Priscilla had turned on her cell phone flashlight, but she flicked it off. "I thought it would be dark in here."

"The windows going up really help brighten the inside, don't they?"

Priscilla studied the circle of red brick surrounding them. She turned her light back on and examined the walls.

"What are you looking for?" asked Trudy.

"A false wall. Or a basement level. Someplace to hide a big box of gold just in case it got found after the lighthouse was built."

"These old chairs." Joan touched one of two ladder-back chairs. "I wonder why they're here?"

"Old fellows sitting and gabbing so the wives don't put them to work," said Gail. "Not much changes, does it?"

They all laughed.

"What a shame it's all so empty and unseen." Priscilla looked around. "Doesn't it seem like an antique treasure like this should be spit and polished?"

"For no one to see?" Trudy made a face. "Who's got that kind of time to waste?"

Maybe people could see it someday, Priscilla thought as they began climbing the wide, winding stairs. They stopped for breath twice, and when they got to the floor beneath the lamp, Joan was in the lead. She reached out, pushed open the thick blue door, and sighed. "You will not believe how beautiful the watch room is."

"Watch room?" Gail hiked an eyebrow as she followed Joan in.

"The room where the keeper kept watch in case of problems. And where they stored supplies to care for the light." Joan moved to the center. Directly below the actual light was a polished blue metal cupboard with glass doors. Inside the cupboard were spare bulbs, old wicks, and tools for repairing the light. Evenly spaced windows looked out in multiple directions, and a broad wooden door, also painted blue, led the way outdoors. "The watch deck." A bright smile lit Joan's face. "All my life I've wanted the chance to walk on that watch deck. And here it is." She opened the door and stepped out. "And it's everything I always hoped it would be. Amazing!"

Priscilla followed her out and sighed. "Breathtaking. I can't imagine a prettier sight than gazing out at the water, seeing it in all its moods."

"She works up a tempest, that's for sure," said Trudy. "A bad nor'easter might make you rue those words."

"Stormy days are ideal for reading, aren't they? Although if winter stretches long here..."

Gail snorted, Trudy looked amazed, and Joan choked back a laugh, which meant winter overstayed its welcome along the East Coast too.

"And I wouldn't want to be hanging out up here in a hurricane, although this lighthouse has managed to stand through five major ones that we know of," added Gail. "I'm not big on history, but storms and weather fascinate me. Folks figured out early that if they were going to build along this coast, they better build strong."

"After many a house washed out to sea," Joan added. "Oh, Priscilla, I am so excited to be up here. Seeing this. I've dreamed about it ever since I was a little girl, but we wouldn't have dared ask Auntie to let us up. She was sure danger awaited at every turn, and having no children of her own, kids made her nervous so there was never the chance. Your arrival has made this day special. Except for the broken car window and ruined living room floor." Joan turned more serious. "You should come stay at my place until things quiet down. Give this newspaper foolishness a few weeks to fade. Once people stop poking around with metal detectors and bothering old churches..."

"Old churches?" Priscilla asked, relieved to hear she wasn't the only target in town.

"Yes, they've been sneaking around the historic church on Cooper Road and the one on Lexington Street. Which makes no sense because that church used to be over by the cemetery and they moved it some sixty years ago to make way for the park reserve, and I expect if someone found a big box full of gold, someone would have heard. The rector had to chase a bunch of folks out last evening. They were snooping in cupboards and corners with no respect for the church or its history. Think about this, please." Joan faced her. "You could sleep at my place and come back here during the day. Break-ins like this aren't the norm for Tisbury, but what if someone is really desperate for money? Desperate people often employ desperate measures."

"I'll lock up tight, and I don't think anyone will try anything while I'm here," Priscilla reasoned. "That's why they broke in this afternoon—because I wasn't here."

"Do you suppose the person knew that?" Joan looked from cousin to cousin. "Did they know you were gone, like knowing your schedule?"

Priscilla stayed practical. "I've got no schedule, and I've only been here a few days, so that's unlikely. But if someone saw my car in town..."

"Or saw us at the inn or walking."

Priscilla arched a brow of agreement, and Joan's mouth dropped open. "The professor. He was there, and he knew we'd be out awhile. Oh, Priscilla, do you think he'd be rash enough to do something like this?"

"I think he's got something up his sleeve, and that's all I can say about that, but his curiosity about me and this property goes beyond the norm. So maybe I'll do some more investigating in the morning. I'll stop by the library again and add to my cache of information, and that way I can bring you up-to-date. I e-mailed the *Boston Globe* reporter, but he hasn't responded, so I'll call him tomorrow. If his work is going to disturb my life, I've got no qualms returning the favor. I'll need help going through the keeper's logs. And tackling the basement."

"Which is a lot scarier than this amazingly beautiful light-house," muttered Trudy. "We peeked down there when we were getting things ready, spotted cobwebs the size of a small car, and shut that door tight."

"I don't mind getting dusty if we can do basement exploration some afternoon," Joan offered. "My last ultrasounds are scheduled for eleven thirty, so I'm generally out of work by noon."

"You think you'll be okay here tonight?" Gail asked. The wind stirred her hair, and she brushed it back out of her face. "There's not an extra room at my house like there is at Joan's, but we have a comfy sofa and that's not a bad place to sleep at the end of the day."

"Dan and I have two empty rooms if you don't mind sleeping with garage-sale clutter. It'll all be gone in a few weeks," Trudy added.

Their thoughtfulness warmed Priscilla's heart and strengthened her reserve. "'I will fear no evil, for you are with me; your rod and your staff, they comfort me.'" She quoted the twenty-third Psalm easily, a longtime favorite. "God and I have got this. And the four of us can work together to figure it all out. With a dog at our side!" They moved back inside and then down the long, curving metal stairs.

"This was a workout going up, and a fright going down." Gail frowned at the open-backed metal steps. "I know I'm going to trip and fall and take you all out."

"Next time we're letting you go first, in that case," Joan joked. "Don't look down. Look straight. Trust your feet to feel the way."

"I'd be more inclined to do that if I didn't know we were several stories up on dangerous stairs," answered Gail. "I'll just grip this railing for dear life and be fine. Maybe."

They reached the bottom, and Priscilla looked around again. "Is there a basement under the lighthouse?"

"Nothing I've ever heard of. And no storage doors anywhere."

"So there really isn't any place in here where the gold could be hidden, is there? The walls aren't insulated, and there doesn't seem to be any trapdoor in the floor."

"I thrive on cleverly hidden doors." Gail's face brightened at the thought. "I've read every mystery series I could get my hands on, and every winter I hunt up a new one. Folks were mighty clever about tucking a secret passage here and the odd door there. But I don't see anything like that in here."

"And it would mean someone found the gold and moved it," Priscilla reminded them. "It was stolen long before this lighthouse was constructed."

"But that gold piece you told us about means that some part of the gold was here at some time. Unless it's a coincidence to have that very kind of gold piece show up in the attic, and I don't believe that for a minute."

"Me either," said Priscilla. "Not after today." She locked the lighthouse door and lowered her voice, just in case she might be overheard. "We'll tackle this together. Agreed?"

"Yes." Joan put her hand in the middle of their small circle. "Who's in?"

"Me." Trudy smacked her hand on top of Joan's.

"I've got little choice in the matter." Priscilla laid her hand on top of Trudy's.

"And I've got at least a decade of mystery-reading experience on my side. In!" Gail's hand finished the pledge tower. "Let's get this solved so our lives can go back to same old, same old."

"Agreed." They broke apart, and Priscilla walked the women to their cars. "If you need anything, call me," said Joan. "And call 911 if anything happens. Keep your phone nearby, just in case. Okay?"

"I will." Once they'd gone, she took the phone charger straight into her room and plugged it in as a reminder because she rarely thought to bring the phone into her room at night. Tonight she would, and every night thereafter. If she remembered.

She double-checked the doors and windows, then went to bed, thinking she'd never fall asleep.

She was wrong.

She fell asleep so quickly that she couldn't remember falling asleep the next morning, and when early light flooded the room, she sat up, invigorated.

Yesterday's antics were a cause for concern, yes. But she was an intelligent, educated woman with a trail to follow, and once she had her first cup of coffee, she intended to do exactly that. Starting with tracking down that reporter and some more local info.

CHAPTER ELEVEN

M ildred, you're being unreasonable."

The raised voice caused Priscilla to stop in her tracks as she walked toward the back door of the museum shortly before nine that morning.

"I'm being no such thing." The stern note in Mildred's reply meant business. "The coin is not for sale under any circumstances, Franklin. It's a piece of island history, and you should appreciate that more than most."

"Then let me see it."

Mildred sighed. "I told you. It's not here. I've put it in the safe deposit box until we have a secure place for it. And I don't want word leaking out about it and all kinds of folks pestering poor Priscilla any more than she's already been bothered. It's absurd."

"Not so much now that she's found part of the treasure on the lighthouse grounds. Where there's smoke, there's fire—we all know that. Did she say where she found it exactly?" the professor pushed as Priscilla marched up to the back door, spittin' mad.

"She did not," Priscilla announced in her best clipped voice, the one she'd used on uncooperative cows over the years. "Nor will she, and she'd be happy for you to know that the next time someone trespasses on her property, she'll have new means at her disposal to shift them quickly."

The professor spun around, surprised, and if Priscilla was reading his face correctly, a little nervous too. Well, good! "The people of Martha's Vineyard don't take highly to threats, Mrs. Grant."

"And I don't take highly to breaking and entering." She faced him squarely. "Or people who damage cars and homes while on a quest to steal something that doesn't belong to them."

"Priscilla, have you had more trouble?" Mildred moved forward and put her hand on Priscilla's arm. "Come in. Franklin was just leaving and taking his demands with him."

"Someone broke into your home?" His eyebrows shot up, but they were always doing that, so Priscilla ignored them and locked eyes with him.

"Yesterday. Right after you ran into Joan and me at the inn, Professor. You knew we were having lunch and that Joan offered to show me around the village. Now that could be a coincidence." She tapped her right foot three times. "Or not."

"You think I could have had something to do with it?" Franklin sputtered. "Why would a man of my renown even consider such a thing?"

"The same reason you came over here, demanding to get your eyes and hands on that guinea Priscilla donated to the museum. And make sure you jot that down as a tax write-off, Priscilla," Mildred added as if the professor wasn't important enough to take more of her time. "I'll give you a receipt. At current value and in such good condition, it will give you a sizable write-off."

"I hadn't considered that," Priscilla told her. She turned back to Franklin. "Professor, I don't know you. You don't know me. But I take threats and danger seriously, so be forewarned. I intend to find out what's at the bottom of this treasure quest, if for no other reason than to reclaim the peace and tranquility my family loved about this island. Now good day."

Faced with the indignant stares of two strong women, the professor walked out, turned, and headed straight for the library, which meant Priscilla would put her own visit there on hold for a while. She waited until he was gone before turning back. "Well. That was fun."

"Oh, Priscilla, all this nonsense your first week in town. What you must think of us!" Mildred tapped the one-cup brewer. "I think straight Colombian should be the choice of the day. Don't you?"

"Strong works for me." She set her purse on one chair and took a seat in another. "I have to admit it felt good to tell him off, though, and while I'm ashamed to admit that, I'm a little pleased too."

"Taking charge of one's life is an important step," said Mildred. She brewed the first mug and set it in front of Priscilla. "We women need to stand up for ourselves and steer our own paths." The tension in her face eased, but Priscilla recognized the quick flash of pain before Mildred busied herself with the next cup. "Especially when we're facing years of being on our own."

"You lost your husband too?" One look at Mildred's face confirmed it. "I'm so sorry, Mildred."

"Well, things happen. We just wander through life unconcerned until they happen to *us*." Her emphasis on the pronoun hit home with Priscilla.

"I wasn't ready to say goodbye," Priscilla admitted.

Mildred set her mug on the table and took the seat across from Priscilla.

"And then when I was faced with the inevitable..." Priscilla drew in an almost painfully deep breath. "I almost caved." She stared down at the coffee, remembering the shock of Gary's prognosis and how quickly he was gone.

"But you didn't."

"No." Priscilla squared her shoulders and sat more upright. "I didn't because what if I did fall apart? What kind of example was that to my daughter? I raised her to be strong and independent. To take care of herself. But after all those months of watching the snow fly and the bare trees bend and dull grass get matted, I had to leave. When the lawyer's notice came about the lighthouse, it was like a door got thrown open. As if the light beckoned me to come."

"And then to face all this nonsense. And to stumble upon a piece of the very gold that's got everyone all riled up! What a coincidence!"

"But what if it's not?" Priscilla asked quietly. "What if this is all part of God's plan? I'm here, the lighthouse is involved somehow, and I found a clue that's been wallowing upstairs for who knows how long. Maybe this is where I'm meant to be after all. Maybe I'm supposed to be part of the solution, Mildred."

"That's an inventive way of looking at an interesting turn of events, and it makes as much sense as any. Perhaps all of us here and all who've gone before aren't bound just by circumstance, but by the accidents of timing, which might not be accidental at all."

Not accidental at all.

Priscilla smiled. "That's exactly how I feel. And on that note, I'm going right back to the beginning. The theft of the gold and Nathanial Claybrook's capture and demise. My daddy loved puzzles. He always said the way to solve a puzzle is to begin at one end or the other. Or both and meet in the middle."

"Well, you're living one end, so you've got that covered." Mildred looked a little excited by the prospect, and Priscilla didn't think the historian let herself get too excited over much of anything. "And with the reporter's research, maybe we can find more facts about the origin. Although finding records that have survived fire and flood over two hundred years later is no easy task. But I'd be glad to help all I can, Priscilla."

Priscilla finished her coffee and stood. "I'd appreciate it, Mildred. Right now I've got to be a little careful with whose help I accept, but yours is a welcome addition."

"Thank you." Her words had clearly pleased the other woman. "And be careful what you say when you stop by the bakery too. The tables have ears, in case you haven't noticed."

"I'll be discreet," Priscilla promised. "Are you a fan of the cranberry muffins?"

"I'm more a fan of the crème horns, I confess. The muffins make me feel far too healthy for my own good."

Priscilla laughed because that was the very reason she got them. The chocolate chip cookies were a whole other level of indulgence. "That's good to know. I'm off to the library, hoping the professor has gotten what he needed and left by now. I'd prefer not to have another run-in this morning."

A text from Dr. Morris's veterinary clinic came through just then, and Priscilla smiled. "And once I'm done with my sleuthing, I'm picking up my new secret weapon to discourage intruders, a shaggy little mutt named Jake. He's about to become my new lighthouse watchdog."

She pulled up a picture she'd taken the day before and held the phone out toward Mildred. "He's a little beat up right now, but I think with some tender loving care, the little fellow will be the perfect companion. If nothing else, a word of warning when strangers come about would be welcome."

"He's so cute, and I think I've seen him roaming about down by Faith Fellowship."

"That's where I found him."

"Pastor Rona liked to leave the odd bite out for him now and again. She mentioned it a few weeks back, and I remember saying she had a soft heart for strays, and that's why the winter homeless mission is so successful. 'Whatever you did for one of the least of my people...'"

"'You did for me,'" Priscilla finished softly. "I'm off. Call me on my cell if you come up with anything, all right?"

"I will."

Priscilla texted the vet's office that she'd be by to pick up Jake at one o'clock and then made her way to the library. Would Clara be there? Would she be able to treat Priscilla normally if she was involved in the break-in?

Priscilla hesitated outside.

She didn't want the single mother to be involved. Lean farm years and a couple of natural disasters had been hard to get through with Gary by her side. How much more difficult it must be alone.

Clara couldn't be involved. Priscilla convinced herself of that outside, walked in as if everything were fine, and went straight to the computer corner of the history section where she found every one of her bookmarked research pages gone.

She stared at the cloud database and plugged in every possible search she could think of, but none of her starred pages remained.

Who could have done this? Who could have accessed her pages and erased her work? When she attempted to do a user history on the computer, the machine groaned a sharp retort, rebuking her for trying something that went against library rules.

Clara hurried over. "Is something wrong, Priscilla?"

"It most certainly is. I had pages of research flagged for"—she stumbled a little because she didn't want to sound like a treasure hunter and then went in another logical direction—"for my family history here. The Lathams, the Howarths, and the Baileys and how we're tied to the Massachusetts colony and the Vineyard."

"You saved it to a folder in the cloud?"

"I did, and the folder's gone. Wiped out. Erased."

"Let me see." Clara slipped on to the seat once Priscilla vacated it. She stroked in a few commands and frowned. "When did you last make an entry? Yesterday? Or did you access the cloud from home?"

"Here. Yesterday. There was no time for further research yesterday because when I got home, I discovered my house had been broken into and my floor destroyed."

Clara's gaze flew to hers and she looked honestly surprised, but Priscilla refused to be fooled. Who else had access to her library files? "You're kidding. Someone broke into the cottage?"

Priscilla nodded.

"Because of this stupid gold quest?"

"That would be my guess."

"That's dreadful." Clara's dark eyes went somber, but her fingers shook as she struck a few more keys. "I can't believe that people here would do such things for money. Probably half the town could use that fortune, but you don't see us breaking and entering to find it."

Exactly what someone would say if they didn't want to be discovered. Priscilla bit back a sigh as she tiptoed into this bit of information. "Money's tight for a lot of folks? Why would they live here with the cost of living so high if it's hard to make ends meet?"

"Because it's home." Clara didn't smile or sigh, but she cast the library a look of love. "I was born and raised here. I'm raising two kids on my own, but I stay here despite the costs, because the island isn't like any other place. It's unique. So yes, we could move and do all right somewhere else, but then I'm denying them their heritage, to be part of something wonderful."

"It's nothing like Kansas, that's for sure."

Clara smiled, pushed a few more keys, then shrugged. "I suppose it takes courage to move away rather than sit tight and hope things get better."

She was right. It had taken courage and a hefty endowment for Priscilla to pack her bags and head cross-country. For a young mother with two kids and no inheritance, relocating would be intimidating. And if the library ceased to exist, where would she work?

Clara stood and looked dismayed. "I can't figure this out. The folder is gone, and the computer history is erased. There are only a handful of people in this town who know the code to erase browsing history here, and all of them have been in the library since yesterday morning. In fact, the professor and his assistant had a short meeting here just a little while ago, but I didn't see the professor on the computer. I'm so sorry, Priscilla."

So was Priscilla, but she was intrigued too. "Why would a summer dweller have the code to the library computers, Clara? That makes no sense."

"It does if you're part of the 'old guard,'" Clara replied. "The Mayweather family roots go back as far as yours. Clarence Mayweather is on the library board, but his health took a bad turn last summer. He's in the adult care facility over in Edgartown, but he assigned his spot to his nephew, the professor. It's an old way of doing things, and trustees and new board members will be elected in November, but until then, the professor is on the board, a fact he loves to brag about."

That sounded like the professor all right. And she'd wanted to check into his personal history, but she'd do that work in a more private setting at home.

"I'm so sorry about your work, Priscilla. If word gets out that research is disappearing or things are bad here, it won't look good for the library or any of us working here, and that can only make our situation worse."

"Then I'll keep it to myself, Clara."

Clara looked instantly relieved, but for what reason? Job security or because she'd just fooled Priscilla? "I'll recreate what I can. It's hard when some things are only accessible in library files, but I'll persevere." Then, to keep Clara from guessing the real motives behind her research, Priscilla added, "I love history, and I never realized how rich our American history was on this side of the country, so this is special for me. I could just hop on to one of those genealogy sites, but doing some of the work myself is rewarding."

Once again, Clara looked relieved. "If you need help, just ask. Although I'm tied up with the Harbor Ladies' Reading Guild for the next hour or so. I did their introduction first thing this morning. They've been conducting their monthly meeting. Once that's completed, I offer direction on the next book they'll read."

Priscilla felt her focus sharpen. "They meet monthly? I love to read, and that might be the kind of group I'd enjoy. What time do they gather?"

"Nine thirty on the second Thursday of the month. And when the meeting's over, they go to a local place to have lunch."

"It sounds delightful!" It did sound nice, but that wasn't what struck Priscilla. If Clara had been in the meeting room, greeting the Ladies' Guild at nine thirty, she wouldn't have seen the professor for some time. He could have easily slipped into the computer carrel and accessed her information. She asked one more question before she packed up her things to leave. "You said only a handful of people have the administrator code for the computers. Who are they?"

"Well, there's me." Clara frowned quickly. "But I'd have absolutely no reason to do any such thing, of course. The assistant librarians both have the password. And the library board. And the mayor, although I don't think he even realizes it, and he's never come to the library in the nine years I've been here. While some patrons love the library, like your ancestors Elodie and Llewellyn, some people find us useless. Like Mayor Whipple."

Clara's voice had acquired a distinct edge when she mentioned the mayor. "Who's on the board?"

Clara ticked off her fingers as they moved toward the doors. "Mildred Pearson, the professor, your cousin Joan, and Alma Whitaker."

She trusted Joan and Mildred. She didn't know Alma Whitaker, so she'd have to check that name. But it probably wasn't a coincidence that Professor Mayweather was on the board, had the code, and was in the library while Clara was opening the Readers' Guild meeting.

She stared at her notebook as if puzzled and shrugged. "Well, clearly not one of them has a vital interest in any of this. I'm going to shrug it off as a computer glitch and move on. That's the best way to handle it, don't you think?"

Clara looked relieved by her words. Maybe too relieved? "Oh, that's the smart thing to do. Technology is getting so advanced, some days I think it thinks for itself. Yes, brush it off and enjoy your day, and I'm so sorry about your house yesterday. That's scary."

"Thank you."

Clara hurried off toward the library meeting room, but she glanced back before she went through the door, and when she saw Priscilla watching, she waved.

But it wasn't a completely friendly wave. The action and her face looked pensive, as if caught in mischief, and Priscilla left the library determined to find out why.

It took little time and virtually no work to learn more about Clara's circumstances, unless she called ordering a muffin, two cookies, and a crème horn work. As she waited for Candy's assistant to bring out a new batch of the bakery's famous crème horns, a snatch of conversation came her way.

"Well, Clara was beside herself after that news yesterday, and who can blame her? Nobody's job is safe these days, and that's a shame."

"Do you think the treatment's that pricey?"

Treatment? Priscilla scanned the bakery counter easily, then swept the occupied table a quick look as she listened while pretending to be very interested in frosted lemon cookies.

A middle-aged woman with upswept hair and a haughty nose sniffed. "Mental health treatments are quite expensive, not that I would know anything about that. My Arthur and Agnes were delightfully healthy throughout their growing years."

"Arthur did burn the Williams's barn down," the first woman noted.

"An accident, of course, and no one was injured."

"Because he let the cows out to run amok first," another woman intoned in a wry, dry voice.

"It was their feeding time, I believe."

The wry woman sniffed and sipped her coffee, gazing off as if bored, and the haughty woman went on.

"Anyway, Clara's son is acting out quite a bit in school, and the therapy has pushed her to seek a new loan on their house. But I heard from Jim Blanc that she's already mortgaged as far as they'll let her go. So what can she do? Hire another babysitter and get a second job?"

Clara needed money for her son's therapy? Was that why she seemed worried about her job and her income? Probably one of many reasons to fret over money for a single mom, Priscilla decided, but therapy didn't come cheaply anywhere, and Priscilla was pretty sure the same was true here on the island. Maybe even more so with the higher cost of living.

"Jim shouldn't be sharing that kind of information with any-one." The final woman scolded the first ones with a strong expres-sion and a firm tone. "And we shouldn't be gossiping about it. In fact, I'm going to stop by Clara's place later with a gift card. If more of us offered a little of this and that quietly, maybe she wouldn't have to worry."

"In my day we stayed married, and that eliminated at least part of the concern," the hawk-nosed woman noted.

The third woman stood, clearly irritated. "And I suppose this is what you'll be thinking about in church this Sunday, Alma? How to draw and quarter another parishioner behind their back?"

She pivoted almost straight into Priscilla, offered a quick apology, and charged out the door.

So Clara attended church with these people? And was the hawk-nosed woman Alma Whitaker? Or was there another Alma in town? And how could two members of Clara's congregation sit here making light of her financial woes?

Priscilla decided she liked the third woman. As for the other two...she'd give them a wide berth. Unless she needed information. In that case, she'd listen with careful ears.

A glance at her watch assured her she had time for a quick stop at Misty Harbor Tours. She spotted the tour bus in what appeared to be a leased parking spot alongside the Harbor Walk. The Lobster Shack was running a lunchtime special, but lunch could wait. She popped into Teresa's tour office, a tiny shop front dwarfed by restaurants on either side, and looked around.

The office was simple, not shabby. It was clean and bright with freshly painted walls. Murals depicting Martha's Vineyard historic sites decorated two walls. Teresa hung up a phone call, saw Priscilla, and came her way. "Mrs. Grant, how nice to see you. I'm so glad you stopped by."

"I saw your tour bus and wanted to see what kind of tours you offer," Priscilla told her. "My daughter will be coming to visit at some point, and I want her to see why folks think Martha's Vineyard is so special."

"Our tours are the perfect way to do that," Teresa assured her. She handed her a pamphlet. "You can see we've got two longer tours and one shorter one each day. Both routes take us past your lighthouse and around the shore. We try to hit all the historic spots we can in a limited amount of time, and a few of the high-end homes as well. I take from twelve to one off each day for lunch and to catch up on phone calls."

Priscilla pulled out her notepad. She flipped it open to a blank, white page. "I'm sure you've got advice on what else we could do when Rachel gets here. Can you offer me a few tips, Teresa? Other than what's on the tour? And do you have a pen? Somehow I've gotten out of the cottage without one." She shook her head as if surprised when in fact she'd left her pens home on purpose.

"I've got a bin of them," laughed Teresa as she handed over an identical match to the pen they found outside the cottage yesterday. "It was cheaper to order five thousand, and I'll be giving these away for years, I'm sure. I'd love to meet your daughter when she comes to visit. I don't think there's anything nearly as nice as our island, but then I was born here and I'm determined to keep things afloat."

Something in her voice tweaked Priscilla's sympathy. "Have things been hard?"

"I prefer the term *challenging*. The island took a hit when the stock market tumbled, and it's been a tricky recovery. Things are better now, but in the meantime, a lot of folks had to leave to find other employment. The Claybrooks are old-time Vineyard, but we're not old money. We tend to stay out of sheer stubbornness."

But at what cost? Priscilla wondered. "Don't take offense, but when people own properties valued at a million dollars or close to it, wouldn't it make sense to sell and do a start-up somewhere else? A person can buy a sweet house for a fraction of that and have money in the bank across most of the mainland. What keeps people here?"

"Love. And some bullheadedness," she admitted. "I'm single, and when you're living here on one income, it's tough. But there's a lot of common sense in what you say, and I don't think we've seen the end of the sell-offs. Luckily tourist numbers are up for this year, and more folks are building and fixing, which means more construction jobs. We may come out of this minirecession better off than we were."

She seemed sincere and hardworking. Just because someone was down on their luck didn't make them a criminal. "I actually found one of your pens outside the cottage yesterday. The color helped it blend in to the grass." She spoke easily as she watched for Teresa's reaction.

She got none.

The phone rang, and Teresa moved to answer it. "I expect these get dropped all over the place, but I figure that's just a way of getting word out. If someone finds a pen and looks me up, then that's cheap advertising, and with the crazy gold story going around, people have stopped by to see if my tours take them to any possible gold sites. As if it's sitting somewhere, ripe for the taking. Crazy, right?" She lifted the handset. "Let me get this call, and I'll give you some ideas for exploring."

"I've got to make a quick run to the pet store, so I'll get them later." Priscilla tucked the brochure into her purse with the notepad. "You take your call and enjoy your lunch."

"I will. Thanks."

Priscilla considered the conversation as she headed back toward the municipal lot. Teresa seemed sincere. Clara seemed sincere and worried. The professor seemed far too obviously insincere, and for a smart person, would he be that obvious if he was the culprit?

Perhaps if he was long on brains and short on common sense.

Sincere or not, Priscilla decided to find out where Teresa had been the day before. Did her one-hour lunch offer enough time to rifle a car and the cottage out on the shore?

It couldn't possibly, not and get back to town in time for her one o'clock tour. So if Teresa conducted yesterday's long afternoon tour, then she couldn't have been the person who tore apart the cottage. But if someone else drove the tour, that left her wide open as a suspect.

How could Priscilla find out?

That one was easy. She'd run by one of the stops listed on Teresa's colorful brochure and ask.

CHAPTER TWELVE

Her phone buzzed an incoming text from Rachel as she approached the museum. *"Mom, how's everything today? Worried about u. Check in when able."*

She didn't want to worry her beautiful daughter, but she did want her decisions respected. Although if someone had broken into Rachel's car or apartment, Priscilla wouldn't be one bit happy about it. *"A beautiful day,"* she texted back quickly. *"I'm learning all kinds of things about the town and I love getting to know my cousins. You'll like them. Also, picking up my dog today. All is well!"*

"You're sure?" Rachel texted back.

"Positive. I'll send you a picture of Jake when I pick him up. Love you!" Priscilla pocketed her phone and lightly tapped on the museum's kitchen door. Mildred came toward the door and spotted the white bakery bag. Her face broke into a wide smile. "You didn't."

"I did, and gladly. It's so good to have someone in town who doesn't seem to be either after me or my family home or the gold. Mildred, thank you for just being you!"

"Not many would say the same. I believe the terms *crusty* and *curmudgeon* have been linked to my name in the past." Then

Mildred's lips quirked in humor. "But generally that's been said by ill-mannered folks needing lessons on propriety. Priscilla, thank you." She raised the bag slightly. "This will be such a treat."

"I'm having supper tonight with Joan and Trudy. Gail's tied up with her dad. Why don't you come by, and we can all eat together?"

"I can't. I have an ailing mother in Harbor's Rest Nursing Home, and I spend Thursday evenings with her. Not that she'd miss me if I didn't show up."

Priscilla winced. "That's a hard row to hoe."

"It is, and I'd feel bad if I got out of the habit," Mildred explained, and Priscilla liked her better for the admission. "I spend Tuesdays and Thursdays with Mom, and then my sister and I swap out weekend visits and adventures."

"Adventures?"

She nodded. "Anytime you take a dementia patient out in public, we classify it as an adventure. Because from one minute to the next, you don't know what's about to happen. But if we didn't do anything...well." She lifted her shoulders slightly. "She took care of us when we were quite a handful, three little kids under age four. It's our turn now."

"The invitation stands. We'll do it another night."

"I'd like that."

Priscilla's phone sounded a musical alarm that meant it was almost time to drive to Dr. Morris's veterinary and pick up Jake. "Gotta run!"

"Give my best to your new four-legged friend."

"Will do!"

She swung by Smith Bodfish & Swift's rustic store and took twenty minutes to pick out doggie essentials. By the time she was checked out, it was time to drive to Southside Veterinary and pick up Jake.

She packed the back of her SUV full, surprised at herself. Was this the quiet, somber widow, filling her car? Was this the frugal shopper who had just spent an inordinate amount of money on dog dishes; collars; leashes; toys; and a big, comfy dog bed?

Yes!

And she felt marvelous!

She pulled up in front of the animal clinic and hurried in the front door this time. "Hi. I'm here for Jake."

"And he's anxious to be let loose," replied the tech from behind the counter. "I had him out a little while ago, and he wanted to be set free in the very worst way."

"Which means I have to be careful to keep him leashed or inside. Unless I put up a fence for him, but the island doesn't allow spur-of-the-moment fences, does it?"

The woman shook her head. "No, but invisible fencing is quite popular here now. It's gotten more affordable and doesn't break any of the island's aesthetics rules."

Rules for appearances. Rules for refurbishing and repairs. Rules for the water, the harbor, the beaches.

She'd never considered farm life simple, but it was, comparatively. Martha's Vineyard was different. It had a historic appeal that should be preserved. She understood that. But the thought of so many rules governing multiple aspects of her choices stung a little.

And then Jake came through the door on the end of his new leash, and she forgot all about rules and regulations as she bent low. "Come here, fella!"

He didn't hesitate. He didn't pause as if wondering who or what she was. He bounded right for her as if somehow he knew they were meant to be together.

Of course, that was silly.

But it didn't feel one bit silly. It felt good and right and normal, and when she paid the veterinary bill and marched out the door with her dog on a leash at her side, she felt better than she had in a long, long time. And when she looked over at Jake a few minutes later, riding shotgun in the front seat of her car...

He looked happy too.

A low growl startled her awake twelve hours later.

Priscilla's heart rate swept up. Goose bumps dotted her arms and neck when Jake growled again from his spot on the floor. He'd turned his red-and-white snout up at the idea of a dog bed and curled up on the throw rug alongside her bed instead. But he wasn't curled up now. He was standing, legs braced, nose pointed toward the window overlooking the east cove.

Priscilla gulped.

She gripped the blankets tighter. She'd assumed it would be great to have a dog around, a friend to warn her of uninvited visitors, but right now, with fear racing up her spine, she wondered if she might be better off not knowing a thing.

Coward.

She winced because she didn't want to be a coward. She wanted to be brave and bold and independent, but fear ruled the moment.

Jake crept closer and poked his head toward the window, staring into the deep, dark night.

She slipped out of the other side of the bed, crept around the pineapple post footboard, and peeked out the window.

Gerald O'Bannon.

Slipping through the far edge of the yard, gripping a flashlight in his right hand.

What was he doing here? Was it Gerald who had skulked through the tall grasses and sand the other night? Was it Gerald who broke into her house? He had the proximity to do so, but he seemed so nice. And he was a Coast Guard captain. A military man would never do such a thing, would he?

Folks in the armed forces need money, same as the rest of us.

She scolded the inner voice, but as Gerald curved around the far side of the lighthouse, the inner voice made a lot of sense. Money and power were huge temptations. Maybe too huge, even for the military, and what did she really know about him anyway?

Not much.

She waited, scarcely daring to breathe, and when Jake began that low-throated growl again, Gerald reappeared, heading east this time.

What was he looking for in the dead of night? Was he simply patrolling the area because there had been trouble? Or was she being simplistic and trusting, the two qualities Rachel had cited as worrisome?

The hackles on Jake's neck rose. He didn't bark. She wondered about that. Was he staying noisy enough to warn her but quiet enough not to alert Gerald? Could a dog know the advantage of that?

Of course not. Especially a young dog. And yet…

She watched as Gerald disappeared from sight, and then she sank down on to the bed.

Jake broke his watch and padded over to her side. He sat quietly and laid his head in her lap. She gave him a nice long head rub while she gazed outside. "Well done, my friend. Well done. But now that I'm aware of the late-night goings-on that seem prevalent along my beach, how will we get back to sleep?"

Jake yawned. Then he yawned again, walked five steps, turned in three slow circles, and curled right back up where he'd been before Gerald walked by. Within two minutes, he was out for the count.

Not Priscilla.

Wide awake, she paced the floor and then realized that pacing was doing nothing but making her anxious. She didn't want to stew. She didn't want to investigate the attic in the dead of night, but she'd brought down a stack of logbooks.

She went out to the living room, opened one of the logbooks, and began making notes. When Jake rolled over nearly ninety minutes later, she looked his way. The pup opened one eye, spotted her, and she was pretty sure he gave her a smile before he rolled over and dozed off again.

Glad that one of them could sleep, she worked for another forty minutes before she stopped and stared at one distinctive name that jumped out at her, a name she'd noticed in her library research.

Bayleigh Point.

She stared at the nineteenth-century ledger, written nearly one hundred years after the gold disappeared, and spotted a clue. A clue that underscored the sudden interest in her lighthouse and her home as people undertook a quest for hidden riches.

Her land had been tagged with a different name originally. A name mentioned in the reports on Nathaniel Claybrook and the disappearance of the gold. Early settlers had called the lighthouse outcropping "Baighlea Point"—only the spelling differed from mention to mention, a common enough occurrence in old, hand-scripted records. In the library archives, it had been "Bayleigh" Point because the Bayleigh family had owned this land as newcomers. Many of the current Bailey families on the East Coast could trace their heritage back to those early Baighleas and Bayleighs, regardless of spelling. In this nineteenth-century mention, the lighthouse keeper stated that the lighthouse was on what used to be known as Bardsley's Point.

And Bardsley's Point was the very place where Nathaniel Claybrook was caught, and caught without a bit of gold in sight. Were Baighlea Point and Bardsley's Point and Bailey's Point all different names for the same place? This lighthouse keeper tidbit pointed in that direction. Perhaps town records would confirm the name change?

The young revolutionary hero had been here—right here—on her land, over two hundred years before, and he'd set something in motion. Something that affected his time and hers. But did he hide the gold here? Or was his capture here a coincidence? Nothing related to the actual timing of events had been uncovered, but come tomorrow morning she'd give the reporter from the *Boston Globe* a call...and she'd check a little more closely on the handsome Coast Guard captain who worked up the beach.

She yawned and looked at the clock. It was almost 3:30 a.m., and when she yawned again, she figured it might be worthwhile to try and grab a little more sleep.

Did Gerald know about the relationship between the lighthouse and the early theft? Did many people?

Probably not, or she'd be even more entrenched in fortune hunters. The fact that local police had been chasing people with metal detectors off of private land implied that most people were searching willy-nilly.

But whoever was targeting the lighthouse seemed to have an inkling that her cottage sat on the site of Nathaniel's capture.

She wrapped the ledger in double plastic bags and buried it deep in the sugar bin. A thief was unlikely to look in such a place, and she wanted this new tidbit of information kept to herself for the time being. She wrote nothing down purposely and then went back to bed.

Maybe Gerald was being a good neighbor.

Maybe he walked the beach in nightly rounds, and she didn't know about it because she was new to the area. Either way, the dog was smart enough to go back to sleep once the captain had gone back the way he came. She'd be foolish not to follow suit.

She called Brandon Scott, the *Globe* reporter, just after 9:00 a.m. Her call went straight to voice mail. She swallowed a sigh of frustration. She'd already e-mailed him twice with nothing to show for it but an automated "out of office" reply. Midsummer was a big vacation time in the Northeast, as evidenced by the crowds of tourists throughout Vineyard Haven, Tisbury, and the other island towns, but was he really out of the office or simply avoiding a huge influx of questions about buried treasure?

She left him a message with little hope of hearing back from him. She ended with her name and her cell phone number, then hung up the phone. She brought Jake to the car and headed for town by way of Joan's house. Joan had the morning off, and she'd tell Priscilla the truth about Gerald. She hoped.

"Priscilla!" Joan had squared her picturesque yard with Austen-friendly English country gardens. Small bushes rubbed shoulders with perennial flowers, and Joan had cleverly tucked old-fashioned trellises here and there. They provided a backdrop and a raised point of interest, giving the garden a carefully orchestrated casual feeling. If Tisbury had a garden club, Joan should be in charge because no one in Wheatfield came up with gardens resembling this. Of course, having the Atlantic Ocean as a backdrop didn't hurt. Joan's property wasn't waterfront, but the water and boat masts were visible from her backyard. "Come on back. Now that it's July, I've got to give the flowers an early drink, or half the water ends up evaporating. How did your night go? Better, I hope."

"I can't say better or worse, but I can still say interesting. Is Jake all right to come out here with me?"

"Oh, he's fine, Priscilla!" Joan patted her leg, and the dog came running. "But you'd best hang on to him or tie him to the house stake over there. I'd hate for him to run off."

Priscilla tied the leash to the stake and returned to Joan's side. "So what happened last night?"

"Gerald O'Bannon was skulking around my house at one in the morning."

"Gerald? Skulking?" Joan burst out laughing and managed to spray two lawn chairs instead of the shaded hostas. "Gerald doesn't skulk. He's never skulked in all the years he's been here. He's about as straight-shouldered a guy as I've ever met."

"I saw him with my own two eyes. And Jake growled."

"Did he?" Joan aimed a smile at the dog while she directed water to the base of four gorgeous bright pink Knock Out roses forming a ninety-degree corner. "Atta boy, Jake!"

"Joan, this is serious."

"I know it is, and I'm concerned by what's going on, but Gerald isn't a skulker or a bad guy. He's a good man who takes his job very seriously and goes out of his way to help others. Why would he be snooping around your property?"

"Does he need money?"

"Oh, honey, most of us think we need more money, and usually we just need to learn to appreciate what we have instead of longing for more. Humans are somewhat ridiculous that way, don't you think?"

"I agree 100 percent, but that greed is showing its true colors all around me right now, and it's worrisome."

"Ask him what he was doing there."

Priscilla was not about to do any such thing.

"You're nervous about asking him."

"Well, I can't just come to town and start throwing accusations around, can I?"

"If you word the request correctly, there's not a lick of accusation about it," Joan told her. "'Gerald, I saw you keeping watch on the lighthouse last night. Were you thinking those treasure hunters might come back?'"

Joan's clever wording did the trick. "That would work."

Joan kept watering. "Of course it would. That way he's got a chance to explain, and you don't sound like you're accusing him.

Although I have to say the timing of the break-in coincided too well with our lunch the other day. So was that someone's good luck that you didn't come back to the cottage and find them? Or did someone see us in town and take advantage?"

"My thoughts exactly." Her phone rang just then, and when Priscilla pulled it out, the reporter's number showed on the screen. "I have to take this." She moved to the far side of the yard. Jake barked once, as if in question, then watched as she walked away. Was he afraid she'd leave him?

She knew that feeling well, so she changed directions and walked his way, rubbing his head as she answered the call. "Mr. Scott, hello. Thank you for returning my call."

"It's the only call I'm returning," the reporter confessed. "I'm being deluged by amateur sleuths wondering what I know about the gold. I never expected there would be this kind of an outpouring of interest about a two-hundred-year-old story."

"A fortune seems to have that effect."

"I'll say. But when I realized you'd just moved into the lighthouse, I had to call you back. You said you had a question about Baileigh and Bardsley's Point."

"Is that the former name of the lighthouse point? I found a reference to it under a different spelling, but also referring to this plot of land."

"I found the lighthouse plot under three distinct spellings of Bailey," he explained. "It wasn't unusual for people to spell things phonetically as generations moved beyond the origins of the Pilgrims. Family names dropped all kinds of letters to ease the spellings and pronunciations. I'm kind of a history geek," he added, "so doing this article was great fun, but I never meant for it to create a problem for you or others. But while I found mention that Nathaniel was captured on Bardsley's Point, I couldn't find Bardsley's Point on any map. That left me with no idea where it was in relation to anything else."

So he didn't realize that Bailey Point and Bardsley's Point were the same place. But someone did, and they were determined to check it out.

"They searched for the gold all over the area, but the English never found it, and subsequent searches failed as well. There is no written record of it that I was able to find. Someone could have found it and kept it quiet. But the most likely spot I found for the British encampment wasn't far from the current site of the Latham lighthouse. If that's correct, then the proximity brings attention right back to the lighthouse owners and the surrounding area. Are you a history buff, Mrs. Grant?"

"I am, but I've never delved into New England history before," Priscilla explained. "I'm from Kansas. I was a long-time member of the Pioneer Sisterhood, a group of ladies who charted the pioneer trails. We examined the good and the bad of westward movement. But that history was quite different from this."

"You do have a respect for history. Good for you." He sounded happy. "Listen, I've got to go cover a story near the Harvard campus, but if you come up with anything of interest, let me know. Not because I'm after the treasure," he reassured her, "but because it would be cool to solve this mystery, wouldn't it?"

"It would indeed. And it might give me some time to sleep at night."

"Sorry." He sounded sincere.

"Not your fault. You go cover your story, and I'll cover mine."

He hung up, and she stroked the dog's head while thinking.

No matter which way she rearranged the mental scenario, her lighthouse was at the middle of the mystery, and whoever was targeting her land seemed to know that.

The basement.

The very thought of examining that rock-lined, crypt-like, cobweb-covered area put shivers up her back.

At that precise moment, Joan turned off the water, looking quite satisfied.

And quite available.

"Joan. How would you like to help me clean the basement while we casually search for gold?"

Joan didn't hesitate a second, and Priscilla realized they might be more alike than looks would allow. "I'll get some old clothes and dust rags. Marjorie wouldn't go into that basement for love nor money, and she wouldn't let anyone else down there either. I believe the furnace got serviced once a year, and that was it. And that poor man probably had to fight his way through cobwebs to do it."

"I'll guarantee you're right." She unhooked Jake's leash from the stake at the edge of the house. "You really don't mind?"

"Mind?" Joan looped the hose around its stand and grinned. "I've been dying to explore the lighthouse and the cottage ever since I was a little girl. What's a little dust and some spiders among friends and family?"

"I can promise you both!" Priscilla declared, laughing. "I'm going to stop at the bakery for treats, and we can gain sustenance for the mission. A cranberry muffin for me and a cream puff for you."

"Taking into account the age of the basement, make that two cream puffs. If I should pass away from dust inhalation, I want to die happy."

Two cream puffs, one muffin, and maybe three chocolate chip cookies today. She waved over her shoulder as she and Jake headed to her car. "Consider it done."

She drove straight to town but then faced a problem.

Parking was essentially unavailable unless she parked blocks away, but she couldn't take Jake into the bakery, and she couldn't leave him in the car. She grasped the dog's leash and walked the three blocks to the bakery, wondering what to do. When she got to the bakery, she stared at the door, flummoxed, but then a familiar voice came to her rescue.

"I see two possibilities here, Priscilla."

She turned quickly, surprised by Gerald's deep voice. His eyes hinted amusement at her obvious plight, and he swept the pooch a quick look. He managed to allay some of her suspicions when he bent low and gave Jake a thorough petting. "Hey, fellow. You've got a new friend, I see."

"We found each other inadvertently two days ago, and I decided he might like a regular place to lay his head at night."

"And three square meals a day isn't a bad thing either." Gerald stood back up. "I'll hold the dog, so you can go in and get whatever it is you need."

"It's want more than need," she admitted but smiled. "You don't mind?"

"Not in the least. I've got a dog."

"You do?"

He nodded. "Sammy. She's a good old girl. She's always happy to see me when I get home."

"Does your wife take care of her while you're gone?" The words were out before Priscilla realized how they sounded, as if she were wondering about his marital state. She wasn't, and the fact that he didn't wear a wedding ring meant little. Didn't it?

"No wife. I've got two grown kids from a marriage that fell apart a long time ago." Regret deepened the crease between his eyes. "We were young and somewhat stupid, but the kids are wonderful. And my daughter Aggie has a precocious three-and-a-half-year-old son named Max and is expecting another baby this winter. And once you get to know Max, you realize that the best things in life really are free."

Such a beautiful testament to love and family and regret. Was he sincere? Oh, how she hated that she even had to question that!

Or was he spinning a yarn to keep her from suspecting him?

She opened her mouth to ask about last night, the way Joan had advised, but he waved toward the door. "Better go in. There's a line, and I've got to be back on duty in ten. I just stopped in town to grab a quick fish sandwich from The Net Result over in the marketplace on Beach. They make the best fried fish around, no matter what other signs might say."

"That's good to know." How could she bring up last night now that the conversation had turned to fresh fish? And with a time constraint attached?

She went inside, procured the baked goods, then added half a dozen lime bars, just in case Trudy and Gail stopped by later.

When she came out, Gerald handed her the leash and smiled. "Good to see you, and it's really nice to see that this fellow has a good home."

"Thank you, Gerald."

He raised a finger to his cap, just one finger. A quiet salute that seemed utterly sincere.

But was it?

How could she know?

CHAPTER THIRTEEN

She called Joan once she and Jake were headed home. "I'm on my way!"

"Me too," Joan answered. "I've got buckets, wash rags, bleach, and a pick and a hammer. Just in case we see anything requiring deeper examination."

"Perfect!"

She rounded the last curve before her cottage, ready to work. Jake smiled over at her when the wind whipped through the fur on his head. She put on her signal to turn into the cottage driveway and came to a quick stop.

A strange car sat in her driveway. As she hesitated about whether or not to turn in or keep right on going and let the police handle this newest intruder, the driver's door opened, and a tall, well-dressed woman stepped out.

Rachel.

Priscilla sighed inside and planted a wide smile on her face as she made the turn and parked next to her daughter. "Rachel! What a surprise, honey. What are you doing here?"

Before Rachel could reply, Joan pulled in. But she wasn't driving her car. Today she'd buzzed up the island on a minimotorcycle with a little red-and-white sidecar attached. She wore a helmet and goggles, and if Priscilla had planned a more ludicrous intro for Rachel's first glimpse of the island, she couldn't have done better.

Joan parked and hopped off the bike with unusual enthusiasm. "The car wouldn't start, and I haven't brought the scooter out in ages!" She peeled off the helmet like a racecar driver at Talladega as she approached. "It's not speedy, and tourists get annoyed when they have to chug along behind me, so I've had it tucked away, but the sidecar was perfect for our mission. Bring on the spiders and mice. We're ready!" She grinned at Priscilla and stuck her hand out to Rachel. "I'm your cousin Joan, and no need to introduce yourself because you look just like your grandmother in the family albums. Tall, willowy, gorgeous, and self-possessed. Nice to meet you, Rachel."

"And you," Rachel replied. The compliment soothed the worry lines between her eyes somewhat, but she'd drawn her brow at the word *mice*, and even the nicest compliment wasn't going to fix that. Rachel hated mice. And bugs. And getting dirty. Growing up on a prairie farm hadn't been the easiest thing for her. She looked at the quaint cottage, then at Priscilla. "Am I interrupting a vermin quest?"

"Nothing we can't put off for a day or two, darling. I'm so glad to see you!" She was *always* glad to see her daughter, but the timing could have been better. And yet she didn't want Rachel to feel like she had to make an appointment to see her own mother.

Rachel aimed a rueful look at the two older women. "That probably won't be true once you hear me out. I know you want to get a feel for all of this island stuff, but the common sense response in this situation is to repack your bags and come home with me,

Mom. Someone has broken into your house here." Rachel turned her attention toward the yard, the lighthouse, and the sea. "It's stunning, but what if something happens to you? I can't live like this. To have you so far away and spending every day worrying about you. I've come to take you home."

"And on that note"—Joan backpedaled toward the scooter—"I'm going to leave you two to figure this out on your own."

"You're leaving?" Priscilla half-squeaked in protest.

Joan kept moving backward. "We'll clean the basement soon. I promise. If you're still here." She hopped on to the small, supercute scooter, pulled her helmet back on, and circled back to the road.

And then she was gone, leaving Priscilla with Rachel, Jake, messed-up plans, and... "The cream puffs!" she shouted down the road, but of course Joan couldn't hear her between the scooter, the helmet, and the wind in her face.

"Cream puffs?"

She turned back to her beautiful, headstrong, worrying daughter.

Priscilla had never been a worrier. She liked to think she faced each day with a resilience inspired by faith, hope, and love. Maybe that was why the grief following Gary's death weighed her down so much. And scared her, she admitted to herself. Should she let Rachel's overblown concerns drag her down? Or worse, lead her back to Kansas?

She reached into the car for the bakery box and then handed it to Rachel before she released Jake. He bounded straight to

Rachel and sniffed her feet, then sat back as if offering approval. Priscilla attached the leash and took him on a quick turn of the property, then led him back to her waiting daughter. "Rachel, meet Jake."

Rachel bent down and gave the pup's silk ears a nice petting. "He's sweet, Mom."

Priscilla unlocked the door and led the way into the house. She'd closed it up tight before she'd gone to Joan's. Which meant, unfortunately, that the musky odor of last night's dank marsh breeze still lingered inside.

Rachel's nose wrinkled instantly. "Nice smell."

"I was downwind of the marsh overnight. They can get smelly in the summer."

"All summer?" She sounded incredulous as she set the bakery box on the counter.

"I have no idea, honey, because I just got here." She turned toward Rachel after she set down her purse. "Which means I need time to get adjusted. To learn things. To get a feel for the island before I make any major decisions."

Rachel raised her right hand. "I respect that, Mom."

She probably didn't, but Priscilla let her talk.

"But after hearing about the break-in, I had to come. If the roles were reversed, you'd do the exact same thing."

"If I thought you were endangered, yes."

"Well, people breaking into one's house does put one in danger," Rachel offered mildly, and she could afford to use that mild tone because she was right. "What's in the box?"

"Amazingly delicious confections from one of the best bakeries I've ever been to!"

"For real?" Rachel undid the plain white string around the box and lifted the top. She sighed, smiling, and picked up a cream puff. "Right here is reason enough to call this trip a success."

"Do you need a plate?"

"I do." Rachel waited while Priscilla withdrew two small china plates from the cupboard. "I haven't had a cream puff in years."

"Remember those cream-puff sundaes we used to get at Terhune's?" Will and Martha Terhune had run a small diner in Wheatfield featuring good, simple food and cream-puff sundaes.

"I was so sad when they sold that diner." The new owners had offered a more haute cuisine menu and hadn't lasted a year before they closed the doors and filed for bankruptcy.

"Don't mess with success."

"If it ain't broke, don't fix it."

They exchanged smiles. Gary had loved the common-sense wisdom in old adages and proverbs. He had a litany of them at his disposal and dropped them into conversations at will. Using his words closed some of the gap between mother and daughter.

Priscilla withdrew her muffin, and Rachel lifted her brows. "No way does that muffin compete with this cream puff, Mom."

"Which is why I have chocolate chip cookies for dessert," Priscilla quipped. She took two forks out of the silverware drawer and pulled out a chair. "Have a seat, darling, and let's enjoy this treat before I explain to you in no uncertain terms why I am absolutely, positively not coming back to Wheatfield right now. Or maybe ever."

Rachel frowned, but as she took a bite of Candy's overstuffed cream puff, even Rachel couldn't maintain a sour look. "Okay. We'll argue once I'm done with this because I don't want anything to mess up my current level of happiness. Even stubborn mothers. Deal?"

Priscilla smiled and broke off a piece of her tender, golden muffin. "Deal."

Joan called about three hours later. "How's the standoff going?"

"We've declared a truce of mutual respect for age and stage."

"Which means she's not quite ready to put you in assisted living, eh?"

Priscilla laughed, but the laugh had a rueful note. "Pretty much. I think she's more relaxed about things for the moment. She's walking the beach, the wind has freshened up since last night's marshy smell, and I'm taking her to the Red Cat Kitchen for supper. It will be crazy busy, so we're heading over early. Can I have a rain check on basement detail? Rachel's heading back on Sunday morning."

"How does Monday look?"

"Sounds like the perfect way to celebrate my one-week anniversary on the island," Priscilla declared. "And a busy one it's been."

"You can say that again. See you Monday when I'm done working. Is twelve thirty good for you?"

"Perfect. But Joan?"

"Yes?"

"Rachel ate your cream puffs."

Joan burst out laughing.

"I couldn't tell her no. And it might have made all the difference, Cousin."

"If it soothes Rachel's nerves about life in the Vineyard, I'm all for it. And as long as Candy runs the confectionery, there will be fresh cream puffs every day. And muffins," she added, and Priscilla was pretty sure that might tip the scales in favor of staying on the island forever.

"That had to be the best seafood dinner I've ever had, Mom." Rachel pushed her long hair behind her ears as a sea breeze sent locks swirling around her face. "And this walk along the harbor is a perfect follow-up."

"Do you think a place can be in your blood, Rachel?"

Rachel lifted her shoulders and looked doubtful. "The practical side of me says no, but then you read about adopted kids who inherit their father's love of fishing...a father they've never seen. Or how a child will grow up loving to bake and cook and create amazing foods, a quality passed down by a mother they never met. So there's something to it, I suppose."

"Dad was born to farm."

Rachel nodded.

"And I loved the farm. I loved him. I loved working with him. But without him and with you grown . . . " She paused and faced Rachel fully. "It's not my place anymore." Rachel started to speak, but Priscilla pushed on. "I know it was your home for a long time."

Rachel's lower lip trembled slightly, but to Priscilla's relief, she firmed it. "Yes. And I've got lots of great memories there."

"Because it was home. But it's not home anymore, Rachel." Priscilla swept the busy harbor, the throngs of tourists, the dappled shade and rolling waves a long, slow look. "And this isn't either— not yet anyway. But there's something here, Rachel. As if, despite the fact that I'm not an islander and some of these folks aren't big on newcomers, there's a draw for me. A draw that goes beyond the beautiful setting and the sounds and the scents of being on the water. Something deeper."

"Roots?"

Priscilla nodded, looped her arm through Rachel's, and started walking again. "Yes, as odd as that sounds. To find my cousins here. To have this house that's been in the family for generations. To know my aunt left me her home at the very time when I felt desperately alone in Wheatfield. I'm staying here, at least for now and probably for good, because in one week here I've had more crazy adventures than I've had in decades. It's not just because I'm a Latham and there are old roots, Rachel. It's because I'm a widow and God's given me an opportunity for something new to chase the grief away. And a new spot for you to visit!"

Rachel sighed, but she didn't argue. "I hear what you're saying, and I don't mean to be selfish."

"You don't have a selfish bone in your body, darling."

"I do. I selfishly wish everything would stay like it was. Like it's always been."

"Life rarely works that way, I'm afraid."

"Maybe that's why I'm fighting this," Rachel mused. She took a deep breath, and her expression changed. "I smell something delicious being fried somewhere nearby, and I'm catching a background whiff of saltwater and flowers. And seaweed. And it all kind of mixes together and isn't as bad as it sounds when you say it out loud."

"Life in a shore town."

"I guess."

Priscilla squeezed Rachel's arm lightly. "I want to figure out what normal is like here. I want to test the waters out there"—she pointed to the ocean—"and here, on land. And we've got all day tomorrow to have some fun, so why don't we do something touristy for the day? We could do a whale watch." She pointed back behind them to the block of tourist attractions along the waterfront. "Or go to Oak Bluffs and see the gingerbread cottages. Or take one of Teresa Claybrook's bus tours."

"The closest I've come to a boat is a cruise ship, and I'm not so sure about those waves." Rachel jutted her chin toward the rolling ocean tide lapping the shore. "Let's do whales another time. But I'd love to take the bus tour and do some exploring with you."

"Then that's what we'll do. We'll take a day to learn a little more about the Vineyard and our family heritage."

She didn't mention that it would give her a chance to double-check Teresa's schedule the day of the break-in. If Rachel thought her mother was getting involved in something shady, she'd start worrying all over again. Priscilla had set a personal goal while Rachel roamed the beach earlier. When she kissed her daughter goodbye at the ferry on Sunday morning, she wanted two things accomplished: one, that her daughter's concern was allayed, and two…she wanted to attend a church service in the village. And she wasn't going to pick a church ahead of time—she intended to leave this to chance. Whatever service began after Rachel was on her way would be the one she'd attend.

She was leaving her first church service on the island in God's capable hands.

That thought made her smile as they took the walking loop away from the water and back into town. "You know what I could use?" she asked Rachel, and she was a little surprised when Rachel guessed correctly.

"An ice cream cone, like we used to eat whenever we walked along the river when I was a little girl."

"Yes! And there's a place just ahead. My treat."

"Speaking of that…" Rachel hesitated before she continued. "How are you doing for money, Mom? I know Dad remortgaged the farm to pay for the Bronson's acreage and the new Morton Building. So you're making that payment every month. Do you need help? Are you okay?"

Talking with Rachel about money felt odd. Gary's family had always guarded financial information like dogs guarded bones. And her husband had been a wise farmer in many ways, but he hadn't counted on death, so the new mortgage was a monthly drain on her funds. "I'm okay for now, but I won't be comfortable until I sell the farm. There will be enough income from that to give me a retirement account and money for the coming years. And I could always get a job here. I'm open to that possibility because I don't want the winter to drag. Last winter taught me that. I want to feel vital and involved. I was missing that last winter in Wheatfield."

"And I was crazy busy with multiple projects and couldn't get out there or even have you come into the city and hang out with me. I actually dove into every project I could because if I kept busy, I didn't miss Dad quite so much." Rachel stepped into the line for ice cream and leaned her head against Priscilla's for a few long, delightful moments. "How different that must have been for you."

It had been a very different scenario, but Priscilla refused to dwell on it because right now she was in a marvelous place with her beloved daughter. Ocean breezes and ice cream were much more pleasant to think of. "I'm having Island Caramel Crunch. How about you?"

Rachel studied the flavors and then smiled. "Parkerhouse Cherry with Fudge Chunks. Because how could that possibly be bad?"

"Your dad's favorite with a chocolate twist."

"Making it the best of both worlds." When they got to the front of the line, Rachel refused to let Priscilla pay. "My treat this time. You can get it the next time I come visit, okay?"

Her words made it sound like she understood her mother's choices a little better, and her smile underscored the words.

Priscilla smiled back. "Deal. Next time's on me."

"Perfect."

CHAPTER FOURTEEN

Priscilla approached the church on Sunday morning with mixed emotions.

It had been hard to say goodbye to Rachel. She hadn't counted on that, not really, but having Rachel here had seemed good and right. And now Rachel was headed back to the mainland and her life there.

On a positive note, she'd confirmed Teresa Claybrook's presence on her tour the other day, meaning that Teresa couldn't have been the one who roughed up the cottage. It felt good to be able to wipe her name off the list because Priscilla genuinely liked Teresa. The farm had taught her to understand the rigors of making a living on shortened time.

She walked into Grace Community for the 11:00 a.m. service on Sunday morning and scanned the pews for a friendly face. She didn't see a soul she knew, but she saw a few familiar faces from the local shops. They sat toward the front, and the island visitors seemed to congregate in the back pews.

Being a property owner didn't make her a native, but she wasn't a tourist either. Where did she belong? She picked a middle pew and slid way to the end.

When the middle-aged minister offered a rousing sermon about the missing lamb in Christ's parable, the message hit home. Not about the gold. Settling that would be good, but more importantly, she wanted to feel like she belonged somewhere. Could she do that here? Or should she click her sandaled heels together, recite "There's no place like home," and head west?

"Priscilla."

Her name came in a hushed whisper from behind her. She turned and spotted Trudy two pews back. Her cousin offered an encouraging smile in a silent gesture of unity.

Priscilla returned the smile as key notes of "Softly and Tenderly" sounded on the organ. The words and the music combined to smooth her choices. Kansas wasn't home without Gary. The farm wasn't a farm without Gary.

But here…

Here she could be herself. She could try new things and forge a new path.

When the service concluded, Trudy and her husband came down her pew, and her cousin grabbed her in a hug. "I'm so glad to see you here! I was telling Dan that your first week here might be enough to scare you off, and I half expected you to follow your daughter on to that ferry this morning. But you didn't, and I can't tell you how happy I am about that."

"Because you don't want me to sell the lighthouse?"

Trudy brushed that off instantly. "A building's a building, Priscilla. But family? Now that's something else again. Auntie felt so bad about the old quarrel with your mom that just having you here has made a difference to us. I don't want you to leave." Trudy tucked Priscilla's arm through hers as they made their way to the exit. "But I don't want you to stay just because Auntie wanted to fix things. I want you to stay because you can be happy here. Life's too short to live it unhappy."

"And if there's anything we can do to help," her husband added, "we're happy to do it. I wasn't born on the island. I've been here for thirty-one years, and I'm still one of the new kids on the block, but it's a great place to live. And being part of the Latham family doesn't hurt," he finished, smiling. "The family tree carries a lot of weight around here."

He was correct, Priscilla realized. As unlikely as it might seem, being a Latham meant something beyond this day and this moment. It meant roots. Old-fashioned, stick-in-the-mud roots.

She liked that idea.

"We're having some folks in for brunch to talk about the situation at the library. The library board will be there, and a bunch of regular patrons. Come join us," Trudy urged. "You can meet more of the locals, and they'd love to meet you. I would have called to ask you, but I didn't want to intrude on your time with your daughter."

The whole library board? Which meant four people who had the code to wipe saved pages from the library computers. Of course she'd go! "I'd love to," Priscilla declared. "I need to go home first and give Jake some time outdoors. We had to hurry out this morning, so he didn't get his due."

"Perfect. If you can get back into town around one, we should be all set. And don't bring a thing. The Monaghan sisters have arranged all the food, and I cannot begin to explain how much there will be. Just come and visit a bit. I can't wait to introduce you to people. They'll be delighted to meet you!"

She squeezed Priscilla's arm, and her happy smile put Priscilla in mind of a puppy again, but in the best way possible. Trudy met her days with refreshing abandon. Why not greet the day with a smile?

It felt good to grin back at Trudy and Dan. "I'll be there. See you soon."

She'd left her car parked a few blocks away, unsure which church she'd attend. As she passed the open doors of Faith Fellowship, a woman wearing a minister's garb waved from the narthex. "Hello there!"

Priscilla paused.

The woman descended the four steps quickly. "Aren't you the one who took that poor dog to the veterinary the other day?"

"I am." Priscilla extended her hand. "Priscilla Latham Grant, newly arrived and now a pet owner."

"Katie Rona." She accepted Priscilla's hand with a firm, quick grip. "I'm the pastor here, and I want to thank you for what you did. He's been dashing about these streets for a month or more. He seemed to be getting on all right, and with some folks down on their luck these days, I wasn't sure if he was a true stray or an old-timer's pet."

Misgiving hit Priscilla square in the chest. "You think he might belong to someone?"

"I don't know." The pastor shook her head. "This corner of town has a more mixed population, and we've got our share of characters. I'm more inclined to think he was a stray or abandoned. He's a smart one, sure enough, because he's avoided being caught for weeks, and that's saying something. No one has come around looking for him."

Since Priscilla hadn't even given this a thought, she was relieved to hear that no one seemed to be searching for Jake.

"If someone does ask about him, I'll get ahold of you. You're Marjorie's niece, aren't you?"

"Yes." Did she sound as concerned as she felt right now? One look at the pastor's face said she did.

"I've worried you, and that wasn't my intent." Katie Rona drew her brows together. "You go home and enjoy that pup and don't fret. I'm sure he's a stray, and I shouldn't have said otherwise."

"Do you really think so?"

"I do." The pastor spoke firmly. "And I apologize for making you worry. I saw you walking toward the water and thought it was a good time to thank you, and I've messed that up by saying too much. You have a good day now."

"You too." Priscilla didn't know what else to say.

She passed the bakery without stopping, first because she was going to brunch and second because the thought of someone claiming Jake had ruined her appetite.

She tried to block it from her mind but couldn't. She drove back to the cottage to take him for a quick run. He raced to the door to greet her, tail wagging, and Priscilla did something she hadn't done in a long time.

She sat right down next to him and cried. She didn't even know why she was crying, but cry she did.

Jake scrambled into her lap. He panted a happy welcome, then seemed to sense that something was wrong. He stopped panting. He sat quietly, staring up at her, and then leaned his head against her chest and sighed.

Oh, that sigh. As if he were the happiest dog in the world to be fed and loved and kept safe from harm.

What would she do if someone claimed her new friend?

A knock on her door interrupted her emotions. She couldn't reach any tissues from where she sat, and she couldn't get up off the floor quick enough to gather her wits with Jake in her lap. When Joan's head popped around the corner of the kitchen door, she didn't hesitate to come right in. "Priscilla, what's wrong? Are you all right?"

"I'm a blubbering old fool is what I am, and I can't believe I'm sitting here on the floor with this sweet dog, positively sobbing over the thought that someone might claim him."

"Someone owns Jake?" Joan didn't hide her look of surprise. "Since when?"

"Well, someone might own him, according to Pastor Rona. I passed Faith Fellowship on my way to my car after church."

Joan reached a hand down and helped Priscilla stand up. "Does she *know* someone owns him?"

Priscilla shook her head.

"And several folks have mentioned he's been wandering around," Joan reminded her, her voice taking on a thoughtful note.

"True."

"So you collapsed in a heap on the floor because of something that doesn't really exist?"

Put that way, it did sound silly.

"Here's what I think." Joan petted Jake while Priscilla snapped the leash on to his brand-new collar. "I think you've had a lot of change in one week. I think when someone becomes a widow, their emotions are on high alert for a long time. And then to come here and have all the adventure of gold diggers and people sneaking about in the dark of night—I'd probably cry too."

"So I'm foolish to worry about Jake."

"Not foolish, but does the good Lord want us borrowing trouble?"

He did not, and He made that quite clear numerous times. "No."

"And were you the sort of Kansas farm wife who looked for trouble?"

The exact opposite was true. "Never."

"Then let's not start here. I expect it was hard to have Rachel here and then harder to say goodbye, and to have worry about the dog on top of it all simply tipped you over the edge. Once Jake has his walk and we have some of the Monaghan sisters' food, this will all look fine in retrospect. Especially if they bring bread pudding."

"Bread pudding?" The term itself was an oddity.

"You've never had it?"

Priscilla shook her head as they walked Jake toward the marshland.

"Then you must try it, warmed up with whipped cream. It's a New England staple, and Charity Monaghan makes hers without raisins, thereby raising her cooking quite high in my estimation."

Another thing they had in common. "I'm not a fan of raisins either."

"Well, there you go." Joan said it as if that solved the world's problems. "I stopped by to see if you wanted to ride into town together. But I'll totally understand if you want to bring your car instead so you can leave when you like."

"You drove out of your way to check on me when you could have just gone on to Trudy's church?"

"That's what friends do, isn't it? And if the friends also happen to be cousins, well..." Joan smiled. "Better yet."

Funny. Ten minutes before, she'd decided to stay right there, just her and the dog, hanging in the doldrums together. But now, with a prickle of common sense from Joan, that idea seemed preposterous. "Yes, let's drive together, if you don't mind having me home by four or so. I want to do some low-tide exploring."

"Oh, that's the reminder I needed." Joan planted her hands on her hips. "I saw you all upset and forgot why I hurried over here in the first place. I have a box of letters to show you."

"Letters?"

"Old ones!" Joan exclaimed. "From one of the small trunks of keepsakes my mother hung on to. Our great-great-grandfather was the original lighthouse keeper, Llewellyn Latham. You've got his harbor logs here, but we also have two boxes of old letters. Some he wrote to his brother and sister who moved to the mainland. At some point they gave them back to my grandmother and my mother got them from her. But many were to his sweetheart, Elodie, our great-great-grandmother. My mother had a thing for old stuff, and she must have passed that on to me because I've kept these in a box in the closet all these years. I have no idea what's in them, but they're worth a look, don't you think?"

"I think exactly that. Come on, fella." She took Jake into the house, washed up, and faced Joan. "Do I look as disheveled as I feel?"

Joan laughed. "Not in the least. Rumpled feelings on the inside are definitely not showing on the outside."

Wise words from a smart woman. Priscilla locked the door of the cottage behind her, but she paused before she climbed into the passenger seat of Joan's sedan. "Thank you, Cousin. For coming over and for understanding."

"Well, I had no intention of doing that, but as I started out, I just got this niggle that it would be good to swing this way and see if you'd like to come along with. And when God sends those niggles, I've learned to follow through on them. And here we are."

They drove back along the curving road toward the welcoming village, and Priscilla was struck by a new reality.

The chances of someone coming to check on her in Wheatfield would have been slim to none. Not because folks didn't care, but they kept to themselves. Maybe that was a Midwestern thing or maybe just a Wheatfield thing, but either way, she'd have been crying lonely tears for a long while.

Not here.

Already there were several people willing to look in on her. To invite her to join in. Folks who reached out, even though she was an outsider.

And that didn't just feel good, that felt marvelous.

Less than an hour later, Priscilla realized that some locals found her something to be tolerated at best, which meant her earlier optimism might have been too quick. And her crime? She'd mentioned her desire to increase the size of the living-room windows to allow a broader ocean view. "If I have to replace the windows to avoid further break-ins, it makes sense to adjust the size to my liking while I'm at it."

"It's not allowed." Eyes narrowed, a sour-faced woman scolded her quickly. Priscilla recognized her from the confectionery. She'd been bad-mouthing Clara a few days before. "You can't just take over a preservation relic like the lighthouse and start changing things. It isn't done."

"Priscilla, have you met my neighbor?" Joan moved alongside Priscilla just then. "Alma Whitaker, this is my cousin Priscilla Grant. Alma lives two doors up from me," she added and then shifted her attention back to the older woman. "I don't think increasing the window size is going to be any kind of issue." Joan made light of the situation. "As long as there are windows already there, increasing their size shouldn't be a big deal."

"If the Preservation Society signs off, then it's fine. But there shouldn't be anything done to a historic landmark without their consent."

"Except they don't own the lighthouse," Joan reminded her. "Priscilla does. And if she's got to replace the windows, it makes no difference to anyone if she makes her water view a little better. It makes perfect sense."

So this was Alma Whitaker, the final member of the library board, and about the least likely suspect who could have messed with Priscilla's library notes.

"I was so sorry to hear that you had trouble." Unlike her mother, Alma's daughter Agnes seemed quite sincere. "What a fright to come home to things torn up like that."

"And most uncommon around here." A younger man joined their group, the man who'd been with the professor at the inn earlier that week. Alan something-or-other. "Clearly an outsider, searching for long-lost gold."

"Gold that probably doesn't even exist," added Agnes. "If it did, I can't believe it hasn't been found long before now."

Not to be swayed by talk of gold, Alma went right back to Priscilla's windows. "You being from outside"—she clipped the words in a strong Massachusetts twang—"means you have no true understanding of how things are run here. For you to make changes to anything concerning that lighthouse is of great concern, regardless of what may or may not have occurred there."

May or may not have occurred? Did this dowager think Priscilla broke into her own house?

"Our *history*," Alma went on, emphasizing the word by drawing out each syllable, "is of considerable importance to us. Of course a Midwesterner wouldn't understand such things."

"Mother, really." Her daughter rolled her eyes, but Alan seemed inclined to agree.

"Respecting the history of the island embraces the history of our great nation." He raised a cup of coffee as if toasting their forebears. "Those original settlers battled for generations to gain a foothold. I can't help but agree with Mrs. Whitaker's take on this. Her sympathies for all things historical have helped secure the island from modern-day transformation."

"Thank you, Alan." Alma bestowed a grand look his way. "It is a rare thing to be understood in current times."

Priscilla understood one thing quite well. This wealthy woman would have made a great royal back in the day, but that day was long since gone. Why be mean when it was just as easy and more satisfying to be nice?

"Priscilla." Mildred joined their small group. "What's going on over here? You didn't have the audacity to think for yourself in front of Alma, did you? Or to make a suggestion without being asked directly for your opinion?" She aimed a cool stare at the dour old woman. "The Vineyard is a mixed bag of people and opinions, as you've seen. Of course, history has proven that those who don't adapt eventually become extinct." She accentuated the final word of the sentence with firm intention.

"I think Alma and Alan have made a good point." Franklin Mayweather had moved their way from another direction, and he seemed ready to face off with Mildred, which seemed foolish when there was good food and company about. "To ensure our future, we must cherish the past, and arbitrarily changing things might set an unwanted precedent."

"If I choose to change the configuration of the windows in my own home, that should be my concern, and mine alone," Priscilla replied. "If I were adding on, then I would understand needing permission. But if I opt for larger windows overlooking the water, that shouldn't bother anyone."

"The historians among us would be most displeased."

Priscilla was pretty sure she didn't care.

"I'm sure out on the prairie, no one would give a thought to your choice, my dear." Alma folded her arms and locked eyes with Priscilla. "But you are not on the prairie. In case you hadn't noticed."

"There is something to be said for maintaining the authenticity and integrity of a historic place like the lighthouse property," added the younger man.

"Property that has been updated several times in the last century and a half," Mildred scolded. "And no one bothers any one of you if you decide to replace old, drafty windows or add insulation. Priscilla's just doing what Marjorie should have done years ago, and you all know the truth in that."

Alma ignored her completely and faced Alan. "You are a true lover of history," she declared. "If Franklin ends up losing his position over that plagiarism dustup, I expect you'll be right in line to take his place. And if you need a letter of commendation, let me know," she added as the professor spun on his heel and crossed the room, clearly agitated by her words.

Could the plagiarism scandal be threatening the professor's job? If it was, finding a hidden treasure would look mighty attractive about now.

"I appreciated your recommendation for tenure, and if necessary, I may take you up on that offer, Alma. It's never a bad thing to have esteemed retired faculty on one's side. I'd expected to add accomplishments to my tenure application this summer, but it's almost mid-July and time is escaping me." He bowed slightly, like a manservant from *Downton Abbey*, then moved to the laden buffet table, where the professor joined him.

"Who is he?" Priscilla asked Mildred as Alma's daughter helped her mother to a chair. The fact that the ornate outdoor chair resembled a throne wasn't lost on Priscilla. "He was with the professor when Joan and I stopped at the inn for lunch this week."

"Alan Napier, an assistant professor who works with Franklin. When you can get him to work, that is." Mildred frowned. "The village board hired him to run the Whaling Museum according to the posted hours, but he thinks nothing of putting the Closed sign in the window and going off to do research."

"Being on a tenure track is time-consuming," noted Joan. "And with the professor's fall from grace, Alan could be a likely replacement, don't you think?"

Mildred shook her head. "Young and brash and hardheaded. He's been at the museum several times already and seems more argumentative than interested in historical fact."

"The passion of youth." Joan almost giggled, and Mildred even smiled.

"Spare me that and give me an honest day's work. Why is it so hard to find someone who would love manning the Whaling Museum at least part-time? Maybe that's the problem—one person, day after day. Unless you love telling the exact same stories, it could get tedious, I suppose."

"Or be absolutely fascinating," Priscilla said. "Imagine putting yourself in that way of life, inserting yourself in the seventeenth and eighteenth centuries. Battling the seas, praying your men home, boys, determined to go off to sea to claim their fortune. Now that's a tempest, right there."

Joan leaned closer to Mildred. "I nominate her for next year. Part-time, of course. She'd have a ball, and people would love to hear her talk about the whaling industry. And why a Kansas farm girl knows all this about whaling is a mystery to me."

"My mother. History books, whaling books, anything to do with Martha's Vineyard or New England. She loved history and her heritage. I expect it was hard for her to never come back here before she died."

"But you're here now, and that makes us all happy." Trudy had come their way and heard her last statement. "Our lost lamb, brought back to the fold."

"Sappy." Mildred rolled her eyes.

"But kindhearted." Joan smiled at her younger sister.

Priscilla brought the conversation back to the two professors. "Am I wrong to wonder how they can both afford to spend a whole summer on Martha's Vineyard with state college salaries?"

"More wise than wrong, if you ask me," Mildred replied. "Franklin's uncle has let him live in his house each summer, and now that he's in Harbor's Rest, Franklin looks after the property for him. That's how he was able to appoint Franklin to take his library board spot. And Alan took the position as a historical docent at the Whaling Museum, giving tours and speeches about the whaling and fishing industry along the Massachusetts coast. The pay isn't great, but it leaves him time to help the professor get things back in order and to work on his own dissertation at the library, although he seems to be setting his own hours lately. Over the years, the museum owner has gotten quite lax about being present during the tourist season, and why have a museum listed if no one can get in to see it? So he offers room and board in addition to the wages to entice people to run his museum for him."

Priscilla heard the gong of the harbor church strike three. Joan raised one hand to let her know she was ready to leave. Priscilla turned to Mildred. "I appreciate the rescue, by the way. Your timing was perfect."

Mildred smiled without glancing Alma's way. "Most folks on the island are good, normal stock. But we've got a few who have their feet firmly entrenched in old ways that the rest of us kicked to the curb decades ago. What's on your sleuthing agenda today? And how is the lighthouse pup faring?"

"He's happy to be there and I'm happy to have him, so it's a wonderful thing. Joan and I are going to have a look along the shoreline at low tide, so we've got to run. I don't know how much we'll discover because I'm sure many others have scoured the area, but I need to see things firsthand."

"Then I'll see you later in the week. And Priscilla?"

Priscilla had started away, but turned back. "Yes?"

"Do be careful." Sincerity marked Mildred's gaze.

"I will. And if there's anything interesting, I'll let you know." She bid Trudy, Gail, and Dan goodbye and met Joan at the car. "Ready for a hunting trip?"

Joan looked downright excited as she shifted the car into gear. "I feel like I've been waiting for this exploit for decades. Today, the craggy shore. Tomorrow"—she grinned, delighted—"the basement!"

CHAPTER FIFTEEN

S horeline, 1. The Latham cousins, 0." Priscilla kicked off her slip-on shoes once Joan appeared at the cottage the next afternoon. "But I did not let our lack of success yesterday dissuade me from being hopeful today. And I bought cookies." She raised a bag from Candy's bakery.

"And I brought the letters from my house." Joan carried in two boxes and set them on a side table. "There has to be well over a hundred letters in there, and I'm sure some food for thought, but speaking of food, let's have cookies now and then more later because tackling that basement will work us up an appetite."

Priscilla handed Joan a fiber mask she'd purchased at the drugstore that morning. "No sense breathing in dust and microscopic critters, right?"

"Oh my word, I can't imagine wearing this thing for cleaning. It's bad enough I have to wear them at work sometimes." Joan held up the mask. "Priscilla, are you serious?"

"I've cleaned many a chicken shed in my time," Priscilla told her. "That fine dust is the worst if you breathe it in, and I don't want to spend my first summer here coughing like a barking seal. I'll leave it up to you, of course, but these things are worth every bit of the over-the-top look they give you. But first, a cookie. Or two," she decided.

Masks on, they descended the staircase slowly. Priscilla had turned on the single light at the foot of the stairs. She went first, waving a dust broom to drag down the closest cobwebs.

"Auntie must have avoided this place completely." Joan aimed her flashlight around and then set a battery-powered floodlight on a small old table. She switched it on.

"Oh my." More webs lined the craggy rock walls. Something might have moved in the far corner, as if startled by the light, but Priscilla wasn't sure and didn't really want to think about it. She moved around the uneven floor, waving her own light here and there.

"The support beams look good." Joan pointed her light up. "No rot, no bugs. That's important stuff around here."

"But there doesn't appear to be anything special down here," noted Priscilla. "And it's smaller than you'd expect." She looked around, frowning as she made a mental measure. "As if only two-thirds of the cottage has a basement."

"And yet this same stone continues around the full perimeter outside." Joan moved past the furnace, a hot-water heater, and a few odd pieces of stacked wooden furniture. She aimed her light and surveyed the far wall with intent, then paused. "Priscilla, look at this." She tapped the stone on one side with a small hammer and then the stone in front of her. The two taps bore distinctly different sounds. "Someone patched this. There's something behind this part of the wall. You can tell because it sounds hollow here." She tapped the stone again. "And not hollow here."

Something behind the wall... "What, I wonder?" asked Priscilla as she moved closer.

"And do we really want to know?" mused Joan. She passed her hand across the stony face of the hollow section. "I can't imagine why it would be walled off or..."

The wall creaked, and a rock-crusted door opened in front of them.

Both women shrieked.

"Joan!"

"Priscilla!"

The door had given way slightly. Priscilla was inclined to dash up the stairs and think good and hard about coming back down again, but Joan had no such qualms. She pushed harder, and the door swung open.

Dank, musty air poured forth. The space before them had no light, but their flashlights pierced the darkness.

Joan's brows drew together above her dust mask, and she stepped through the door, but not before looking back at Priscilla. "Under no circumstances are you to come in here and risk us both getting locked inside with no one to save us. Like, ever."

"I'll stand right here in the doorway, keeping it open," Priscilla promised, but when Joan's light caught the outline of a more standard door on the opposite side of the room, she grabbed a small table, wedged it in the doorframe to keep the rock-faced door open, and followed Joan into the new room. "Another door."

"But to what?" Joan's face looked gray in the shadowed reflection of the flashlight beam.

"A root cellar, maybe?"

"Or a secret room where we'll find a stash of gold?"

"I'd be lying if I said that wasn't my first thought, but I didn't want to say it out loud," Priscilla confessed. She reached forward and turned the handle with her gloved hand. Nothing happened.

"Locked or stuck?"

Joan studied the wall after she tried the door. "It feels locked, but it's hard to know. Hold my light, okay?"

Priscilla aimed both lights at the door area as Joan ran a finger along several small rock edges. "You think the key would be close by?"

"It could be, or it could be hidden, and that means we'll have to break down the door."

"Like with an ax?" Priscilla's voice squeaked.

"Yep." Joan moved left, then right, as Priscilla followed with the dual lights. "I'm going to get the floodlight and see if that helps us find the key. And if there's no key, then we go to Plan B."

"Which is?"

"A trip to the hardware store."

Priscilla was afraid that's what her no-nonsense cousin meant, and while it made sense, the thought of crashing through a door was a trifle unsettling. "Couldn't we get someone else to do this part? The door-breaking part?"

"We could, but what if there's something that bears thought on the other side?" Joan replied, ever practical.

"Like the gold."

"Or old bones."

"Oh, I hadn't thought of anything like that!" Priscilla bobbed the light as Joan moved past the wedged table to procure the larger light.

"Ouch!"

Priscilla couldn't quite bite back a gasp. "What's wrong?"

"I smacked my leg against the table in the dark. Are you sure you're okay? I don't want to make you uncomfortable."

Despite minor qualms about taking axes to doors, Priscilla quickly reassured Joan. "Having lurkers skulk around my house makes me uncomfortable. Having people break into my house and wreck my floor makes me uncomfortable too. And having bossy old ladies crab at me because I'm going to replace my windows wasn't exactly fun. But this?" She couldn't believe she was about to say this, but she did. "This is actually kind of exciting, isn't it? Like those girl sleuths I loved to read about when I was a kid."

Joan's laugh said she understood. "You can be Trixie, and I'll be Honey. Or Nancy and George." She set the light down on the table in the doorway and aimed it toward the wooden door. The beam of light helped brighten the entire wall. "Much better."

Priscilla moved forward and reached up. She slid her fingers across the wooden frame, and when she felt a small object, she directed her attention back to Joan. "I think now that I've got more light… Here we go. I've got it." She pulled down an old metal key and then paused. "Are we ready?"

"Ready and waiting," breathed Joan.

Priscilla slipped the key into the lock. She turned it slowly, letting the metal find its old path, and when they heard a distinct *click*, she turned the handle.

The door opened toward them. As they edged it open, Joan trained the double flashlights on whatever was on the other side.

A tunnel lay before them. And somewhere at the end of the tunnel, light penetrated the darkness.

"Are we going in?" Joan stared into the tunnel, eyes wide.

Priscilla crouched low. The sound of water lapped the tunnel, which meant either water came up beneath it or maybe that the tunnel ended at the water's edge. And yet they'd examined the area just yesterday and found no evidence of any opening. "Would it be safe, Joan?"

Joan winced. "A fellow got buried a while back by digging too deep into the sand. I honestly don't know, Priscilla. I'm game to explore, but what if it's dangerous?"

"It must be above the water because it's dry."

Joan nodded. "But is it lined with good old bedrock? Or eroded shale, waiting for our weight to tip us into the ocean or onto a rock?"

Close. So close. But it would be foolish to go crawling into the tunnel, not knowing what kind of support they'd find. "We need to reexamine the shore area and see where this ends. We must have missed something, Joan. We can hear the water..."

"And smell it, so we're aiming toward the cove, absolutely. But how did we miss an opening? What were we doing?"

"Talking, I expect."

"Obviously." Joan's dry tone made Priscilla laugh. "Okay, we reexamine the shoreline and see if we can figure this out. And I expect Trudy and Gail would love to be in on this little mystery, don't you think?"

"Absolutely, so let's make a plan and set it in motion. If the girls can come over for supper tonight..."

"Not tonight. Gail has Bible study at her place at six thirty. But tomorrow night would work, wouldn't it?"

"Low tide is at five forty tomorrow evening."

"We gather at four thirty for sandwiches, then we go exploring. With four of us, we have to be able to find something if there's something to be found."

Priscilla agreed. "Ida Jones gave me a call this morning. I'm having her come by tomorrow so we can figure out what to do about the cottage gardens. A proper cottage needs proper gardens, like yours, and Ida seems like the right kind of gal to help do the job. She and I can tackle those reeds and tall grasses. It's possible that the opening might have been covered by them."

"She's a sweetheart and hardworking and can use the money," Joan agreed. "Okay, you and Ida see about clearing things in that area. We'll come by ready to search from outside." She shut the door firmly, locked it, and tucked away the key. "For now, we go upstairs, clean up, and pretend we found nothing while we take Jake for a walk and munch on cookies."

A wonderful plan from beginning to end. As they closed up the basement, Priscilla's phone rang with Rachel's ringtone.

She let it go to voice mail. She didn't dare answer it and try to pretend like they hadn't just stumbled on what could be the hiding spot for a cache of gold coins worth millions. Better that Rachel think she was busy—which she was. She'd text her daughter later.

Would she sleep tonight?

She didn't know, but if they could solve this puzzle, she was pretty sure interrupted sleep would be a thing of the past.

Priscilla had not properly appreciated quiet, uneventful nights in Kansas, but when she woke up Tuesday morning after a night of quiet, uninterrupted sleep, her appreciation for such a simple thing grew.

"Jake, let's have a quick walk with our coffee, eh?"

He trotted to her side and sat while she attached his leash. When they got to the beach, they walked along the coved edges, their tracks the first ones to break the smooth sand path that morning. "Of course, our tracks will get washed away when the tide comes up," she told the happy dog. "But we'll just make new ones tomorrow. You and I." The thought of making daily marks in the sand with her new friend pleased her, as if marking the sand helped stake their claim to the island...and each other. "We've got a busy day ahead of us, Jake."

The dog perked one ear, listening.

"We've got to gas up the car, stop by the library, get some fudge at Murdick's, get cream for coffee, and I think I'll get fresh cold cuts in town. The gals and I can make our sandwiches and then go exploring. What do you think?"

He yipped and spun in a circle before settling into a brisk walk alongside her. Priscilla was no Dr. Dolittle, but she was pretty sure he approved of her plans. She gave a quick look along the water's edge as they circled around, but she saw nothing that looked like an opening. And yet if they saw light at the end of the tunnel, it had to be entering somewhere, didn't it?

Why a tunnel?

Her history-loving brain jumped in multiple directions. Smuggling? If new windows created a stir among the old and gilded, imagine what besmirching the Latham family reputation would do. But why else would there be a tunnel leading from a secret basement room?

She took Jake back to the house, settled him inside, and almost caved when he whined to go with her, but she had multiple stops this morning. Leaving Jake in a hot car wasn't an option, and he needed to know he couldn't always ride along. She closed up the cottage, double-checked the locked door, and headed to the library.

"Priscilla, so nice to see you!" Clara's words meant one thing, but Priscilla noted the concern in her eyes. "Did you have a nice weekend?"

"Busy and nice," Priscilla assured her. "I've come to have a quick look at two volumes about my genealogy."

"Do you need my help?" Clara raised a long-handled duster. "I'm just finishing this week's dusting detail, but I'm at your service."

Priscilla took a moment to survey the historic pictures along the foremost wall. "I should be fine. I just need a quick glance. Am I related to some of these people?"

"Several." Clara used the duster as a pointer. "By blood and marriage because your family tree has a lot of branches, but we do give a special place of prominence to Llewellyn. He was a great proponent of history and literacy and wanted everyone's children to have a chance to learn."

"A magnanimous heart."

"So it would seem." Clara reached up to run the duster around the perimeter of one of the framed portraits. Three people had sat for this particular painting. Llewellyn, Elodie, and an older woman.

"Who is the older woman?" Priscilla asked.

Clara tapped the card encased in plastic below the oil painting. "Priscilla Soule Latham."

Priscilla couldn't hold back a smile. "It's a family name, indeed."

"As is Johanna, Gertrude, Emmeline, and Abigail," Clara told her. "Each generation has had at least one of each, although current generations are using derivatives. Of course, they're spread out now, but it's a lovely tradition, don't you think?"

It was, and how special to learn that she was part of a tradition she never knew existed. Her mother had loved her birthplace and her family, despite their later differences.

"If you need help, just ask. And were you able to recreate your lost files, Priscilla?"

Clara seemed uncomfortable as she asked the question. Why? And if she was hiding something, why would she bring it up? That made little sense. "I did, thank you. And I've backed up all my notes as well. If I'd done that in the first place, there wouldn't have been a problem."

"True. But there shouldn't have been a problem at all, and I apologize for that, Priscilla. I feel like I let you down."

Priscilla had a light-bulb moment.

Clara wasn't uncomfortable around her because she'd sabotaged Priscilla's research. She was worried because she'd let a customer down, and in tight times, a bad review or complaint could cost someone their job. "Oh, Clara, don't fret about that, please. Whatever happened was not your fault, and I never thought it was. This won't go any further than you and me, all right? It's over and forgotten."

Relief brightened Clara's dark eyes instantly. "Really?"

"Of course! I've got a list of chores today, so if I miss you on my way out, have a great day." She hurried off to the local history area, pleased to have lightened Clara's stress. She stopped in front of the shelf she'd frequented for several days and stared.

The Latham family books were gone.

Priscilla searched high and low, thinking someone might have misfiled them, but they were nowhere to be found. First her notes and now the family history?

That made no sense, except that in the case of millions of dollars' worth of gold coins, it made perfect sense. "Clara."

Clara handed a patron a book and then hurried to Priscilla's side. "What's wrong?"

"The family books," Priscilla kept her voice soft and pointed to the shelf. "They're gone."

"No." The worry that Priscilla had erased earlier returned to Clara's face with full force. "They can't be." She examined the shelf, then the one above and below, much like Priscilla had done before her. "Those books can't be loaned out." She turned to face Priscilla. "Which means someone stole them."

Priscilla winced. "This treasure-hunting nonsense has folks all in a dither, but why steal the library's books when someone can simply come in, sit down, and gather their facts?"

"But then they'd be noticed," Clara whispered. "And folks might think they had a track on the gold. Taking a few books might not seem huge to some people, but it worries me, Priscilla. I'm afraid whoever is trying to find this gold will stop at nothing."

Priscilla hated that Clara could be right.

"This corner is blocked by the computer carrels and the history section. I can't see what's going on over here, and that hasn't been a problem in twelve years. But apparently it is a problem now."

"We'll figure this out," Priscilla promised, and she meant every word. One way or another, they would find out who was either trying to find the gold or thwart her attempts to find the gold. With each passing day, Priscilla was becoming more aware that her adversary meant business, and that realization sent a cold shudder down her spine. Was the professor that callous?

And what if her suspicions of the professor were off base? Who could walk around town, checking things out without raising suspicion of any kind? A police officer or...

A coast guard captain.

Her heart dipped.

Gerald was in and out of town all the time. Folks greeted him when they saw him. And he'd been at her house in the light of day and the dead of night.

She hated to think any such thing about a member of the military, but right now she couldn't afford to assume anything. She left the library none the wiser than when she entered, but doubly suspicious. Whoever was sabotaging her work had a clear idea of what she was doing and when. Just enough to delay her progress.

Priscilla had never claimed to be an athlete, but in a battle of wits, she would not be outdone. Determination firmed her steps as she walked through the village. No one should put greed and fortune ahead of others' well-being.

She stopped at the bakery after she bought a pound of mixed fudge. Candy took one look at her as she moved to the front of the line and bagged two chocolate chip cookies without being asked. "On the house," she declared and handed the cellophane envelope to Priscilla. "My prescription for whatever put that look in your eye."

"Letting aggravation show is not a usual occurrence for me, but I consider myself called out," Priscilla admitted. She raised the cookies. "Thank you for this. Can you package me another dozen for dessert tonight, one loaf of your tender multigrain bread, and one cranberry muffin? With nuts this time."

"With nuts." Candy lifted her eyebrows as if nuts raised the stakes, and today they did. Priscilla intended to go home, make ham salad, check the reeds, and take a little time to examine Joan's letters while Ida planned a garden makeover.

She headed back to her car, irked but energized. She knew things the would-be thief didn't. She knew about the tunnel. She knew where she'd found the lone coin. And if the two were related, she needed to plug in all the pieces of the puzzle and examine the full picture.

A text from Dr. Morris's veterinary office came through as she paused at the Stop sign next to the village playground. She glanced down, saw the text, and didn't dare keep driving.

Inquiry from mainland about red-and-white young Australian shepherd lost Memorial Day weekend. Family taking ferry in a.m. Possibly Jake?

Her breath caught square in her chest, and she pulled the car off to the side of the road as her heart raced, paused, then raced again. She gripped the phone tightly, staring out, willing the words to disappear from her screen. But when she finally gathered the nerve to glance down again, there they were, plain as day. And just as ominous.

CHAPTER SIXTEEN

Of course it was Jake. Why wouldn't it be? How many stray red-and-white dogs wandered around an island?

Her chest ached. Her hands twitched as an adrenaline buzz coursed through her system.

Rachel was right. Getting a dog was a stupid thing to do. She'd put herself into the line of fire by falling in love with this little dog, and if he was snatched out from under her, she had no one but herself to blame.

Dismay thickened her throat as reality loomed.

Jake, staring up at her, so pale against the slate-gray roadway.

Jake, legs braced, warning her that someone lurked on her property at night.

Jake, spinning in circles, happy to see her.

Oh, her heart.

She gripped the wheel, staring forward. Kids raced around from apparatus to apparatus in the adjacent playground, swinging, leaping, climbing, sliding. Did they think it odd that she sat there watching? They might, but they didn't realize she wasn't seeing them. Not really. She was seeing another dream go up in a whiff of smoke.

She could get another dog. She knew that. But she'd been all set to believe that Jake was meant to be hers, that their destiny was linked. And who waited seven weeks to come looking for a lost dog? Wouldn't they have reported the loss to the local dog warden before they left? If they didn't, what kind of people did that make them? Was possession nine-tenths of the law?

Indignation warred with sadness. Did she have to let them take the dog?

You know the answer to that if Jake is their dog.

Maybe she did. And maybe she didn't. She had shifted gears to finally continue driving when a troop of little boys let loose a whoop. A handful of little cars zipped along a flat stretch of playground. Two of the swift-moving vehicles veered to the side, but three of them raced along the smooth surface, hit the end, and flew off into the grass.

Her brain replayed what she'd just seen. She parked the car, climbed out, and watched as the boys raced the cars again. When two of the boys dashed to the side of a thirty-something mother, Priscilla followed them.

"Good morning," she said.

"That's the one," whispered the older boy. "She was watching us."

Oh, merciful heavens, could this day possibly get any worse?

Priscilla faced the mother. "My name is Priscilla Grant, and he's right, I was watching them." She smiled down at the boys. "The remote-control cars they have. Do you know where I can get them?"

"You can order them online," the woman said.

Priscilla hid her disappointment. Getting them to the island would take days.

"Or if you go to the Tisbury Pharmacy, they have a toy section just beyond their soda shop."

"There's a soda shop in the pharmacy?"

The woman nodded. "One of the most popular retro stops. You might be able to find these there. They've carried them in the past."

"I'll check it out. And thank you."

"You're welcome."

"Welcome!" The smaller boy grinned and waved, mimicking his mother's words, then moved around his mother to pet the mid-size dog she'd tied to the fence. The dog nuzzled the boy's hand, then his face, and Priscilla's heart froze once more.

What if the people coming to look at Jake had a child?

Could she keep Jake from a child who loved him? From a child who might have spent long nights crying himself to sleep, missing his puppy? But the time frame still bothered her. What dog lover would waste so much time before trying to locate the dog?

It made no sense.

She circled back through town, and when she spotted a parking space just right for her small car, she grabbed it and hurried into the quaint pharmacy. The soda bar slung off to her right. She walked past it and got another surprise. The store actually opened into another space, where racks of toys dominated the near aisles. She found the remote-control cars and picked up four, then made it five, just in case. She made it through the cash line and was on her way back to the lighthouse in just a few minutes.

She couldn't think about what might happen tomorrow. It wouldn't do. She'd focus her time today on solving one mystery. Tomorrow she'd face whatever might come her way.

But she'd make sure that Jake had the best possible day any dog ever had. Just in case.

Ida arrived at noon, and Priscilla had just enough time to get her started on reed cleanup before Joan pulled in.

"Ida! Hello!" Joan crossed the yard and gripped Ida's hand. "I was so glad when Priscilla said you were available to help out over here."

"I jumped at the chance." Ida gave the open yards surrounding the cottage and the lighthouse a fond look. "I had so many ideas for what could be done here, but as Marjorie got older, she didn't want to fuss."

"Whereas I have fallen in love with Joan's gardens and want to fuss, but I don't have the eye to plan it out," Priscilla told them. "I love the look, and I don't mind weeding and laying mulch, but I'm not the garden-planner type."

"And that's where we come in." Joan exchanged a smile with Ida. "Auntie was set in her ways for a decade..."

"Or two!" added Ida.

Joan's smile deepened. "There's truth in that. Ida, I have all kinds of bulbs and perennials I can share."

"And both gardens will be better for it, yours and Priscilla's." Ida popped open the trunk of her car. "I'm going to start by clearing out that shaggy grass and some of the reeds. There's no sense having the view hogged by Mother Nature's generosity. Then I'm going to stake out the areas around the cottage and the perimeter. That way you can see if the spacing is what you're thinking, Priscilla. And we want the yard to be dog friendly, of course, so we'll leave walking areas between the gardens and save Jake the trouble of leaping over."

Jake must have heard his name because a distinct whine came through the side door.

Joan heard the whine and read Priscilla's expression. "Is Jake all right?"

"He is. I'm not." She explained the note from the veterinarian and sighed. "I keep hoping it's the wrong dog, and then I realize the unlikelihood of that, so then I imagine ways to justify keeping Jake and refusing to give him up."

"Seven weeks is a long time," noted Ida.

"I thought so too."

"But things happen in life, so perhaps the time gap is explainable."

Leave it to Joan to be gently sensible when Priscilla would prefer to be staunchly possessive. "Of course we'll wait and see." Priscilla didn't sigh. She'd done enough of that on the ride home. "That's the best choice."

"In the meantime, you and I have some old family papers to sort out."

"And I'll get to work out here." Ida hauled wooden stakes, heavy twine, and a mallet from her trunk. Using Priscilla's key to the small garage, she rolled out an old-style rotary lawn mower. "I've mowed this yard with this old boy many times, but I wouldn't mind a power mower at some point, Priscilla. Although pushing this does give me quite a workout."

Priscilla added *new lawn mower* to her list of necessities, and then she and Joan spread out the cache of letters inside. When Gail and Trudy joined them for an early supper, they'd only gotten through half the box.

"It seems Llewellyn was a letter writer." Gail tapped the still unread stack of logbooks from their ancestor's years of manning the lighthouse. "Trudy and I can start on these. We should be able to get through all of them before low tide." They took seats on opposite sides of the table as they each selected a journal.

"He has a winsome style." Joan read from one of his early letters to Elodie.

"'Three seasons may separate us, my dearest, but the ropes of true love know not time or age. They bind from within, hearts entwined.'"

"Oh my." Priscilla made a face. "I'm not sure if I should be dismayed or grateful that Gary never in his life said anything half that romantic."

"I think it's absolutely enchanting," said Trudy. She uttered a feminine sigh, smiled, and put a hand to her heart.

Gail's skeptical look underscored the difference between them. "I'm going straight to sappy."

"I'm more in line with Gail's assessment too." But as soon as she said the words, Priscilla wondered, *Why aren't I more drawn to the romance of the nineteenth-century epistles?* Was it because she didn't like romance or because it lost its sheen when she lost her husband?

Joan rolled her eyes. "This is from the woman who cried all the way back from the village because of a dog…yet she scoffs at the thought of a romantic suitor writing tomes of love. Keats, Shelley, and Wordsworth are not to be insulted, Cousin. They are to be enjoyed."

"All right, it's fine." Priscilla raised a hand in defeat. "Maybe it's just not my style."

But by the time Priscilla had read half a dozen more of Llewellyn's letters, she'd half fallen in love with the wordsmith herself.

"He really loved her." She folded a letter carefully and slipped it back into its aged envelope.

"He did," agreed Gail. "These logs are downright poetic. Our Llewellyn loved to record stories about the water. The land. Ships at sea. He had a talent, for certain."

"He took his job seriously." Priscilla held up a letter citing a shipwreck between the island and the coast. "In this one, he's praying for lost souls, but also for those that were rescued because he worries for their guilt at being saved when so many lost their lives."

"A gentle heart. It's pleasant to know we have such a thoughtful soul in our ancestry, isn't it?"

It wasn't something Priscilla had ever thought about before, but it did seem nice. She opened the next letter—a shorter one, and much more pragmatic—and when she read the contents, she understood why. She stood and couldn't stop her hand from shaking.

All three cousins looked up and then stood with her. "What's happened?" asked Gail.

Trudy tucked her hands together. "Are you all right, Priscilla?"

Joan reached for the letter. "What have you found?"

"The answer," Priscilla whispered, as if someone might be listening.

Joan took the thin, aged paper and read it softly.

> "'I cannot in good conscience bear weight of that which is not mine, nor secured in such a wrongful manner.
>
> What then, am I to do?
>
> We've conferenced, we three, and have made our decision, and Lo! It is as if the hand of God directs us thus.
>
> A tunnel for freedom begets a new day in ways unthought.
>
> May God be with us, every day.'"

"What do you mean, that's the answer?" Gail frowned in confusion.

"I don't get it. What's the hand of God directing him to do?"

"I'll show you." Priscilla had removed the little cars from their packaging earlier. "We've a race to run. Trudy, can you and Ida go down below the reeds? We're going to release the cars from the secret room in the basement, and let's see if any of them can find their way to the light."

"Secret rooms, buried treasure, and tunnels? What is happening to our island?" Trudy didn't waste a moment's time. "Ida and I will stand guard. Give us a few minutes to get in position, okay? Those steps down to the beach are a little rough."

"We'll head downstairs and get things set up."

"There's really a secret room?" Gail asked as she followed Joan and Priscilla down the basement stairs.

"And a secret door," Joan assured her. "You'll love it!"

"But why would anyone dig a tunnel? Do you suppose our ancestors were doing something illegal?" she wondered as Joan switched on the portable light they'd left set up in the first room.

"In some eyes, yes," Priscilla told her. "But not immoral, and if I'm correct, we have reason to be proud. For the moment, let's go to the races!"

She pushed open the hidden door. Gail and Joan waited as Priscilla set up another work light. When it clicked on, Gail studied the room and the door leading to the earthen tunnel, eyes wide. "No one would ever know this was here."

"A perfect design," declared Priscilla. "Are we 'go' for launch?"

"Let's do it one at a time so they don't bump into each other." Joan held up her metallic blue car. "Ready?"

"Do it."

Gail peered into the tunnel before Joan set her car in motion. "That's odd."

"What's odd?" Priscilla leaned in from behind.

"I saw light, then no light, then light again."

"Like a blinking light?" Joan asked doubtfully.

"No, sunlight. You know, natural light. As if it was there, then something blocked it, and then it was there again. Look, it just happened again, as if something's blocking the light."

"The grasses, no doubt."

Gail looked unconvinced. "There's no way this tunnel comes out near the reeds. It angles to the right up there, and from where we are, it has to come out on the near side of the cove. It's simple physics, ladies. There's nothing on the bluff side of the water, so this must go to the craggy side of the cove."

"Joan and I checked there thoroughly."

Gail sent Priscilla a knowing look. "I'm the storm geek, remember? I don't care much about history, but when it comes to erosion and sedimentation and how Mother Nature gives and takes away, I'm your gal. My guess is this comes out beneath a rocky overhang that isn't really visible from the ground. And might actually land square in the water because of wave erosion."

"Let's see." Joan released her car. She worked the controls to the right, crashed the car into a near wall, then managed to flip the poor thing on to its back, wheels spinning.

"My turn." Gail positioned the lime green car in the center of the tunnel, and with the skill of a master, sent the car rolling straight and then to the right. "Aiming for the light," she muttered, then pressed the accelerator control hard.

The car careened out of the flashlight beam and around the shallow bend. They heard it crash into a wall, and as Gail cranked the control left, then right again, they heard the wheels rev and then...

"What!" A deep male voice rang out in the distance as if someone was there...in the tunnel!

A groan followed, just as deep. Just as low. And far more scary.

"Shut the door!" Priscilla pulled back and tugged Gail with her. She slammed the door shut and applied the key with shaking fingers.

Someone was in the tunnel, and that meant they could get into the cottage if the door was left unlocked.

"Trudy!"

"Ida!"

"To the beach!" The three women raced up the stairs and out the side door. Jake joined in the action. He raced toward the beach, barking a stern warning, but when a woman screamed bloody murder, Joan and Priscilla almost kept pace with the dog. "Trudy!" Joan shrieked her sister's name as they crested the knoll.

"Here! With the professor. Oh, hurry, girls! Hurry!"

The professor. Just as she suspected.

Priscilla and Joan hurried down the uneven steps. Gail followed just a bit behind. And when Priscilla and Joan rounded the craggy point, there were Ida and Trudy, heads bent, kneeling beside the inert, bloodied body of Professor Franklin Mayweather.

Priscilla's heart stopped. Her breath caught. This wasn't the scene she expected to find, and just as that began to register, a small boat came racing around the corner.

Startled, all five women turned toward that way.

The boat reared up as the driver gunned the engine, then slammed down on to the shallows. The high-throttled engine refused to grip in such minimal water, which meant whoever was driving lacked skill.

Jake raced back and forth in the sand, barking a warning.

Joan hit 911 in her cell phone and didn't mince words. "We have an unconscious man in the cove just east of the Misty Harbor Lighthouse, and there's a boater behaving dangerously just offshore. He's traveling at a high rate of speed in shallow waters. We need an ambulance and the police and the Coast Guard. Stat!"

Priscilla dropped to her knees and felt the professor's neck. "He's got a pulse. And he's breathing. Professor! Professor, can you hear me?" A large bruised bump protruded from the professor's forehead and upper cheek. A trickle of blood stained his hair and his left ear, and his shirt sleeve was torn from his shoulder.

"We were here, right here, waiting to see if one of your little cars came through, and then we heard a scuffle and a shout. Then another shout, two men arguing. We weren't sure we should even peek around the bluff, but then there was a loud groan and a smack and then nothing. And we peeked, and this is what we found."

"Oh, this poor man," added Ida. "I can't believe someone would do something like this. Where is that ambulance?"

"Coming," Joan assured her.

Sirens sounded from land and sea. They screeched toward the lighthouse from multiple directions.

Jake wasn't sure which way to bark or which growl would suit the moment, so the young mutt scrambled here and there, alternating noises. "Oh, the poor guy, he'll get himself all worked up. Priscilla, I'm going to tuck Jake into the house so he's not as agitated." Gail lifted the young shepherd and escorted him back to the house.

That helped some, but as the sirens screamed into the area, Priscilla was pretty sure the little dog would be going crazy inside. But better there than here, she reasoned.

"Professor. Professor, can you hear me?" She leaned down as two boats pulled up to the dock. One bore the insignia of the Tisbury police, and the other displayed the bold red stripe of the US Coast Guard.

Gerald O'Bannon jumped off the second boat, hurried across the dock, then ran to the women. "What's happened?"

"We're not sure," began Priscilla. "We were exploring the grounds around the lighthouse, and we found the professor unconscious…"

"We called for help," added Joan.

"And someone with little knowledge of boating took off in a smallish boat, sixteen or seventeen feet long, blue hull and split windshield," Gail explained.

The ambulance crew trundled a gurney their way just as the professor began to move. "*Ohhh*… My head. My head!" He moved a hand to his rapidly swelling lump, and Priscilla couldn't help but feel a little sorry for him, though what he was doing on her property was anyone's guess.

"Can you hear me, Franklin?" Gerald leaned down. "What happened? Who did this to you?"

"Alan."

"Alan Napier, your assistant?" Priscilla sat back, surprised. "He was here with you?"

The professor winced, moaned, and winced again. "We were investigating a new possibility concerning the gold. Alan discovered some information indicating an old tunnel leading from the lighthouse and that the Bardsley family owned the lighthouse property for a short while. We felt sure the gold must be tucked in the tunnel because Nathaniel Claybrook was captured on Bardsley's Point. For that little bit of time, this wasn't Bailey Point, so we knew we'd tracked it down. Finally."

Priscilla was about to announce that the gold wasn't here when the professor stopped her with his next words.

"We found the chest full of treasure, and it took both of us and no small amount of ingenuity to get a chain attached to winch it out of there."

Priscilla sent a look of warning to the cousins. "You found the gold, Professor?" The paramedics were moving into place at the base of the rocky cliff and would take the professor for examination soon, so she needed to glean whatever information she could—the faster the better.

He nodded and gave a grimace of pain at the same time. "We were working it through the mouth of the tunnel when a noise startled me. Like something chasing me in the dark. I turned to look, but couldn't see anything. The noise came again, with twin lights like glowing white eyes. I tried to hurry out of the tunnel, but the opening is small." He pointed up, and sure enough, if you laid on your back and had a good imagination, you could discern part of an opening above the rocks. "I got wedged. Alan had put the crate into the back of the boat. When I got loose and tried to scramble after him, he grabbed hold of my arm and shoved me backward off the boat. I fell and hit my head on the rocks, and that's the last thing I remember."

"You saw the gold?" Priscilla leaned closer. "You opened the chest and saw the gold?"

"Why do you keep questioning me?" He scowled up at her, and Priscilla was pretty sure he wouldn't be bothering her with any more leering smiles, especially once he found out there was no gold. "I'm hurt, and I can't concentrate on anything. And shouldn't someone be chasing down Alan and putting him under arrest for assault and battery? Or something? And no." He turned agitated eyes toward Priscilla. "The chest was locked, of course, and the lock well-rusted. We didn't see the gold, but we hefted it, and not much else is that heavy."

"Gerald." Priscilla moved away and motioned the Coast Guard captain her way. "We have to get to Alan before he hurts someone else trying to save gold that doesn't exist."

"Say what?" Gerald's eyes narrowed. He leaned closer, and there was no missing the spicy scent of his aftershave, like one of those old-time commercials with the handsome seaman coming home. "What do you mean?"

"The gold was found a long time ago," she whispered. "We just found evidence of it, so no one else knows, and if Alan thinks he's protecting a fortune in gold, he's liable to hurt someone. Or worse."

"Let's go."

"Me?"

He grabbed her hand and hurried back to the Coast Guard cruiser with her in tow. "You're the one with the information. It might come in handy, Priscilla."

"Isn't this against the rules or something?" she asked, but with a backward glance at her gaping cousins, she quick-stepped her way onto the boat. Within seconds, Gerald's crew had the cruiser undocked, turned about, and on its way.

And just that quick, Priscilla Grant was chasing down a criminal on a speeding Coast Guard vessel, and no one in Wheatfield would ever have predicted such a thing.

CHAPTER SEVENTEEN

Priscilla turned her face into the wind. Fresh sea air cooled her warm cheeks and made a wild mess of her hair, but she didn't care. It felt marvelous to be on the water, racing across the narrowing waves of a fairly calm Atlantic Ocean.

"Do you get squeamish on boats?" Gerald had been busy as they got the boat underway, but now he came to her side as if regretting his quick maneuver.

"Apparently not!" She smiled at him.

"This is your first time on the water?"

"But not the last," she promised. "This is fun! And look, over there." She pointed ahead. "I think that might be the boat we saw. It was that color."

He lifted a pair of binoculars, his mouth grim. "That's him all right. What was he thinking? That he could get away with stealing someone else's property?"

"Treasure hunters don't see the object of their quest as belonging to anyone. To them, it's there for the taking if you can find it."

"How do you know the gold is gone? What makes you think that?" asked Gerald.

"Llewellyn Latham found it long ago. He and his family decided to use it for the good of mankind and funded the library."

"That guy whose picture is on the wall?"

"With his wife and mother, yes. The answer's been here all along. It was simply a matter of putting the pieces together. Alan must have been dogging my search because every time I uncovered a clue, it disappeared. There is something good about all this though." She angled a glance his way as the captain curved the craft to follow Alan's course. "I can take you off the suspect list."

That got his attention. He tipped his sunglasses back and stared at her. "Me?"

"Yes, you. I saw you prowling around outside my house one night, keeping to the shadows."

"Well, one should keep to the shadows if he or she doesn't wish to be seen, Priscilla." He sounded quite sensible, but also amused. "So you thought I was skulking around your place, searching for gold?"

"You made the list, that's for certain."

He laughed before he lifted his binoculars again. "We're closing, Seeley."

"Aye, sir!"

"So what were you doing if it wasn't searching for gold?"

"Still she doubts." He grinned now, facing forward, and Priscilla found his grin to be absolutely charming, and that surprised her more than anything else that had happened today. "We've been notified of a few smugglers or drug runners using the island for a drop point."

"When we have thousands of miles of Atlantic coastline, people are using Martha's Vineyard for drug drops? That seems unlikely." She scoffed.

"It's quite likely, actually, because there are so many folks on land and in the water during the season that it's painfully simple for a boat to blend in."

"Hiding in plain sight."

"Exactly." He smiled as if proud that she recognized the maneuver. "We've caught a couple over the last year, but there are always more ready to take their place. And as you said, with all that coastline to cover, it's open season for the drug trade. The more uncomfortable we make it for them to use Martha's Vineyard as a drop site, the more likely they are to move their trade elsewhere. So what you saw that night was me checking out the twin coves below the lighthouse. I stayed close to the houses on my way back, but Seeley and I did the shoreline on foot first."

Well, now she'd done it. She'd put a nice military man on her suspect list because he had the audacity to do his job well. "Gerald, I'm…"

"Hold that thought and the possible apology I sense coming with it." He raised the microphone to the ship's loudspeaker to his mouth. His voice boomed out over the waves. "This is Captain Gerald O'Bannon of the United States Coast Guard. Stop the boat, Mr. Napier."

Mr. Napier did no such thing. He gunned the engine and took off like a shot.

The Coast Guard vessel followed but not at breakneck speed. "I'm trying to avoid an accident," Gerald said softly below the noise of the engines and the cool, moving air. "If he heads toward shore, we could put others in danger."

"Perhaps if we get close enough, I can tell him he doesn't have the gold." Was she foolish to make such a suggestion?

Gerald must not have thought so because he considered her, then the boat chase, and nodded. "Worth a try."

He ordered Seeley to draw in. The navigator did so, lessening the distance between them without being aggressive. When they'd gained some ground, Gerald pulled out his cell phone. With a couple of moves, he'd secured Alan's number and made the call.

"I was hoping to use your cool megaphone," Priscilla told him.

"This is my attempt to minimize the drama and avoid the interest and encroachment of all those boats." He indicated the crowded shoreline to their left. "Let's try the old-fashioned yet new-fangled telephone first, shall we?" He completed the call and waited.

No answer.

"You get your wish." He raised the megaphone as they drew closer. "Napier, stop the boat. You don't have the gold. I don't know what you have, but it's not the British coin."

A police boat began closing the distance from the opposite direction while a third boat approached from the ocean side.

"Mrs. Grant can explain this to you."

"Me?" She stared up at Gerald as he handed off the megaphone.

"It's your party."

She lifted the megaphone to her mouth. Her heart rose into her throat about the same time, but she took a deep breath and hailed Alan. "It's not the gold, Mr. Napier. The gold was found a long time ago. I've got proof. Whatever you have there isn't worth risking your life or anyone else's."

He'd slowed the boat as the other cruisers began to hem him in. "I don't believe you!" He looked their way, a desperate man.

Priscilla kept her voice calm with effort. "I wish you would," she called back. "The gold was found over a hundred years ago and used to finance the town library. I don't know what you found in that tunnel, but it's not filled with gold from the Revolutionary War. That was found and emptied long ago. Please, Alan. I know you don't believe me, but if you take a moment and check the chest, I'm sure you'll find that I speak the truth."

"It's a trap to capture me!" He sounded incensed and worried, but Priscilla detected a note of regret as well.

"I would like you to stop because I don't want anyone else hurt, but mostly I want this gold nonsense to be a thing of the past so I can get on with my life in Tisbury. We'll back off while you check the chest."

"Why should I believe you?"

"I'll vouch for her," Gerald said. "You know me, Napier. I'm a man of my word."

A long stretch of silence ensued.

Priscilla held the megaphone. Seeley trolled the boat motor to give Alan time. And Gerald lifted his binoculars to survey the scene in the other boat as the two additional cruisers quietly ringed Napier's small boat. He gave her a thumbs-up about the same time that Alan yelled in frustration. "I don't believe this!"

"Alan." Priscilla didn't know this man, she didn't know his story, but she couldn't imagine working in close proximity with the professor and not going a little bit mad, so she kept her voice easy. "You didn't know. And the professor told us you didn't attack him. He said you shoved him, and he fell and hit his head. Now that you know you don't have the gold, I think we should end this right here. Before it gets any worse, correct?"

He groaned, a sound of regret.

"Let us come aboard," Gerald proposed. "Come on in with me. Let's sort this out. Mrs. Grant is right. Things could be a lot worse than they are right now, Alan. Let's put the brakes on this before something else happens."

Would Alan agree? Or would he take off in a futile attempt to escape them and risk lives in a chase?

It seemed like a long time before Alan spoke, and when he did, he only said three little words. "I give up."

"That's what I was hoping to hear." Gerald didn't make a big deal of it. He kept things calm by staying calm himself. They pulled the Coast Guard boat alongside Alan's speedboat. An officer with a badge that said Chzchavosky crossed to Alan's boat. He and Seeley put handcuffs on Alan, then Seeley helped ease the professor's assistant onto the Coast Guard vessel.

"Chickie, can you bring that boat in for us?" Gerald asked.

Chzchavosky nodded. "Yes, sir." He moved to the wheel of the smaller craft.

Seeley and another officer took Alan below and stayed with him while Gerald took control of the Coast Guard boat. He notified the other police departments of the outcome and his intent, then aimed the boat toward the harbor.

"Can't say I get the allure," he said to Priscilla once his duties were done and the boat was in motion.

She raised one brow. "Of possible millions?"

"Of wanting more, always more. It's impossible to serve two masters, God and money." He guided the boat around a buoy then slowed the engine. "I made my most grievous mistakes a couple decades back. I learned a tough and valuable lesson: do your job to the best of your ability and find joy in the little things."

"Like that new grandchild coming."

"Exactly like that." He smiled, still gazing forward. "Dogs, grandkids, good friends, and the sea." This time he flashed a smile her way. "It's a good life."

"Simple is best."

"Ayuh." He grinned when she smiled, and as he pulled the boat up to the dock, he tossed a rope to the waiting policeman. "Well, Mrs. Grant." He took her hand again to guide her off the boat. "I hope you found your first boat ride enjoyable."

"Enjoyable and exciting," she assured him. She smiled up at him as she crossed on to the dock. "Thank you for answering the call so quickly, Gerald. It's nice to have you on my side."

He said nothing, just tipped the brim of his cap lightly. "I'll let you know what happens."

"And the chest Alan took from the tunnel?"

"We'll process the contents, and the district attorney will decide if we need to hang on to it until trial. If Alan goes to trial," he corrected himself. "Once they sort this all out, it might come down to a list of misdemeanors unless you press charges for the breaking and entering. Napier might come out of this better than he thinks."

Priscilla wasn't sure if that was good or bad. "I've got news I need to share with the town, but I'm not sure how to do it. What would you suggest?"

"We're big on town meetings here. I'll call the mayor and the town board to get it set up. I expect people will want to hear what you've got to say."

"I think they will," she agreed. "And I'm interested to see what the chest contained."

"Rocks!" Alan almost spat the word in disgust as the two younger officers led him on to the dock. "Some stupid trinkets and letters and a kid's rock collection."

He'd hurt a colleague, messed up his reputation and his career, and would now have a criminal record, and he had nothing to show for it. *"For the love of money is a root of all kinds of evil..."* Wise words from Timothy, and a good daily creed.

They started to walk by, and Priscilla saw what might be her last chance to talk to Alan. "Alan, why? Why the mad hunt for the gold? What made you do it?"

The officers paused.

Alan didn't look at her at first. He looked out to sea and then drew his eyes back to hers. "I've done everything the university asked me to do. I've put up with being Franklin's assistant, which in Franklin's world means I do all the work and he gets the big paycheck. I worked, published, was cited by good reviewers, and I tried to make my mark in history, and after all of that, they sent a letter last week while I'm working in that horrible, wretched, smelly Whaling Museum that said I would not be granted tenure. Eight years I've spent there, dealing with cost cuts and pay freezes. Four years more than in most places and still denied. I didn't want to start over and have to deal with another professor. I'd found the information about the tunnel right after the *Globe* story broke. Llewellyn had mentioned it later in life, but it got overlooked as time went on. And then forgotten. But the minute I read it, once I realized that Bailey Point was also known as Bardsley's Point in the eighteenth century, I knew it had to be somewhere on your property."

"And it was. But it was found nearly a hundred and fifty years ago."

She watched in silence as Alan was led to a waiting police cruiser, and when the escorting officer closed the back door with Alan inside, she breathed easier. "Well. That was an adventure."

Gerald laughed softly. "Not exactly Kansas, is it?"

"No." The cruiser pulled away as her phone buzzed in her pocket. "But I like the differences. I like them a lot."

"Enough to stay?"

She turned his way. His eyes met hers. He arched his left brow and waited quietly.

Her heart made a funny turn in her chest, kind of like the lock on that old chest must have felt when it creaked open. She could wait to make her decision. She didn't know what the morning would bring, but as gulls swooped and cried overhead and people milled about the lakefront walks and elongated docks, she realized she'd already decided. "Enough to stay."

"That's good to know." Gerald fell into step beside her as she moved up the dock. "I'll stop by and update you on everything."

"Thank you, Gerald." She put out her hand.

He gripped it lightly. "You're quite welcome. And I have to say, we made a good team out there." He indicated the water with a glance.

She blushed.

Priscilla could not remember the last time she'd blushed or had a reason to blush, but she felt the heat rise to her cheeks and knew her fair Midwestern skin was staining bright pink. Of all the schoolgirl things!

She ignored the rush and focused on his words because she couldn't remember a more exciting moment than racing across the swelling waves of seawater. "An unforgettable experience for sure."

He grinned. "Acknowledged." He motioned to the Tisbury policewoman who had come to the cottage the week before. "April, can you see Mrs. Grant back to the lighthouse? Paperwork goes hand in hand with an arrest, and I expect she'd like to return to her company."

Her company and her four-legged friend whose future lay in flux.

"Glad to." The middle-aged woman opened the door of her SUV. "Hop in. I'll have you back home in no time. And I can't wait to hear what the excitement was all about."

"It's a story that could have had a far worse ending. I'm glad for everyone's sake that wasn't the case." Sincerity underscored Gerald's tone. "I'll see you soon, Priscilla."

"Thank you, Gerald."

He tipped that finger to his cap once more, a small salute that meant more than some shouted accolades.

CHAPTER EIGHTEEN

By the time Priscilla got home, the cousins had compiled information from various friends and family, leaving Priscilla little
to tell. "I'm not sure if I should be dismayed or elated that folks
can spread that much information to so many in such a short space
of time," she told Ida and the cousins as they gathered around a
feast of ham salad and potato chips an hour later. The evening sun
slanted light over the yard, and the ladies had set up a folding table
and chairs outside.

"It's definitely in our favor if help is needed," offered Gail.

"And not so much when one of your kids throws a party when
you're out of town," noted Trudy. "Luckily they've all grown
beyond that nonsense, but it taught me that there are precious few
secrets to be found here."

"And yet we just uncovered a major one that was right in front
of our eyes," Priscilla replied.

"True."

"Which means there might be more." Joan sprinkled fresh dill
on to her sandwich. "People are often most oblivious when things
are most obvious."

Gerald's car pulled into the drive. Priscilla rose to meet him as
he crossed the yard. "Your paperwork is set, then?"

"It is, and while there are still details to figure out, I had the powers that be schedule a town meeting like you suggested for tomorrow at noon."

Noon?

Priscilla winced inside, but then she took a deep breath and agreed. Tomorrow would go on as needed regardless of what her morning brought. "Noon will be fine. We can fill folks in on what we found out and set the treasure hunt officially to rest."

"And everyone in law enforcement will thank you." He sounded quite assured about that. "Our tourists are not generally the law-breaking sort, so this has created some interesting confrontations and more overtime pay than our little towns have in their budgets."

"Is there an update on the professor?" Ida asked. "He was trying to refuse treatment, mostly because he had no good explanation for why he was trespassing on private property and searching for something that didn't belong to him."

"They expect he'll be fine, but I don't know what professional repercussions might come his way," Gerald told the group. "He already had a scrape with the legal system concerning his book. This can't possibly help matters."

"Both times trying to take the easy way out." Joan held out the platter of sandwiches. "Gerald, I know you're still on duty, but take some to go. We'll never eat all these, and I have to give credit where credit is due. Priscilla makes the best ham salad I've ever had, and that's saying something in New England."

"Do tell." He accepted a sandwich on a paper plate and raised it slightly. "I'll let you know my opinion tomorrow."

"And I'll look forward to hearing it," declared Priscilla. "Thank you for arranging the meeting."

"Glad to help. Ladies?" He raised his free hand and turned to leave. "Have a nice evening."

Jake whined at the door. He planted his paws on the screen, tail wagging, and peered at them. Priscilla let him out, gave him a corner of a sandwich, and watched as he moved around the yard. He made particular note of the garden stakes, and when Priscilla frowned, Ida laughed.

"To be expected, I suppose. We'll have a bonfire when the work is done and burn them. A dog likes to let the world know who he is and where he is."

The ladies stayed until dusk, planning what would be said the next day and electing Priscilla the speaker. When they left, she took Jake inside.

She curled up on her bed, half-drained and half-excited.

She would stay on Martha's Vineyard.

She'd made a firm decision earlier today as she raced across ocean waters to nab a criminal mastermind who turned out not to be that masterful after all.

She'd face whatever tomorrow brought with all the Midwestern resolve she could. She couldn't bear to think of losing her newfound friend, but she'd shown herself a few things these past days.

She wasn't fearful. She wasn't in the doldrums, not when she was here on the island. Here she was herself. A different self, without Gary and without the farm, but her own person. Priscilla Latham Grant, ready to take this bend in the road and any others that might come her way.

She'd call the Realtor in Wheatfield after meeting with the folks who'd lost their dog. One way or another, she would move on, just as she'd always done. Just as her mother, Charlotte Latham Ingerson, had taught her.

She reached for the clock and realized she didn't need an alarm here. The sun and the sea and the surf had called her awake each day. She'd let them do the same again.

She left the alarm alone, and when she awoke bright and early in the morning, she made coffee, took Jake for a brisk, cool walk, then settled in with the last of her stack of Llewellyn's letters. After reading the fifth one, she had to set the letter aside and blot her eyes. Llewellyn wasn't just a soulful writer. He was a soulful man, and she was proud to claim him as an ancestor. She pocketed the letter to reference at noon.

When a white sedan pulled into her driveway at fifteen past nine, she took a deep breath, squared her shoulders, and walked to the door, ready for whatever was about to happen. She let Jake outside and prepared for the worst.

"Is this him?" Priscilla asked.

A man with an affable manner had exited the driver's side. He bent low and called Jake softly. "Charlie! Come here, boy!"

Jake didn't hesitate. He raced toward the man, licked his hand, and then waited with just a hint of a shiver for the expected petting the man quickly provided.

Priscilla's heart didn't just break. It shattered. She knew it was ridiculous, but as a young woman climbed out of the passenger side, she bit back the slew of questions she longed to fling their way. Why had two healthy, young, comfortable people left a dog behind to fare on his own for so long and not come looking for him?

A newborn's cry sounded from the backseat. The tiny, plaintive voice begged for attention, and the young mother turned instantly. Her look, her concern, her attention, locked on her child.

The man didn't stand right away. He continued petting Jake—or *Charlie*—while Priscilla fought the lump rising in her throat.

The baby cried again, and the young mother leaned into the backseat to pick up the infant. "There, there, it's all right. Look here, your first trip to the island, sweetness." The mother's words made it sound almost like a benediction. "We'll have to get a picture for your scrapbook, won't we?" She came toward Priscilla with the baby. "Mrs. Grant?"

"Yes."

"I'm Amelia Hayes. And this is my husband, Jason Hayes."

"It's nice to meet you." It wasn't nice. It was the exact opposite of nice, but when she looked down at the baby, realization dawned. "I was wondering why it took so long for you to get back here to look for Charlie."

"Elizabeth June Hayes, that's why." Amelia spoke with the pride of all young mothers in her voice. "Five weeks early and a fighter, but it took us this long to get her home from the hospital and strong enough to bring across. We never expected me to go into labor while we were here, and we'd only just picked up the puppy, so the timing was wretched all around."

It was, in more ways than one, but Priscilla clung to the advice Joan had offered. "I've found it's always best to look on the bright side of these things. A healthy, beautiful baby is a wonderful thing."

"Oh, it is. I consider it a miracle of the highest order, but I suppose every mother feels that way."

"I expect most do."

Amelia smiled at her and then over at her husband and Jake. "He looks wonderful, Mrs. Grant."

"Thank you. He's a dear boy. Clever as can be, knowing when to bark and when to stay quiet. And comes on command, such a rarity for a young dog. You'll be impressed with his intelligence."

"Impressed?" Jason stood up, and Amelia looked at her.

"By how smart he is," Priscilla explained, barely able to get the words out around the lump growing in her throat. This young couple hadn't abandoned Jake on purpose. They'd gone to the mainland to give life in a whole different way, and no one could hold that against them.

"You think we've come to claim him." Jason stood rooted in place, looking surprised.

"Is that true?" Amelia raised her brows. "Oh, Mrs. Grant, nothing could be further from the truth."

"No?" Had her heart just hit a new sinus rhythm? Priscilla was pretty sure it had.

"No, we wanted to come and thank you and make sure he's all right. We felt so bad, and we knew we couldn't get back here, and there was no one to call. We tried the shelters and animal control, but they hadn't seen him, and we didn't want to pester the police by calling repeatedly. We're happy to know he has a good home and someone who loves him."

"We panicked when Amelia went into labor," Jason explained. His features were a mix of embarrassment and honesty. "We'd gone to an open field to give him a little run-around time."

"The veterinarian had told us not to take him to the dog park because he hadn't received all his vaccinations yet, you see. But he ran off, and then everything that could possibly go wrong did."

"Amelia's water broke, and her contractions started, and we didn't know what to do. I had to get her home. And then we pretty much lived in the NICU for the next month."

"We wouldn't dream of taking Charlie away from you." Concern deepened Amelia's words. "I'm so sorry you thought that. We should have made our intentions more clear."

Jake was staying here, right here, with Priscilla. Life had just taken a wondrously blessed upturn. Gratitude and joy nudged open another corner of her widowed heart.

"When Elizabeth gets a little older, we'll get another puppy. Or maybe an older dog in need of a home," Amelia continued. "Right now we need to concentrate our attention on this little one, and as long as Charlie..."

"Jake," Priscilla told them and couldn't help if she sounded a little proud and relieved rolled into one.

"As long as *Jake* is fine, we're thrilled. He looks absolutely delighted to be here with you, Mrs. Grant."

"That makes two of us." She wouldn't cry. She would not! But she wanted to, she was that relieved she wouldn't be saying good-bye to her scrappy friend. "Do you want to stop in and feed the baby?"

"You wouldn't mind?" Amelia smiled in relief. "I didn't want to impose, but we've got a two-and-a-half-hour trip back home, and I'd love to get her fed and changed."

"Come in, please. I've got cookies and coffee and comfy chairs. What more could a person want?"

"What more, indeed?" Jason smiled. "The little things mean everything, and there is nothing like praying for your child's life to remind you of that."

They didn't stay long, but long enough to cement a ready friendship and an invitation to return any time. "When you come vacationing, make sure you stop by," Priscilla reminded them as they bundled the baby back into her seat. "The door is always open to you."

"We will!" Amelia waved out the window as Jason backed the car around. "Goodbye, Priscilla! Goodbye, Jake!"

Jake dashed right then left, as if assuring them he was fine, and when Priscilla gave him just the tiniest piece of a cookie, he sat down and offered a doggy smile.

For her. Just for her.

She hauled in a deep breath, tucked Jake inside the cottage, gathered her materials, and drove into town. She didn't expect a large turnout for their hastily called town meeting, so when they had to move the meeting from the library's meeting room to the great room, Priscilla was surprised. And when every one of the one hundred and twelve chairs was filled, she was astonished. Island residents did take their town meetings seriously.

Clara led Priscilla to the front while the mayor explained Alan's arrest. "Now, I'm not sure what we want to call this whole *kabobble* about gold and treasure and old secrets," he commented once the facts were presented. "I'm going to apologize to Mr. Scott over there." He pointed out the reporter standing off to the side. "I considered his story to be irresponsible journalism at first, inspiring all kinds of treasure hunters to bother folks. But then I got to thinking." He paused and played the room with a thought-provoking gaze. "In a town and a place and a state with such a rich past, we'd be *foolish*"—he stressed the word to flesh out his point—"to brush that off. Here on the island, we revel in our history and thank the Lord Almighty for the here and now, so if learning about our past causes a little dustup now and again, I say that's all right. Long as no one gets hurt, of course. And here to tell us what *really* happened with the treasure is one of our newest residents from one of our oldest families. Priscilla Latham Grant, would you come up here, please?"

Priscilla moved forward, shook Mayor Whipple's hand, and faced the crowd. "Llewellyn Latham found the gold over a hundred and fifty years ago."

An emotional wave coursed through the crowd, a mix of understanding and disappointment.

"My cousins and I have searched our family records. We discovered a letter written by Llewellyn to his future wife, Elodie. They chose their words with care while they debated what to do. There was a lot at stake concerning their decision, and they didn't want people snooping around, hoping to find more."

Folks shared knowing glances, recognizing the wisdom behind that long-ago choice.

"They conferred with Llewellyn's mother, also a Priscilla." She smiled at the group, and they smiled back. "Together they decided to use the money for the good of the community." She pointed off to her right. "When you check out books here, you stand right over there, beneath the picture of Llewellyn, Elodie, and Priscilla. And beneath that is a short note thanking them for their generous support of the library."

"They built the library." Clara put a hand to her heart as she realized where Priscilla was going with the story. "I had no idea that's what happened. In fact, some people wanted that picture taken down and replaced with a smaller version because it gave the Lathams too much notice. I don't expect there will be any more talk of that now."

"I expect you're right about that, Clara." Priscilla shared a smile with the librarian. "And maybe no more talk of closing the library down," she added. She didn't aim her look at the mayor, but the rest of the folks did and that was good enough. "They built this beautiful facility and made sure it had the finest wood, the best seating, and they even left a fund for updating it. We found the original library costs in the archived records, and there was over two hundred thousand dollars left in the fund after paying for the library construction completely."

"And they wanted no credit for their generosity," added Joan from the side. "Which is why no one put two and two together."

"I think we all assumed that the library was funded with a grant or state funds," said Clara. "I never gave it a thought that someone had come up with that gold after all that time. I think most folks figured the gold was more fiction than fact."

"Then what did that Napier guy and the professor find by the lighthouse if it wasn't the treasure?" asked a middle-aged woman halfway back.

Gerald moved forward and brought a large antique wooden box with him. "This. It might be the original box from the gold. It's hard to know without doing extensive testing. So it may have been filled with gold at one time, but now it's filled with some notes and letters written in various hands, a couple of old toys perhaps owned by one of Llewellyn's sons, and a rock collection."

"Rocks." The old man in the front row couldn't hold back a laugh. "Folks went through all that stuff and nonsense for a box of rocks. But where was it hid?" he asked. "Because it ain't like this is the first troop that's gone looking for gold on the island."

"In a tunnel leading from the basement beneath the cottage to the cove," Gerald replied.

"A tunnel? Why would someone need a tunnel to get to the cove unless they were doing something they shouldn't be doing?" Alma

Whitaker hiked her brows and narrowed her eyes in Priscilla's direction. "Sounds like shady dealings with the Lathams to me."

Priscilla stepped forward again. She withdrew a letter from the pocket of her favorite sundress. "This is a letter dated 1859 from Llewellyn to his brother in South Jersey. 'Some may think it bold. Some, foolish. Some, dangerous, and I cannot deny any of these claims, but to sit by and do nothing would disgrace the Latham name and legacy and my soul. The tunnel is done, the stop secure, and all that is needed now are passengers, bound for glory.'"

"The Underground Railroad." Clara moved forward and gripped Priscilla's arm. "Llewellyn Latham didn't just give away a mountain of gold to build a library for the public good. He risked life and limb to help slaves to freedom."

"Yes, he did." Priscilla held up the page for all to see and pointed out the hash marks below. "It seems Llewellyn's brother kept track of their very special passengers. Over seventy souls went into the cottage basement and through the tunnel to waiting boats where they were taken to Canada or a train heading west. Llewellyn Latham found the gold in a fairly invisible niche when he was digging a freedom tunnel to save lives. I'd say our first keeper of the light was a rare and wonderful man indeed."

"A true light in the darkness," remarked Gerald loudly enough for the crowd to hear, and the gathering agreed.

Mayor Whipple stepped forward. "I have to say that this information puts our beloved library in a new historical light. Clearly it must be preserved for posterity, and we need to commission a new plaque explaining the library's rich history. Mrs. Grant, on behalf of the town, we'd like to thank you as well as Trudy, Gail, and Joan for your diligence. And we'd like to officially welcome you back to Martha's Vineyard."

"That's a motion I can second!" called out the old man.

"It wasn't a motion, Fred, it was a gesture," fussed an equally aged woman.

"Don't rightly care, I'm seconding it anyway." The old man grinned up at Priscilla, and she couldn't help but grin back.

"We've got cookies and punch in the small meeting room," called Candy Lane from the back of the room. "And fresh coffee, courtesy of Candy Lane Confectionery."

Priscilla was greeted with handshakes, hugs, and congratulations. All the cousins were there, and when folks had been tempted into the adjoining room for refreshments, Joan took her arm. "And Jake?"

"Jake is happy as can be back at the cottage, where he will live out a long and happy life, I hope!" Delight filled her. She would have fretted about today more if her cousin hadn't offered gentle words of wisdom. "They are the sweetest young couple with a premature baby, and they came back to make sure he was all right. Their little girl is so cute and delicate that I can't describe her in words, and still they wanted to personally make sure Jake had a home."

"And he does."

"Yes."

"This ended so well." Trudy came up on one side and Gail on the other. "Who'd have expected such things to go on here?"

"Well, things do go on, but we're rarely a part of them," observed Gail. "But I have to say, it was a pleasure working this out with you ladies. My brain hasn't been exercised to this extent in far too long. It was positively invigorating!"

"I concur." Trudy clasped her hands together, smiling. "I feel young again."

"As do I." Priscilla faced her three cousins and new friends. "And I have a proposition for you all."

"This sounds intriguing. Or frightening," Joan added, teasing.

"Let's have a supper meeting, and you can explain the proposition," suggested Gail. "Father's got a cold, so let's do it at the cottage, but I'll bring supper this time."

"Which means pizza," noted Trudy.

"But it's excellent pizza, so that's never a bad thing."

"Six o'clock?" Priscilla asked.

Three nods of agreement settled the timing. Now she'd have to see what her three island-rooted cousins thought of her idea. Change made a lot of island folks nervous, so the thought of changing an artifact like the lighthouse might make people downright apoplectic.

CHAPTER NINETEEN

Priscilla had just taken Jake for a brisk walk when she heard the sound of her doorbell through the open front window. She popped around the side of the house. Gerald stood at the door, clutching the heavy wooden box. "There you are."

"I was walking Jake," she explained and had to keep herself from reaching up to smooth flyaway hairs. "We are happy to report no bodies or treasure hunters on the beach this afternoon."

"Wonderful."

She opened the door and followed him inside.

"Where would you like this, Priscilla?"

"The living-room table would be perfect. The girls are coming by, and I want them to see the box close-up. You're certain the police don't need it for evidence?"

"The evidence crew has what they need, and there were plenty of eyewitnesses. The DA said it could be released to you, mostly because if there's anything of historic value, she doesn't want her department to be held responsible if something goes awry."

"A sensible woman."

The crunch of tires on the driveway announced the cousins' arrival. "I'm headed home to let the dog out," Gerald said. "Have you had Jake to the dog park yet?"

"I haven't, no."

"I'm off tomorrow. I like to take Sammy there on my day off, give her a different run about and some other dogs to visit with. I generally go about ten in the morning. If you'd like, I can introduce you and Jake around. You said you wanted to meet more people."

"I do, yes." Nerves hit her square in the chest. It wasn't as if Gerald was asking her out on a date, for heaven's sake. He was going to walk his dog and invited her to come along. Not exactly an outing under the stars. And still she hesitated.

"No worries." He backed up a step, unaffronted. "It's at the far end of town, just off Dawson Place, and stretches a good long way. You'll find your way there at some point."

He stepped out the side door as Trudy pulled in behind Gail and Joan. In three seconds he'd be out where any conversation they had could be overheard, weighed up, and probably misconstrued, so if she was going to make a move, she'd better make it now.

"I'll meet you there at ten. All right?"

"Yes." He didn't smile. He didn't grin. He just gave her a look of easy contentment, and that was just another reason to like him. "See you then."

The girls piled in the side door as Gerald made his way down the back walk.

"Priscilla, he brought the box!" Gail said.

"Family treasure," exclaimed Trudy, "of the very best kind!"

"And pizza from Offshore Ale over in Oak Bluffs."

"Mashed potato pizza?" Joan pretended to swoon while Priscilla crossed her arms in disbelief.

"There is no such thing."

"Oh, there is, and I brought an extra large, and you will love it, Priscilla. Cheesy mashed potatoes, chopped up scallions, and peppered bacon…to die for," declared Gail as she set down the box. "And best eaten hot!"

Priscilla had laid out paper plates and napkins, and as the women devoured the entire pizza, she was pretty sure she'd never had a better one in her life. When they got done, they tossed the plates and pizza box into the bin before following Priscilla outside.

"I want to show you something," she told them. She crossed to the lighthouse, opened the door, and invited them all in. "When I look at this lighthouse and read things like Llewellyn's letters, I realize that we—all of us"—she swept her hand to indicate the three cousins—"are part of something big. Bigger even than we may realize."

"What do you mean?" asked Trudy.

"Well, first, we're here. By the grace of God, we are all four here. I have this house, we all have old family names, and we've been brought together. Now maybe that's coincidence, but I don't think it's just that. I think time has brought us together to explore our history and lay down roots for the future."

"So far, so good." Gail's gentle smile invited her to continue.

"I'd like to share the Latham history with others. I'd like to turn this first floor of the lighthouse into a minimuseum with the artifacts we've found so far."

"The letters and the rocks?"

"And the journals and the ledgers and a few pieces of furniture from the nineteenth century. With a tribute to Llewellyn for what he dared to do to help others, and what he and his family did to help the town. I've been thinking about the bus tours too, and I think I might be interested in doing that next season. Opening the lighthouse could give Teresa a boost, and who couldn't use a boost now and again?"

"You wouldn't mind the commotion?" asked Gail, and Priscilla shook her head.

"I've come to realize I don't like the quiet all that much, and a little commotion is good for the heart, while prayer and thanksgiving can feed the soul. It occurred to me as we uncovered all those secrets that maybe secrets aren't always the best choice. A teacher shares their knowledge for the benefit of many, and I think that's what I'd like to do next summer. But I won't do it if my family here objects because Marjorie may have left this to me, but it's a family heirloom, and I recognize the value in that."

She waited while the cousins exchanged glances, and when Joan clapped her on the back and smiled, Priscilla finally breathed again. "I think it's a marvelous idea, and I'll be glad to help."

"Me too." Gail patted the thick, polished wooden rail that ringed the circular first floor. "We can spend some time getting everything just so, and you're right, Priscilla." She smoothed her hand along the arched wood. "Keeping things overly protected does no one any good. What do you think, Trudy?"

"I think it's a wonderful idea, and I know Mildred will be thrilled. She always thought it was a shame that no one could ever get into the lighthouse to see how unique it is. Brilliant, Priscilla." She beamed that bright open smile at Priscilla. "Absolutely brilliant."

Priscilla wasn't sure about the brilliance, but she was 100 percent sure that it was the right thing to do...and that was good enough.

AUTHOR LETTER

Dear Reader,

I cannot tell you how much fun I had writing this book. I first saw Cape Cod and the Vineyard a few years ago when my son did graduate work at Northeastern University. We took a weekend and visited the coast, the people, the fun, quaint shops, and the beaches. How marvelous it would be to live there! Like Priscilla in the book, we live on a farm (although ours is in upstate New York, near the shores of Lake Ontario), so the crazy fun of tourist season and reams of people in and out for five months of the year would be quite different for me too.

What would you do if you opened a letter and discovered you'd just inherited a historic lighthouse and cottage on Martha's Vineyard, a property worth millions? Would you have the courage to start anew and alone in your fifties?

Priscilla Latham Grant stepped onshore as a fairly new widow, examining her options, knowing she needed to make choices. But they weren't easy choices. By selling her family farm, she would be shutting a door on a big part of her life and the husband she lost.

In the sweet town of Tisbury, Massachusetts, faith, family, and friends help Priscilla shape a new road, a path that bonds her to a new normal. And if her "normal" includes a previously undiscovered talent for solving mysteries, well...she's come to the right spot! Enjoy!

Sincerely yours,
Ruth Logan Herne

ABOUT THE AUTHOR

Ruth Logan Herne is the award-winning author of over forty novels and novellas. She loves God, her family, her country, coffee, dogs, and chocolate. When the snow finally melts in western New York, you can find Ruth doing garden therapy because flowers are pretty and they don't talk back.

She lives on a farm with her long-suffering husband (Ruth never stops talking). She's got a slew of kids and grandkids (and the advice to go with it), and she loves meeting readers. Friend her on Facebook, visit her website, ruthloganherne.com, or stop by her blog, ruthysplace.com, or the cooking blog she shares with several other authors, yankeebellecafe.blogspot.com. She'd love to meet you!

AN ARMCHAIR TOUR OF
MARTHA'S VINEYARD

The West Chop Lighthouse
Tisbury, Massachusetts

Who doesn't love a lighthouse? There is something hopeful in the image of a beacon, shining through the storm, beckoning those in peril, lighting the way home. While the rooster may be a quintessential sign of the "country," the lighthouse brings our minds instantly to the shore. And on the island of Martha's Vineyard, we're surrounded by shores!

Come ashore from the ferry at Vineyard Haven, the village within the town of Tisbury, Massachusetts, and if you head north on Main Street, a seven-minute drive will bring you to West Chop and the lighthouse there. It is this lighthouse that serves as the basis for Priscilla's fictional one in the Mysteries of Martha's Vineyard series.

What's a "chop"? you're wondering.

A chop was the old name for a channel entrance, and if you look across the channel, you'll see the East Chop light marking the point. Between the lights, boats could sail into harbor safely, bringing their catch or their people back to land.

But West Chop is more than a lighthouse. We've got two keeper's cottages, very similar to the one you'll find in this series. There's a garage, added in 1935 once cars became a reality. And the original lighthouse, built in 1817. When it was threatened by erosion and construction, it was rebuilt and relocated near its original site. The two cottages are still in use too. One serves as headquarters for the officer in charge of the Coast Guard station, and the other is used as a vacation cottage for all branches of the active military.

Today the West Chop Lighthouse still serves as a nautical guide to travelers and is closed to the public.

SOMETHING DELICIOUS FROM OUR SEASIDE FRIENDS

*Cranberry-Orange Walnut Muffins
from Candy Lane Confectionery
(One of Priscilla's favorites!)*

Muffins

2 cups flour

2 teaspoons baking powder

½ teaspoon baking soda

½ teaspoon salt

1 cup sugar

¾ cup orange juice

1 egg, beaten

2 tablespoons vegetable oil

1 cup cranberry-orange relish

1 cup chopped walnuts
  (optional)

Streusel Topping

1 cup flour

½ cup brown sugar

½ cup white sugar

6 tablespoons soft butter

2 teaspoons vanilla

Muffins: Mix flour, baking powder, baking soda, salt, and sugar together. Add orange juice, egg, and vegetable oil to the dry ingredients. Mix well. Add cranberry-orange relish and nuts. Mix well.

Spoon into paper-lined muffin tins to about two-thirds full. Bake at 350 degrees for sixteen to twenty minutes. (Candy Lane likes to set the muffin pans on a cookie sheet, so they don't get too brown on the bottom. She's slightly overprotective of her baked goods, but then that's why they're so popular!) Cover with streusel topping.

Streusel Topping: Cut butter and vanilla into dry ingredients with pastry blender or two knives, sliced diagonally, until mixture looks like "meal." Spoon or sprinkle on tops of muffins.

Read on for a sneak peek of another exciting book
in the series Mysteries of Martha's Vineyard!

Like a Fish out of Water
by Janice Thompson

Ready to head home, boy?" Priscilla Grant glanced over her
shoulder at the dog in the backseat of her car. She grinned
when Jake's tail thumped against the leather. "I'd say we've had
quite enough adventure for one day, wouldn't you?"

Adventure, indeed. She and Jake had shared a wonderful day
exploring Martha's Vineyard, her new home. Though she'd only
been on the island a short time, Priscilla still couldn't get enough
of the breathtaking scenery or the kindhearted people. She'd grown
to love it here.

Jake seemed to agree. His energetic tail wagged in merry fashion as if to say, "I'd like to stay put too."

"Good boy." She reached back to pat him on the head, and he
settled down, ready for the ride home.

Priscilla turned the key in the ignition and then pointed her
car toward her cottage at Misty Harbor, her thoughts shifting back
to the island and its colorful residents. Could she have landed in a
more idyllic spot? To all who dreamed of white picket fences,
American flags waving in the coastal breeze, and a quaint life along

the 120 miles of exhilarating seashore, this was the place. One could scarcely find a fault with Martha's Vineyard, unless the cost of living was factored in. Owning a home on the island could squeeze the pocketbook, no doubt about that.

Not that Priscilla wanted to fret over finances—not after a day like today, when she'd enjoyed a blissful tour of the island's historic homes. She would ponder the cost of updates to her cottage later. Right now, basking in the glory of this peaceful, picture-perfect day took priority. And eating a crème horn she'd picked up at the local bakery, of course. The take-home bag sat in her passenger seat. The sugary goodness permeated the air around her even now, but she would have to wait until after dinner to enjoy her treat.

Priscilla followed the road past several luxurious homes, beyond a local bed-and-breakfast, and past one of the island's many graveyards with its sloped grounds and massive, overhanging trees. She kept her gaze on the road as she rounded the bend toward her cottage, which always reminded her of one she'd seen in a children's picture book. At certain points, gorgeous, expansive trees cocooned the street and seemed to swallow her whole. At other points, they disappeared altogether, and she caught a glimpse of the harbor in the distance, rippling under the late-afternoon sunlight.

Like most stretches of water on the island, the harbor still caught her by surprise. She could curl around a bend in the road to a sudden viewpoint that took her breath away. There, in front of her, a glass-like sea in all its brilliance. What a magical experience, one that always made her want to hit the brakes.

When she did have a chance to stand at the water's edge, Priscilla always found herself captivated by the sheer number of boats. Everywhere, boats. Some to sail, others to fish, still others to impress folks with their sheer beauty.

Would she ever grow tired of her new home?

"Guess what, Jake?" she said as the revelation took hold. "I just called Martha's Vineyard *home*." A contented sigh slipped out. With each day that passed, another piece of her heart took root on the island, and she didn't mind one bit.

When the cottage that Aunt Marjorie had left her came into view, Priscilla eased the car into the drive and paused to give the magnificent adjoining lighthouse a closer look. The tower was a bright white, capped by its black lantern room and encircled by a railing. Her gaze traveled to the small window about halfway up the lighthouse, which was also trimmed in black.

Soon, if she had her way, the bottom floor would morph into a small museum, complete with the Latham family history. Perhaps by next spring or summer, if all went well.

She shifted her attention to the waters of the cove, giving them a closer look.

"We're not in Kansas anymore, Toto," she whispered. No, indeed. A far cry from it, in fact. She turned off the engine and basked in the beauty of it all.

A glance to Priscilla's right revealed sailboats, fishing boats, and ribbons of late-afternoon sunlight dancing on the waters. What a brilliant display of God's handiwork. She wished she could spend a few quiet moments on the dock with her legs hanging over its rickety wooden frame. In that quiet spot, she would find time to reflect, to ponder life's complexities. To pray.

Unfortunately, something distracted her from the beautiful view—Tommy Townsend, the handyman she'd hired to replace the cottage's windows. He stood to the side of her driveway, worry lines etched across his forehead.

She climbed out of the vehicle and then opened the back door to let Jake run free. The hyper pup bounded toward the water's edge, tail wagging.

"Careful, boy," she hollered. "Don't get…" She didn't have time to add the word *wet* before he dove headlong into the reeds.

Oh well. She'd just hose him down later.

Priscilla took several steps in the handyman's direction. "Everything okay, Tommy?"

He shook his head and shifted his weight from one foot to another. "I hate to break it to you, Mrs. Grant, but I've uncovered some problems with the cottage."

"Besides the floorboards and windows, you mean?"

"Yes. When we pulled out the old window frame, I noticed the clapboard underneath had rotted."

"Can't you just replace it?"

Her question garnered another look of concern from Tommy. "Sure, but the more I got to looking, the more I realized that whole section needs to be replaced. It's one of those things that you need to do all at once."

"I see." She swallowed hard.

"And once the new siding is up, it's got to be painted, which brings me to my second point."

"There's a second point?"

"Yes." His nose wrinkled, and he swiped at his forehead with the back of his hand. "The original clapboards have really weathered over the years. So if we replace a section of the siding and give it a fresh coat of paint, it won't match the rest of the house."

"Ah."

"Common problem here on the island. But if we're really going to do this, we might as well do it right. With your permission, I'll replace all of the rotting clapboard, give it a fresh coat of paint, and then paint the rest of the exterior of the cottage as well."

"Paint the whole house?" Priscilla could almost hear the dollar signs clicking.

He nodded. "Yes, but it's not really that simple. If we're going to go that route, I'll have to sand and scrape beforehand to get rid of a hundred years' worth of buildup. We're talking a pretty big prep job here, and a lot more money than just replacing windows and a few floorboards. I hope you don't mind, but I've put together an estimate." He passed a piece of paper her way, and she gasped as she read the number he'd scribbled down.

"Twelve thousand dollars?"

"Roughly. That's just an estimate."

She gripped the paper, her thoughts in a whirl. "Tommy, I thought this was just going to be the windows and some refurbishing of the living room floor. You know? I'm not sure my pocketbook is prepared for a full-on home renovation job."

"I know." He pulled off his ball cap and raked his fingers through his hair. "You don't have to give me an answer right away. But let me know when you can because the siding has to be brought over from the mainland. That cost is factored in, by the way."

Priscilla couldn't help herself. She groaned. "I'll think about it and let you know, I promise."

"Thanks. And sorry about the bad news."

"Me too." She sighed. "But thanks for your hard work on my behalf, Tommy."

"You're welcome."

He headed to his truck and pulled away moments later, his oversize tires turning up gravel in her driveway.

Priscilla turned to examine the sea-blue cottage with its weathered clapboard siding and trim. The white shutters gave the place a fairy-tale look, and the flower boxes underneath really brought life to the old place. How she adored those beautiful rose-colored geraniums, framed out by elephant ear and lobelia. If only the old home didn't require so much work.

"Thank you, Aunt Marjorie," she said. "Thank you for leaving this lovely home to me."

A lovely home in need of repair, but a treasure nonetheless.

Treasure.

She couldn't help but think of her recent find in the attic, a trunk filled with old diaries and journals. What mysteries they had unraveled. Did this old cottage hold even more stories? Perhaps they would reveal themselves in time.

Priscilla turned her full attention to the dog, who was chasing something around the side of the house. "Jake, get over here." When he refused to cooperate, she let out a piercing whistle. He bounded her way and jumped up on her, covering Priscilla's clothing in mud. Ugh. "Now look what you've done." She continued to scold him as she turned on the hose. "I can't very well hose off out here, but you? You're getting a bath, here and now."

She bathed the dog then watched as he rolled around in the grass to dry off. So much for keeping him tidy. Now he was covered in grass and dirt.

Priscilla clucked her tongue as he shook off some of the loose grasses. "I think you were meant to be a farm dog." She could almost picture him chasing the horses and bounding through the wheat fields. Right now, though, she needed to think about other things, like getting the rowdy pup cleaned up once again and then heading inside for her own bath. Afterward she would take a closer look at Tommy's list and then brave a glance at her bank account balance to see where things stood.

Priscilla bathed Jake once again and then headed indoors. As she made her way through the bedroom, a framed piece of art on the west wall caught her attention. This wasn't the first time Priscilla had zeroed in on the odd painting of a battle sword, of course. She'd wondered about it from the first time she'd seen it. It wasn't her style, not even close. Still, removing her ancestor's cherished belongings just felt wrong. On the other hand, could she live with all of the cottage's knickknacks for the long haul? Something to think about.

She headed to the small bathroom. Minutes later, she settled into the bubbly waters of the claw-foot tub and leaned back to rest her head and neck. How many years had this old tub stood in this same spot? From the rust on the claw feet, too many. Longer than that old sword painting, maybe. But how could she trade in an antique for something shiny and new, especially one with so much history behind it? Seemed sacrilegious somehow.

A sigh wriggled its way out as Priscilla realized that was exactly what she'd done with the farm. She'd traded it in for a new home in Martha's Vineyard. Her daughter's words ran through her mind: *"Come home, Mom. Come back to Kansas where you belong."*

Did she really belong on the farm, or was this a new chapter in her life, one that only led to newer, different adventures? In such a short time, her affections for Martha's Vineyard had taken Priscilla by surprise. The island now felt as cozy and welcoming as this bubble bath. No wonder Aunt Marjorie had made the island her forever home. No wonder Joan, Gail, and Trudy chose to stay. Her cousins could have lived anywhere, but Martha's Vineyard held them in its comfortable embrace.

And now it held her too. This was home now. As it had been for many generations for the Latham family. This little cottage by the sea had provided shelter for her family for over a hundred years and was starting to show the effects of that.

A dark cloud passed over her, one that troubled her heart and threatened to shift her mood. Though she tried to avoid dwelling on it, the reality of her situation took hold. Would repairs on the cottage continue to snowball, eventually bankrupting her and forcing her back to the farm in Kansas?

This, of course, would delight her overprotective daughter. How many times had Rachel uttered the words, "You're in over your head, Mom"? A dozen, at least. Now with this repair bill looming, Rachel's words rang true. Still, every time Priscilla thought about going back to the family farm, a pang of grief pierced her heart. To leave now would be to admit defeat.

On the other hand, staying would require a financial commitment that could very well escalate even further once renovations got underway. Would this old cottage turn out to be a money pit? If so, could she really afford to keep it in shape?

"I don't want to go back to Kansas, Toto," she said to Jake, who'd curled up at the foot of the tub. "No matter how impossible this seems."

The dog opened his eyes, yawned, then dozed back off. Clearly, he wasn't losing any sleep over this.

Perhaps she shouldn't either. Priscilla resolved to keep a positive outlook. No looking back. But how, with financial woes looming, could she possibly move forward from here?

A NOTE FROM THE EDITORS

We hope you enjoyed Mysteries of Martha's Vineyard, published by the Books and Inspirational Media Division of Guideposts, a nonprofit organization that touches millions of lives every day through products and services that inspire, encourage, help you grow in your faith, and celebrate God's love.

Thank you for making a difference with your purchase of this book, which helps fund our many outreach programs to military personnel, prisons, hospitals, nursing homes, and educational institutions.

We also create many useful and uplifting online resources. Visit Guideposts.org to read true stories of hope and inspiration, access OurPrayer network, sign up for free newsletters, download free e-books, join our Facebook community, and follow our stimulating blogs.

To learn about other Guideposts publications, including the best-selling devotional *Daily Guideposts*, go to Guideposts.org, call (800) 932-2145, or write to Guideposts, PO Box 5815, Harlan, Iowa 51593.

Sign up for the
Guideposts Fiction Newsletter
and stay up-to-date on the books you love!

guideposts·fiction
Inspiring reads chosen just for you!

What's New
Mysteries of Martha's Vineyard

Come to the shores of this quaint and historic island and dig into a cozy mystery. When a recent widow inherits a lighthouse just off the coast of Massachusetts, she finds exciting adventures, new friends, and renewed hope.

On the quaint and historic island of Martha's Vineyard, just off the coast of Massachusetts, Priscilla comes face-to-face with adventure—one that includes rediscovered family, new friends, old homes, and head-scratching mysteries that crop up with surprising regularity. Learn More

Reader Favorite
Tearoom Mysteries

Take a quaint New England town... add some hidden treasures... a few suspicious characters... and a good measure of faith and friendship and you've brewed up Tearoom Mysteries!

Come explore this quaint village with its picturesque mountain lake surrounded by wild blueberry bushes, at your leisure. Like the people who come to Elaine and Jan's tearoom, you'll find yourself feeling relaxed. Learn More

From Our Editors
Sugarcreek Amish Mysteries

Sit back and enjoy a vacation for your soul with Sugarcreek Amish Mysteries. These well-written stories of the strong bond that develops between two women of vastly different backgrounds and traditions will tug at your heartstrings and provide hours of entertainment, intrigue, and wonder. In addition to Cheryl's keen insight and excellent riddle solving ability, you'll love experiencing Naomi's proverbial Amish wisdom and exploring her down-to-earth faith. Learn More

A perfect blend of faith, family and fun!

You'll get sneak peeks of new releases, recommendations from other Guideposts readers, and special offers just for you . . .
and it's FREE!

Just go to Guideposts.org/Newsletters today to sign up.

Guideposts. Visit Guideposts.org/Shop or call (800) 932-2145

Find more inspiring fiction in these best-loved Guideposts series!

Mysteries of Martha's Vineyard

Come to the shores of this quaint and historic island and dig into a cozy mystery. When a recent widow inherits a lighthouse just off the coast of Massachusetts, she finds exciting adventures, new friends, and renewed hope.

Tearoom Mysteries

Mix one stately Victorian home, a charming lakeside town in Maine, and two adventurous cousins with a passion for tea and hospitality. Add a large scoop of intriguing mystery and sprinkle generously with faith, family, and friends, and you have the recipe for Tearoom Mysteries.

Sugarcreek Amish Mysteries

Be intrigued by the suspense and joyful "aha!" moments in these delightful stories. Each book in the series brings together two women of vastly different backgrounds and traditions, who realize there's much more to the "simple life" than meets the eye.

Mysteries of Silver Peak

Escape to the historic mining town of Silver Peak, Colorado, and discover how one woman's love of antiques helps her solve mysteries buried deep in the town's checkered past.

Patchwork Mysteries

Discover that life's little mysteries often have a common thread in a series where every novel contains an intriguing whodunit centered around a quilt located in a beautiful New England town.

**To learn more about these books,
visit Guideposts.org/Shop**